CITIZEN
CÁRDENAS

June 2016

Alice

CITIZEN CÁRDENAS

A NOVEL

I hope you enjoy this story as I have enjoyed your friendship   Steve

STEVE COLE

NORTH LOOP BOOKS ~ MINNEAPOLIS, MN

North Loop Books

322 First Avenue N, 5th floor

Minneapolis, MN 55401

612.455.2294

www.NorthLoopBooks.com

NORTHLOOP
BOOKS

This is a work of fiction. Names, characters, businesses, places, events and incidents are either the products of the author's imagination or used in a fictitious manner. Any resemblance to actual persons, living or dead, or actual events is purely coincidental.

ISBN-13: 978-1-63505-056-1

LCCN: 2016902549

Distributed by Itasca Books

Cover Design by Alan Pranke

Typeset by B. Cook

Printed in the United States of America

For E.V.M.
and all who are or have been homeless,
struggling for their survival and dignity

PROLOGUE
GATO 2005

I call him my "Dadi." Of course, he not my father. I'm fifty-eight; he fifty-six. Actually I think I trick him. I call my real father, *mi padre Cubano*, "Papi." I think this Anglo or Greek don't know the difference, especially since I call his wife "Mami." I call my own mother "Mami." His wife I give respect because she don't believe my bullshit. He help me, he cash my check, he bring me back to life, so I give him respect. But I know how to fool him, so he don't get my full respect. Back when I'm somebody, when I have rank, I have some girlfriends. They call me "Dadi." See what I mean, how I trick him?

But he don't always take my bull. Then I have to listen to his. Then I have to do what he say. Sometimes it like he put a bullet up my ass. Like he tell me I have to move in two days. I have to do my laundry in ten minutes. Who is he to wake me up with this news? But I get up, get dressed, wash my face, and remember, "Gato, play this guy like a string." That's what Memo say.

Back then, Memo and I, we drink together in the park. I tell him this guy give me change, a dollar or two, if I hold his dogs when he go in the video store. He might buy some junk radio or tool I find in the garbage. Five bucks, ten bucks. This is when I am in the rooming house, but my check won't last, so I sweet talk and hustle so I can eat, drink, whatever. Then they throw us out of that place and I have to live in the park. So now he let me clean his yard for ten bucks, one time twenty. So I think, OK, I move out in two days, two weeks, what's the difference? He say the city will pay the rent at the hotel. Then I'll have the whole check. I'll give my Dadi some excuse so he'll give me one hundred, two hundred all at once. Play it up, stretch it out, stretch him out before I go to the hotel.

Last time I live on the street is when I'm "dead." I always remind Dadi, "Remember when I run across the street telling you and Mami, 'I'm dead. I'm dead.'" Then I show them the letter from Social Security. Let's see, I memorize the first line, "We are sorry to learn that JESUS CARDENDAS, the person for whom you were receiving Supplemental Security Income payments, died July 30, 2002." My eyes are burning, I read it so many times. The paper is so crumpled from folding in and out of my back pocket. How can the government do this to me when I fight in their war and become a citizen? Just because they say so, don't make it true. But I no can prove it because I have no ID, and without ID, Social Security say they can't give me a check. I ask Dadi, "Do I look like I'm dead?"

I figure showing this letter to Dadi is good for ten bucks, it good for two, three, five from almost anyone I show it to. Why you think I run from inside the park and across the street by the school where Dadi and Mami are? You can never just get money from him. There have to be a reason. He read that letter, Mami read it. I explain it, my payee died. I don't know if they know about a payee. He start asking questions like a machine gun, ask one question, ask another, he don't even give me time to answer. Who your payee? When he die? You go to Social Security? You lose your ID? The payee have your ID? Mami, she slow him down so I can tell the story before he interrupt me with another question. Then he get political. Say it is messed up, they can't do that to me.

But Dadi do something. I don't know exactly what, make some calls to the bank, to Social Security. Mami write a letter saying she know me fifteen years. They say I can stay with them till everything is straight and I get my back pay.

That was just in time. October the weather is getting bad, real bad, rainy, cold. Mami, she nice, she cook for me. For an *Angla*, she know how to cook rice and *gandules* real good. But she don't want me there when Dadi at work. I leave with him in the morning and look for him coming home from the train, or walking Bruno and Domino, their dogs. "I get them," I say, take their straps. I want to do something useful, but not too much. I ain't picking up after no dog. But then if I see someone else, I give him back the dogs. "I be back in a minute." I don't know how long it been when I get back. Maybe I drink a couple of quarts with another *Cubano*, find a VCR in the alley, sell it for two bucks. First time I show up 'bout nine o'clock, Dadi he mad, he tell me, "You ain't here by eight, you can sleep somewhere else." OK, he let me in once after eight, but I don't try my luck the time I find out it almost ten. Mad is one thing. But I don't want to listen to him lecture. I have to be responsible, give respect; no wonder I'm homeless. Who's he think he is, my Papi?

DEBATING GEORGE
ALEXIA 2002

From the time Jesus came running across the street proclaiming his highly exaggerated demise, George and I debated how much we should get involved with him. As usual, George wanted to take on the bureaucracy, this time on behalf of Jesus, or as everyone except me called him, Gato.

"We can't let them get away with this, treating Gato as if he doesn't exist."

"Of course I agree, but you could spend days trying to get to the bottom of this."

"Let's take it one step at a time. Tomorrow I'll go to the currency exchange with him. Maybe I can get a better idea of what really happened with his check."

That tomorrow led to another tomorrow and another and another and another. How George was able to get any work done on his job was a mystery to me and a source of worry. Ever since he had been transferred to the IT department, things had been going downhill on his job. He would boast that the new managers of the department depended upon his technical and business expertise. "They need me more than I need them," he would say. Yet he also made it sound like his manager was a bit threatened by his knowledge, know-how, and nonchalance attitude toward her authority. Now he was spending hours on the phone at work trying to cut the red tape at the Social Security Administration.

But he was getting closer to the truth. Jesus's now-deceased payee would receive his Supplemental Security Income check at the currency exchange on North Avenue. Five business days after the beginning of the month, the currency exchange was required by law to return the check to the issuing bank if by then the addressee had not picked up the check. In this case, the check was returned to Corpus National. The currency exchange provided George a copy of the form they sent to the bank, but the copy was so bad you could hardly read it.

It took him a couple of days and countless unreturned messages before he tracked down someone at the bank who was knowledgeable about the procedures and with enough authority to even research Jesus's case. Then George got the bank official to agree to a conference call with Social Security.

George's tenacity in getting to the root of Jesus's death by red tape motivated me. What could I do to right this wrong? A thought began to percolate in my mind: if George could get the bank to tell Social Security that it was their fault in assuming it was Jesus who died, surely his benefits would be reinstated, most likely with back pay. It would take awhile before the check would arrive. In the meantime, would Jesus have to continue sleeping in the park as the fall weather became colder and wetter? The words of another Jesus came to my lips, *"For I was hungry and you gave Me food . . ."* Yes, I could cook extra each night and give him . . . our leftovers?

Is this what I wanted to teach our son Nick, who accompanied me to church every Sunday? I wanted Nick to be grounded in values. Not the "holier than thou" values of the evangelicals, but the "last shall be first" and the "good Samaritan" values I learned as a child at our Greek Orthodox Church. It wasn't written that Christ said it, but he easily could have. *"For I was homeless and you gave Me shelter."* What would George think of letting Jesus stay with us until he found an apartment, once Social Security decided to reinstate Jesus with back pay?

So the night before the big conference call, as we drank our after-dinner coffee at the kitchen table, I asked him.

George looked at me as if I had told him I had been abducted by aliens. His eyes bulged. "You want to let that lunatic stay here with us? You're as crazy as he is."

"It's not summer anymore; it's been raining every other day. We can't just let him stay in the park."

"Why not? He's been homeless on and off now for four years, ever since they sold the rooming house," George said as he pushed away from the table, the screech of the wooden chair legs on quarry tile amplifying his anger. "You didn't seem to be too concerned last winter. You thought I paid him too much when he shoveled our walk."

"Don't you think we could help him turn things around? With a few months' pay he could finally afford a room, including security deposit."

Now George was up and pacing almost in a circle as he often did when agitated. "And where is he going to get a room? It's not like there are rooming houses on every block anymore. Are you going to drive around with him looking for a place? You know that will be my job. I say, once he gets his check, he's on his own."

"You're such a man of the people, George. You never want to really help anyone; you just want to tilt at windmills. It's not about

Jesus. It's all about you, the big fighter for the people."

"Come on, Alexia. You know that's bull. You always want to help people, but this isn't like helping a mother carry a stroller up to the "L" platform, or teaching Vickie to read. And taking him into our home isn't like taking in a stray cat or dog. You look into their eyes, and that's all you need to know. What do we really know of your Jesus? He's no saint. And aren't you the one who told me to avoid him and called him 'a bottomless well of need?'"

"OK, you have a point," I said, giving George an opening to sit down again.

We'd seen Jesus around the neighborhood for years. He had hustled us and others we knew, but he would do something for a few dollars as soon as he would ask outright. George had conversations with him whenever he did yard work for us. Of course Arianna, my old precinct partner, knew him. But given her history, her reference would raise more issues than they would resolve, especially for George. "I still think we should give him a chance. We can keep it open-ended. At least let's give him a chance to clean up and have a few nights' sleep without worrying that someone might assault him in the park."

"I'm just thinking about you and Nick. How are you going to get your work done if he's here all the time? You think Nick will want to practice his music with Gato hanging over his shoulder? And where's he going to sleep? You want him in Nick's room?"

"We can set up the cot again in the spare room, like we did when Marty stayed with us that summer."

"Let's not compare him to Marty. No matter what Gato calls me, he's not my son."

Marty, George's son from his first marriage, was a sensitive subject between us. I liked him as a six-year-old, when George and I first started seeing each other. I was even paying his child support when George was out of work. But once George started a new job, his ex-wife took George to court for more child support. There was more legal haggling around Marty's choice of college because George was cut out of the decision making but was expected to share the costs equally. George and Marty's relationship suffered, resulting in a two-year period when they didn't talk.

When Marty asked a few summers ago if he could stay with us for a couple of weeks, I was against the idea. "We don't even know him anymore," I protested, thinking about his body piercings, tattoo, black garb, and trips to Scandinavia. Eventually I relented and was pleased when the two weeks went well. Marty connected again with Nick, and having him around buoyed George considerably.

"Remember how you were all over Marty whenever something was out of place, or he looked around in your books and supplies? Once again, I'll have to enforce your rules."

Indeed, several rules came to mind in rapid succession that George, man-to-man, would have to convey to Jesus. He would have to be out of here each day when George went to work. He could not be alone in the house or alone with either me or Nick. He'd have to keep himself and his sleeping room clean and organized. He'd have to be in each night by eight p.m. and retire to his room by nine p.m. He'd have to clean up after himself in the bathroom and help out with chores—garbage, sweeping, yard work, and walking the dogs. Liquor and drinking anywhere on our premises were out of the question. Needless to say, he would have to leave his alley pickings in the alley.

My unstated but absolute rule was that if anything became missing, Jesus would be out of the apartment and out of our lives forever. I was no sap. I didn't believe him for a second when he said, a few too many times, "I'm no tief."

"What about a time limit? How open-ended do you want to make this?" George asked as I enunciated my list.

This was George loosening up, so I pondered it a bit. I realized that after a couple of weeks our nerves, if not our lives, would be shattered. Listening to Jesus's incoherent ramblings day after day might drive me to drink. November 1, the start of the next rental month, was about three weeks away. We circled that day on the calendar with a red marker.

STAYING THE NIGHT
GATO 2002

Dadi tell me to meet him by the park at five thirty. He work downtown, so he pass the park to get home. OK, I figure at least I can get $5. All I have to do is walk the dogs with him. But he say he have news. He talk to the bank, he talk to Social Security, and Mami write a letter saying she know me fifteen years. So they agree, I'm not dead. He say I get my back pay in about two weeks. I think maybe he lend me $50, $100, 'cause I got back pay coming.

I walk with Dadi to his house. He tell me to wait until he get Domino and Bruno for their walk. He go up, then Mami come down and she ask me if I want some dinner, some *habichuelas*.

I'm hungry, but I'm thirsty more. I never go upstairs before. How I go up there if I feel dirty, or maybe I smell, or maybe they have a fancy house? I have to see somebody, I tell her. Now I really need a drink 'cause I'm feeling bad. She trying to be nice to me, she and Dadi they helping me, and I'm too dirty to go up.

Then Dadi is there. The dogs have to go, so they pull down the stairs. I take Bruno; Dadi take Domino. Dadi surprise me more than

Mami. He say Alexia and he talk about it and I can stay with them until I find an apartment.

"What? You crazy? I appreciate it. Believe me, I appreciate everything you and Mami do for me. But I got respect, so I don't want to interfere your privacy." I don't know if he believe me. I don't know what he think. They help me. Do they want something? Everybody want something—even from somebody with nothing.

"Gato," he says, "tell you what. You come up, take a shower, have something to eat."

I'm thinking it real cold and wet in the park from all the rain yesterday. He say I can stay the night and see what I think the next day when he be home all day.

When I tell him I have to meet someone, he give me a few bucks but tell me to come back after I meet my friend. He must know my friend is Miller High Life and how much I owe him.

Soon I'm by myself. I'm cold. I'm shivering. I throw up, lucky I miss my shoes. But I keep going. I go in the liquor store, and right away the Arab ask, "You have money?"

I play cool, but I want to jump him. I flick my hand so he sees my three dollars, walk to the cooler. "We can party tonight, if you like," I say to the two fine girls reaching for wine in the cooler. They look at each other with their eyebrows and walk away without giving me respect. It not like that before, when I have a certain way with the women.

I open the quart bottle right out front of the store. I don't care. I take another hit when the Arab tells me to move on. I give him my "screw you" look. Then I walk in front of the video store, take another hit before I walk past the Arab toward Dadi's, take another hit. Screw him. Let him call the police. I'll be gone.

Soon I have the nerve to ring Dadi's bell. Nick, Dadi and Mami's real son, open the door. I follow him all the way up to the third floor. I wish they live downstairs. I'm out of breath. I don't have my spray. I smoke too much, too long, maybe I start when I'm ten. And the Cuban cigarettes are strong, more strong than Camels. Now I smoke shorties I find, somebody else start. Dadi, he give me some of his smokes—too light, but better than nothing.

The upstairs is nice. All the pictures on the wall, the dining room table, the old cabinets—comfortable but not modern. Not too expensive. Remind me of *mi tía's en Cuba*. Her husband a doctor so they have money, before Castro. Mami is in the kitchen. I use my soft voice, the one *mi tía* taught me to use when I stay with her, 'specially with her women friends. "Mami, your home is as beautiful as you." I learn on my own to flatter the ladies. "It smell real good," I say as she stir the *habichuelas*, bubbling just right. "You cook Cuban?"

She tell me she learn from a Puerto Rican and she hold out the spoon for me to taste.

"Oh Mami, that good, even better than *mi tía*," I tell Mami. I tell myself, real good, but not better than *mi tía's habichuelas*. Mami say I can eat after I take a shower. I hear Dadi calling from the little room next to the bathroom.

He hand me a towel, underwear, socks, pants, and in the bathroom he show me a razor and cream for shaving. "What about this? My neck itch real bad. You got electric?" He dig around in a drawer and he pull out a leather bag. He tell me I can keep the electric razor 'cause it was from an old friend who die.

When I'm done with the shower, I shave, find witch hazel for my face in the cabinet, put on Dadi's clothes, pull the belt tight.

"Jesus, you look good," Mami tell me.

"Mami, I feel good. I can't remember when I feel this good."

Now I remember almost everything from that night. I don't know if anyone ever treat me like that since I left Cuba and *mi familia*.

WHO IS THIS GATO?
GEORGE 2002

Alexia and I wondered, Who is this cat, Jesus Cárdenas, really. Alexia raised doubts right away when we started to intervene on his behalf with the Social Security Administration. Of the two of us, Alexia had encountered him first in the neighborhood while registering voters during the 1987 Washington campaign. She didn't remember registering him to vote when she went through the rooming house on Hoyne. She vividly remembered his persona—how could you not—but didn't remember the name Jesus Cárdenas. To prove her point, she dug around the house until she found an old poll sheet listing the names of all the voters from the rooming house. There was a Felix Cárdenas but not a Jesus.

My encounters with Gato were, at first, more informal. He'd be hustling change or trying to sell me items he'd found. Perhaps he'd offer to hold the dogs when I went into the video store. I've made it a point not to summarily dismiss street people asking for money. Not that I feel for coins whenever I'm asked, but I do when the face becomes familiar and the pitch has a certain quality.

I think of panhandlers as street entrepreneurs. As with most businesses, it's the marketing that counts. The big corporation advertises on network TV, national magazines, the Internet. Local businesses on radio, newspapers, and billboards. Neighborhood stores have the signs attached at their location and sometime distribute circulars door-to-door. The panhandler has nothing but his or her pitch and presence.

"Can I ask you a question?"

Please don't, I think as I walk past a street person with that tired query.

There are likely to be three or four questions before the meaningful one, "Can you help me out with some change?"

"Do you have 36 cents?" That's an inventive one, makes you wonder why such a precise amount.

"Help the homeless." Sure, if you helped this one possibly homeless person you would be helping all the homeless.

The most successful panhandlers, at least with me, employ a technique that I used when I sold display space for community publications. These rags had such small circulations that no advertiser would ever gain from a placement. I'd talk about the interesting stories, local community struggles, and campaigns we wrote about to gain a sympathetic ear. Anything but the advertising value of their buy.

Gato approached me by commenting on the dogs, "Hey, I bet that black and white one's smart. Who's older, the brown one?" He'd follow up with the dogs themselves. They seemed to like him. Of course our dogs were used to cats; we had as many as five at one time.

Over the years we'd encounter each other now and then. I can't say for sure when we exchanged names or he started calling me Dadi, but it was well before I became his payee. Sometime in 1998, after his rooming house was boarded up, Alexia and I ran into Gato, again while walking the dogs.

"Hey, man, where you staying now? Still in the neighborhood?"

"I'm in the park, Dadi; can't find no place on my pay."

"You may have to move west of Western," Alexia offered. "The yuppies haven't taken over there yet."

"Too much gangbanging over there."

"What about down by Chicago and Noble?"

"Don't know nobody over there."

"Well, you can't stay in the park forever."

"I know a lady on Wolcott. She got a room for $200 a month, but I'm short now."

"George, don't we have some yard work Jesus could do for us?"

"How about it, Gato? I'll pay you $20, but there's a lot of work. You'll have to hack through the tall grass before you can mow. It won't be easy."

"I appreciate any work you give me," he said as we walked through the gangway to the yard. "You'll see I do a good job. You got a machete?" He broke out into a big smile, then a laugh. "I cut lots of sugar cane."

"No machete, but you might like my sickle." He seemed to admire the wooden-handle tool with its curved blade. In a minute he was cutting a wide swath through the grass, almost a foot high in places. Next time I looked he was mowing. By the time I brought down some lemonade, he was ready for a drink.

"No beer?"

"You know it's really not good to drink beer when it's hot like this. You still have some more to do."

As we settled into a couple of lawn chairs, Gato leaned forward and asked, "Hey, Dadi, how long you in the neighborhood?"

"About fifteen years. You?

"Longer than that. Ever since I come to Chicago."

"When was that?"

"After Nam."

"You were in Vietnam?"

"How you think I get so crazy? That place mess me up real bad."

I was surprised he was so forthcoming. "Where were you from originally?"

"Cuba."

"When did you leave, before or after Fidel?"

"In '61, when I was fifteen."

He didn't strike me as coming from one of the wealthier Cuban classes that came over in the early years of the revolution. "So you came over with your family?"

"I come on a boat, just me and some guys I know from my hometown, Guantanamo."

"Kind of young, weren't you?"

"Not too young to know bullshit."

I was curious. My sympathy for the Cuban revolution had led me to visit the island in the early 1970s to learn firsthand its brand of socialism. Ever since, I admired the wiliness of Fidel outlasting ten US administrations, all trying to undermine his rule and the Cuban economy. Now here's Gato, not your typical Cuban refugee from the early '60s and certainly not one who found much of a livelihood here in the United States. Could I ever get to know his view of the world? I'd have to gain his trust before I revealed mine.

So I stayed in the yard to take advantage of Gato's openness as he alternated sitting, working, or pacing the yard.

"Where did your boat land?" I asked at one point.

"Land? That leaky boat? Its motor go out; we drift two days. The water almost fill it up. When I see the land, I jump, start swimming. Next thing I remember, I'm on the beach, some sailors standing over me. Coast Guard."

"What happened to the other guys?"

"I don't know, I never see them again. Coast Guard say they found them still on the boat."

"So you think they sent them back to Cuba?"

"How do I know? All I know I reach shore so they have to let me stay. But they ask me all kind of questions. 'Do you have family here? Do you know anyone here? How old are you? What kind of work you do?'

"But I'm thinking, why I tell them the truth? So I tell them I know no one. I lie, I tell them I'm eighteen. I tell them I do some construction work in *Habana*."

"Did you do construction in Havana?"

"What? You think I leave Cuba if I have a job? But I get one in Miami."

The contours of our yard were taking shape, just like Gato's past. But I sensed him getting anxious about something.

Leaning against our blue mower, he asked, "Dadi, what time you got?"

"Two thirty. You got to be somewhere?"

"I told that lady on Wolcott I'd come by there at three. I'll finish up now."

All of a sudden he was working double time. He had this funny way of scooping the piles of grass and weeds into the yard-waste bag. He'd spread his legs with the bag behind him and hike the grass into the bag like a football into the hands of a quarterback. In five minutes he was done. It would have taken me a half hour.

"What about tomorrow?" I asked, wanting to hear more of his story more than I wanted to pay him to trim our front yard.

"What, the front just need a trim? I appreciate you want to help me, but you do it yourself, maybe you need the exercise." As he said that his hand made a rounding motion in front of his own flat stomach. Similarly his mouth turned round. "Hey, Dadi, let me ask you a question. You play chess?"

"I used to, but it's been awhile. Why do you ask?"

"I see a box of chess on the shelf when I get the mower from the basement. You no believe it but I'm good."

"You want the chess set? You do the grass in front tomorrow it's yours, plus ten dollars."

"I don't need the set; I need someone good to play. You smart, maybe you good. I come by tomorrow, I mow the grass, we play chess. You beat me, you owe me nothing for the grass. But I kick your ass, you owe me twenty."

Now he had me interested. We shook hands on the deal and scheduled our match for three p.m. that Sunday. I, too, was looking for a good game and was waiting on our front stoop with the mower, rake, and yard bag at hand when he sauntered around the corner right at three p.m.

"So you ready for an ass-kicking?" he says, smiling slyly.

"First things first, my friend," I said, extending my hand for a shake. "You mow the grass; I'll set up the board in the yard."

I returned from upstairs with some iced tea as he was coming through the gangway. He put down the bag of yard waste, put the mower and rake away in the basement, then carried the bag of yard waste to the back gate and garbage cans. Before putting the bag in the can, he took a quick look inside, raising an old desk lamp like a trophy.

"Hey, Dadi, you need this lamp? I can use this in my new room."

"Congratulations, you worked something out with the lady on Wolcott."

"All I need is $20 more for the first month." A wink accompanied the smile this time.

He let me be White, and I opened the game in standard fashion. I thought I was doing fine after about the fourth move, and he seemed to be concerned what to do next.

"You know, my Uncle Carlos teach me," he said, while out of nowhere he trapped my Bishop. "My parents send me in summertime to Santiago to stay with my aunt and uncle. He a champion when he a teenager."

I couldn't prevent the loss of my Bishop, so I went after one of his Knights. "You sure you want to do that?"

Was he trying to distract me? "I'm good." Actually, I wasn't; my capture exposed my Queen for his taking. So I tried turning the tables. "Isn't Santiago in Oriente province? Wasn't that where Castro's revolution started and had a lot of support?"

"What? Don't you know Santiago de Cuba is its own province now?" As he talked, we each made a couple of moves. "I don't know why, but *mi tía* and *mi tío*, they like Castro. But he make them go in the mountains because my uncle a doctor. I ask them, can I go with them, but they have to leave before they answer me. Check."

I blocked his rook. "Check," he said with a move of his Bishop.

I moved a Pawn to block. "Check," he said, threatening with his Knight. But when I moved my King to the only available space, I knew I was out of time. His Knight moved again. "Checkmate."

He had no trouble beating me a second time, even if no money was on the line. I managed to hang on a little longer, perhaps because this time I was distracting him, peppering him with questions.

"How long did you live in Miami? You worked construction there? How'd you wind up in the army?"

Over the course of the game, I found out that by 1967 he had lost his job, his prized Catalina, the girls he used to party with, all replaced with a rap sheet and a choice: a Florida state penitentiary or Vietnam.

After the game, he didn't want to talk about Vietnam or anything else. He wanted his twenty dollars and seemed aggravated that I had to go upstairs to get it.

Later that afternoon as I was walking the dogs in the alley, I saw Gato hanging in front of the liquor store. I stopped to pick up after Bruno, then looked up, expecting to see Gato sauntering toward me. He was nowhere in sight.

BACK PAY
GATO 2002

I'm back at Mami and Dadi's house now. But what a headache I have from everything that happen in the last three hours. Dadi, he mad 'cause I'm late, after eight p.m. He say it happen again, I can sleep in the park. I tell Mami I'm too tired to eat when I get home. So I close the door to the little room I stay in. I see the little tape recorder on the shelf with the books and think that maybe I tape what happen today in case Salvador do something. I use a recorder before so I know how it work.

All day long I think about what to do with my back pay. Sixteen hundred twenty-nine dollars. That number is good for back pay Social Security owe me. Dadi, he's already tell me he hold my money so it stretches. He know money go through me like spicy food. He's right. I can spend $300 as fast as I spend $30. No difference when it's all gone.

Who do I pay back, who do I put off? Hector I got to pay $200, $300. I probably owe him four. But he from Guantanamo like me, so I pay him first. Forget Memo. I'll just buy him some beer.

Keep him high and he won't remember much. Rodrigo, OK, $100 right away and maybe he won't pull a knife.

Dadi, he'll keep $600, $700 till he know my rent, if I need security. Salvador, he'll have to cash the check, he'll take $170 off the top. If that tief try to take more, I'll kill him.

See why my head is burning? Only about $350 left, less after I get drunk with Memo. It won't stop with the beers. We'll go to Marta's or the Cuban place on Milwaukee for sandwiches, probably run into someone else I owe, have to give them $10, $15.

Dadi better give me $100 for my sock. No, I'll need more. I'll talk real quiet with Dadi, make sure Mami can't hear. Tell him man-to-man I need another $40 to clean my rifle. I know just the lady to do it.

I'm adding the numbers, one way, another way, on the way to Salvador's, in the elevator to the seventh floor, even when I knock on 705 and look through the eyehole. The runt open the door. I can see in, but he tell me to wait. He got all this space: three rooms, but nothing in it. Kitchen table, two chairs, dirty dishes in the sink. Next room his bed; look like my bed if I had a bed. Dirty sheet, holes from cigarettes. Something is wrong, I can tell the way he shuffle around in his slippers. Why he don't want me to come in? Then he come out of the bathroom and hand me a roll of bills.

"I'll see you next month," he say, trying to shut the door, but I'm leaning on it.

"How much you take?"

"The usual, 10 percent. And what you owe me."

"What I owe you? I don't owe you nothing."

"You eat my food, you drink my beer, take my smokes, sleep on my floor. You think that doesn't add up? I should take more."

I push in all the way now. I grab him, push him to the floor, pick up the chair. I want to mess him up real bad. But I don't hit him with it. He lie on the floor like a baby, almost in a circle. I think, If I hit him, I go to jail. What would I tell Dadi? Maybe Dadi be my payee, he won't rip me off. I throw the chair all the way into the other room, slam the door so hard it bounce back open. I don't look back. I know he still on the floor. I don't hear no noise from the elevator so I start running down the stairs. Two flights I'm wheezing. I don't have my spray. How long I rest in the stairs I don't know, but when I get to the street it already dark. The wind is bad, maybe it going to rain. Behind the bush in front of the school across from the senior building, I count the roll he give me. Eleven hundred eighty dollars.

My inside feel real empty, hungry, but not for food. Same time I'm angry, ready to go back up, rough up that *gusano*, find my money. Angry at Salvador, angry at myself, how I get into this mess. If I don't drink, if I don't leave my ID with the payee, I'm not dead for four months.

On the sidewalk now, I'm on my knees. I don't pray too much. I don't know if I believe, but I'm praying now. "¡O, Señor, *dime qué hacer, dime qué hacer!*" I remember I have money and the liquor store is two blocks away.

LATE ARRIVAL
GEORGE 2002

He came to the door that night after our eight p.m. curfew. He was supposed to have received his back pay, a sum he shouldn't be walking around with or, worse yet, sleeping with in the park. Too much money on a homeless person can be a magnet for assault. Gato himself told me of a man found dead in a local park, a story confirmed by the neighborhood paper not long afterward. He could have been a great neighborhood crime reporter if he had his wits about him as much as his whiskey.

I invited him up to our third-floor apartment despite the liquor on his breath. But he wanted to linger on our stoop. He wasn't as lively as he often is; he was looking down most of the time and spoke in hushed tones, harder to understand than usual. It's not that English was his second language or that his tongue has few teeth to press against or even that alcohol slurred his words. Rather, his words assume you know his world, his journeys in time and place, what is a hallucination, what is not.

I suspected it was coming, a story about his back pay. The possibility of being back at square one with him, that his entire check was already gone in the few hours between his payee's mail delivery and 8:45 that same evening was not far-fetched. How could we get him out of our apartment and into his own place without that money? And we needed him out of our apartment.

He followed our rules, he cleaned up after himself, and usually he was on his best behavior. But not always. He'd show me the quart or pint hidden in the inside pocket of his coat or pants he was wearing beneath his pants. He thought it was only Alexia who insisted on the no alcohol in the house rule. Maybe he thought he could level with me or that I'd wink OK. At least he didn't think I'd share it with him.

But we worried that a burst of rage would shatter the idealism that led to his staying for three weeks on a cot in our spare bedroom. We didn't worry that one of his violent streaks would be directed at us, for we knew his gratefulness for helping him was real and he would be forever loyal. Our real fear was losing our privacy, losing our ability to relax in our own home, losing the relative sanity of our lives to the craziness of his. Yet putting him back on the street was not an option we would feel good about.

The story came. Salvador, his new payee, had taken out over six hundred dollars. Less than $1000 of the $1629 was left. "Dadi, I almost kill him, but I can't," he said, recalling his anger at Salvador. For my part, I wasn't sure his anguish was for the "almost" or because he "couldn't." Or was it merely for dramatic effect?

In a way I was surprised that there was anything left, but I didn't believe Salvador took the money. That was just more bull from a master in BS. But I had yet to meet Salvador. Two weeks later, Jesus would have to restrain me when Salvador tried taking more than $50 out of the next and last $543 SSI check he would receive on Gato's behalf. I saw firsthand what a worm he was and wished then that I had believed Gato.

Incredulous as I was, I was also relieved. With the money he had left and another check due on the first of the month, there would be enough to pay a month's rent as security for some kind of accommodation. But where? The neighborhood was not what it once was. The rooming houses and transient hotels that once were themselves characters in Nelson Algren novels were no more in gentrified Wicker Park.

CORTEZ ARMS
GEORGE 2002

The Cortez Arms Hotel was a grandiose name for a flophouse. Like many other single-room occupancies and transient hotels in Chicago, its name seemed to hark back to the pre-depression glory days when it was built. A few of these hotels, like the Flossmoor, were classy joints in the old days, but most were built for the immigrant men who came to Chicago without their families. The Cortez fell into the latter category. Its rooms were small and bleak, though a step up from the worst of the flophouses where the rooms were actually cages, with plaster covering the wire on the walls but not the ceilings.

With our November 1 deadline for finding Gato a place quickly approaching, we were lucky to find the Cortez. For hours over several days, Gato and I drove around following vague leads. A neighbor suggested a building on North and Rockwell. A garbage-picking partner of his heard there was a place on Armitage and Maplewood. Rumor had it a rooming house at Western and Thomas had vacancies. We zigzagged the neighborhood in an ever-widening circle, hoping a For Rent sign would appear on an appropriately shabby-looking building or basement apartment.

The lack of places was not our only obstacle. Like most felines, Gato was choosey. "Not this street; too many gangbangers." But three blocks away he'd be calling out from the car to someone he knew. "Hey Bones, where you been?" or "Cuatro, what's up?" When his friends thumped their chest with the double "L" of the Latin Lords, I'd get nervous, fearing a pullover from cops spotting the gang gestures. Gato swore he was no longer affiliated with any gangs. "I'm too old for that. Besides, I'm already dead."

At work, I scoured the Internet and Yellow Pages. A website on the history of SROs in Chicago mentioned an organization of SRO landlords. The phone book had a listing. On the eighth ring of my fourth call someone finally answered. Noise in the background kept me from hearing the greeting. All I heard was something, something hotel. I asked, "Is this the Transient Owners Association?"

"Hold on a minute." I waited for five. "Who wants to know?" It was the same voice, less noise.

"I'm the payee for an SSI recipient. I'm looking for a room for him to rent."

"You could have just asked if we had rooms to rent," she sassed back.

"You have rooms there?"

"You could call them that. Eighty-five bucks a week. Three forty monthly. You better come over soon; we got just two vacancies now. One week security."

"What's the security if you rent by the month?"

"Same thing. Eighty five." It was getting noisy again when I got the address: 1640 W. Cortez. "Yeah, Marshfield and Cortez. Office closes five thirty." I couldn't believe it; we must have driven by that place three or four times.

I left work early and practically ran to the park from the "L" station. Now when I needed to find Gato, he was nowhere to be found. I saw one of his drinking buddies and asked if he had seen him.

"*¿Quién?*"

"Gato."

"Oh, Gato. You his Dadi, right? He said if I see you to tell you he'd be at Best Burger."

I found Gato lounging in a Best Burger booth, his back against the window wall, feet up on the seat. A half-eaten Doubler and six or seven cigarette butts soaking in the melting ice of an orange drink showed he'd been there at least a couple of hours. The manager tolerated Gato hanging out there as payment, with a Doubler, fries, and a drink, for picking up litter strewn across the parking lot.

As he saw me enter he started, or more likely resumed, flirting with the attendant as she wiped the tables around him. "Where you get such a pretty smile, Maria? I know you happy I'm here." I think he was trying to impress me more than her. He had to know he wasn't getting anywhere with her. I'd seen this routine before.

When I told him about the apartment, he started computing how much rent he would have to pay. He knew he had $740 left: $425, one month plus security. Then he refigured. He knew the back pay would soon be gone. "How I going to live on $197 a month after the rent? I don't have food stamps. I don't have medical card. How about you pay them one week at a time?"

"Gato, if you want me to be your payee, we're going to do it my way. I'm going to pay $340 each month up front. Let's get the place, then maybe we can get you food stamps and a medical card." I knew something about food stamps. I had even been on them for a stretch in the early '70s. First regulation, you have to have a place to live. Food stamps go to households, and you can't have a household without a house. You can't cook without a stove.

I could tell he was still figuring. I told him to wait for me. I'd be back in ten minutes with the rent money and we'd go over to the Cortez Arms Hotel. But he wasn't there when I got back to the Best Burger. It was almost 4:45. I circled back to the park. He wasn't there. Back to the Best Burger; not there. I waited. Reluctantly, I drank their coffee. I stood out in front and started pacing. I was getting mad. "You don't show up in five minutes, you can forget about me being your payee." Ten minutes went by. I was pacing back and forth to the corner so I could see if he was coming from the park, walking the other direction, to see if he was coming from the Walgreens side. "Five more, that's it." I was talking out loud to him, but he wasn't there.

"Dadi, Dadi." He was across the street coming from the north on Milwaukee Avenue.

"Where you been? I told you to wait here."

"I went to check out this place up there. Somebody say they have rooms for $325."

The smell of booze told me he had room for $3.25 worth of beer.

"What's it going to be? Am I wasting my time or what? You want to check out the place on Cortez?"

"You're my Dadi. If you say the place on Cortez, then OK. You told me ask around, to try to find a place myself, so I look for the place on St. Paul. I come back because I saw some bangers."

It was 5:10. I had parked the car on the other side of the park; it would be tight getting there, just six blocks away, by five thirty with the rush hour traffic. But forget about walking with Gato. He'd run into at least five or six people he knew on the way. With each, he'd walk away a few steps so I couldn't hear them talk.

I drove past the Cortez Arms looking for parking. Finding

none, we wound up two blocks away. It was 5:20, so we had to hustle. I didn't doubt for a second that the office would close promptly at five thirty.

From the street, more than a few clues revealed the kind of "hotel" this place was going to be inside. A small sign on the corner of the boxy building read Rooms: 773-555-4242; numerous single windows lined the way to its single street-side entrance; the signs peering through the Plexiglas door window and surrounding panels said it all.

OFICE CLOSES 5:30 PM MON-SAT, ALL DAY SUNDAY
VISITORS MUST BE ACCOMPANYED BY RESIDENTS
NO LOITERING IN FRONT OF PREMISE

Four loiterers engaged each other in animated conversation outside the front door. One nodded at Gato as we pounded on the acetate-covered door window, finally getting someone to open up at 5:26. That someone was probably seventy-five years old and had a straw and grey-colored beard sticking five inches out from his chin. I wasn't sure at first if the musty smell was coming from the bearded one or from the lobby itself. I also wasn't sure which was older, the bearded one or the lobby rug, a faded threadbare oriental. Behind the desk were wooden cubbies, with unretrieved letters sticking out here and there. To the right, on the back side of an open closet door, keys hung from hooks, room numbers hand-painted in black. Recent cigarette smoke and cigar smell from hours ago hung in the air, obscuring the No Smoking sign. I'd seen and smelled plenty of places like this before on the south side of Milwaukee, where I grew up; in Uptown, where I'd done community work; and in the various neighborhoods I traveled through in Chicago.

"She'll be down," were the only words muttered by the bearded one, who later I would know as John Welch.

"She" was Gloria—thirty-five or so, owl-framed glasses, maybe half Latino, half Polish. "You the one who called?" I didn't have time to respond. "You can go up to 214; it's open. Stairs are behind that door."

Coffee cups, coffee stains, cigarette butts, and cigarette burns highlighted the mud-colored carpet covering the stairs, which creaked and sunk a bit when you stepped on them. In the narrow second-floor hallway we squeezed past a fat white guy in a white shirt and tie and a tall, light-skinned, heavily made-up African American woman in tight, very short denim shorts. She was tall, broad, and rough-complexioned enough to be a he. Outside the floor's common washroom the rug was soggy.

Room 214 was indeed open, the door half off its hinges. Inside, more carpet, more stains. Heat would not be a problem here; the room had to be 80 degrees. But the basics were there: a bed, small dresser, sink, a shelf above a mini-fridge, a stove. Gato looked under the bed and then looked at me, resigned. "I can live here."

I wondered whether he would die there, in the Arms of Cortez.

HOLIDAYS
ALEXIA 2002

Call me old-fashioned, but to me the holidays are special. Thanksgiving, Christmas, Easter. They represent the most important aspects of our lives. Family, friends, and faith. Since Nick was born I've tried to follow the traditions of my family growing up. Church was a given, especially during Holy Week. Each holiday also had its traditional foods centered around the main course. Turkey at Thanksgiving, ham for Christmas, lamb on Easter.

Neither George nor I had family nearby to celebrate with, so the holidays became a time to extend our family. My parents were deceased. George's mother, a widow since the early 1970s, had moved to California to live with George's sister and her growing family. We always had guests, neighbors, old friends, or unattached coworkers from George's jobs.

We were nervous this Thanksgiving. George's mother flew in from San Diego to stay the entire week, and joining us for the holiday dinner would be my oldest friends, Louise, my Italian bridesmaid, and her Czech husband Art. What was making me anxious was that Jesus had engineered an invitation for himself when we checked up on him after he was newly settled at the Cortez Arms, where he met us in the lobby.

"Mami, you and Dadi going somewhere for Thanksgiving?"

"No, not this year."

"You know I make a good chicken and rice. I don't have much room, but you can come here; Nick too."

I could barely imagine spending five minutes in Jesus's room after George had described it, let alone eating, not just any meal, but his definition of a Thanksgiving feast.

"Yes, the chicken and rice you made when you stayed with us was *muy sabroso*. But George's mother from California will be with us and our friends who stood up at our wedding. We'll be having turkey and all the fixings."

"What? And you didn't invite me, your third son?"

George tried damage control. "Gato, you didn't give us a chance. That's one of the reasons we came by today, to ask if you wanted to come for Thanksgiving."

"OK, you won't regret. I bring the sweet *maduros*, Cuban style. How you say Grandma in Greek? I think I hear someone at Gus's say 'yiayia.' My *yiayia* going to like it."

On Thanksgiving Day Jesus showed his pleasure at our invitation by showing up on time, dressed in a herring-bone suit and a cream-colored knit shirt, a small silk floral arrangement in one hand and a bowl covered in aluminum foil, smelling of sweet plantains, in the other. Not a hint of alcohol was on his breath. Of course we had forewarned Dimitra, George's mother, giving her the story of how we became involved with him and laying out a range of behaviors she might encounter that afternoon. Nonetheless, we were nervous.

Jesus was charming. When Dimitra came out from the kitchen to meet our first guest, he didn't wait for an introduction.

"Hello," he said with a bit of a bow. "I am Jesus Cárdenas," in a distinct Spanish flourish. "You must be the sister of *Giorgos*."

Of course Dimitra took Jesus's flattery with a smile and a hint of a blush. "Call me Dimitra, but I am too old to be anything but George's mama. What do you have in that bowl? It smells good." Taking the bowl, she peeked under the foil, inhaled satisfyingly, winked at Jesus, and brought it into the kitchen. Jesus had met his match.

When Louise and Art arrived, he took their coats, made sure they sat in the only two really comfortable chairs in our living room, and brought them appetizers from the kitchen. While Dimitra and I finished our dinner preparations and George began bringing plates to the table, Jesus had become the host.

I could hear him telling Art and Louise the story of how we saved his life when Social Security declared him deceased. "They bring me into their home, they treat me with respect." He didn't mention the nervousness that accompanied our generosity nor the lapses in his behavior that caused us to question our sanity.

Once again George and I debated our course of action, though this time on a smaller scale. In the kitchen, I was already sipping my favorite Greek sweet wine, *Mavrodaphne*, to ease the tension of the meal's preparation. "Should we offer drinks to Louise and Art?" I asked George in little more than a whisper.

"They'd think it strange if we didn't."

"What about Jesus? We made such a point of his not drinking in the house when he was staying with us."

"Not to mention my lectures."

Dimitra offered her opinion, "We are Greek, we have wine with our meals, even if it's not a holiday. He's either going to have just a little like everyone else, or he's going to have too much, no matter what you do."

"Mami, you need help with anything?" He was in the doorway to the kitchen on "anything."

"No, you just keep Art and Louise entertained."

"That's why I am here," Jesus replied. "They like a little wine. Louise wants white, Art red."

While we were debating, he was taking orders, the consummate host.

"George will bring them out. Here, you bring in this plate of cheese and crackers."

"Your wish is my command."

After George delivered the wine, he finished carving the turkey, arranging the slices of white and dark meats, surrounded by the drumsticks and wings. By this point Louise, Art, Jesus, and Nick were all poking their heads in the kitchen, volunteering to carry platters, bowls, and casseroles to the table: sweet potatoes, mashed potatoes, cranberry sauce, *fasolakia* and *yigantes* beans, gravy, and of course the turkey.

After everyone but George and I were seated, somehow with Jesus at the head of the table, I brought in my glass, and George followed with bottles of white and red in his hands. He filled glasses for Dimitra and me, refilled for Louise and Art, raised his glass of water for a toast and to proclaim his sobriety, when a throat clearing interrupted George's "*Yia mas!*"

"Excuse me, did somebody forget something? Is everyone going to toast but me? I don't seem to have a wine glass."

George was turning rosé. I turned around to the hutch, grabbed two glasses, and chastised George for not setting the table carefully enough. "Red or white?" he asked Jesus.

"I start with the red."

As George poured one for himself as well, Jesus rose. "*Gracias el Señor por la comida, nuestra familia, y amigos nuevos. ¡Salud!*"

As the meal progressed, Jesus became looser with each glass of wine. When the red was gone, he kept his promise and moved on to the white. Surprisingly he kept both his charm and food intact. But another surprise was in store. When he finished the white, he brought a half-empty pint of cheap vodka from his jacket. "Everything else too expensive, 'specially when I have to share with my friends."

After dinner we insisted that he did not have to help clear the table or wash dishes (our best china). "Jesus, this is your evening to relax and enjoy. You men watch the game; we women will tackle the dishes."

"Sister, you are a saint," Louise proclaimed out of earshot of the fans on the electronic fifty-yard line. "I would never imagine doing what you have done with Jesus."

"You can see, we have our doubts."

Dimitra removed the doubts. "This is the Greek way. We offer friendship to strangers."

"Well, despite his drinking, you have his respect. What's more, you'll have his loyalty. In the old neighborhood, on Taylor Street, we had a few guys like him. Of course, like the rest of us they were Italian, but they drank too much and couldn't hold down a job. But if you did good by them, they'd watch out for you."

Assured by Louise's insight but getting tired, I suggested to Louise that the day was getting long. In turn she prompted Art, who offered halftime as a good breaking point. A few head gestures later and a touchdown given up by Art's team and he was ready to go, somehow getting the message he should offer a ride home to Jesus. Everyone mused at the possibility of an encore celebration the following Thanksgiving. Dimitra, George, Nick, and I were happy to be alone again, even with half the cleanup still to be done.

One of the last things Dimitra told us before returning to

California was that she was proud of us. "I know now we raised George right, and you were too, Alexia. Something good will come from helping Jesus, even if it's hard, and you don't know what the good will be."

That holiday season we continued to "do good" by Jesus, though for Christmas we decided not to mix guests or drinks. Marty was in from New York, but as usual, his schedule was dictated by his mother's plans. The highlights of our celebration were two: Jesus learning to say *Kala Christougena* and the pleasure he took in the presents we gave him, especially the tape recorder he had found and fooled around with during the time he stayed in our spare room.

George suggested that Jesus record his life's story. That got a laugh out of Jesus. "Hey Dadi, how many cats like me die then tell their story?"

TESTING UNO, DOS, TRES
GATO 2003

Testing, *uno, dos, tres, uno, dos, tres. Estoy el Gato* coming from the Cortez Arms Hotel, Chicago, Illinois, taping on the machine I get from my Dadi. Five minutes ago I'm in Robert's room down the hall. I'm glad his door open 'cause after last night I need something.

Now I'm hungry as a dog. That rice and chicken on the stove looking good for last night's chicken and rice. So excuse me, I'm going to eat.

Rustling noises, some chewing noises, spoon scraping the bottom of a rice pot. More chewing. Throat clearing.

My cooking is good. This is Gato again. Dadi say, tell my story. Just talk into the recorder. Not sure what to say, so I'll tell you about my day so far.

I wake up sweating. The light is on, shade down. I don't know is it night or day. The clock is blinking 6:42, 6:42, 6:42, 6:43, 6:43, 6:43. Maybe the power go off. Probably I turn too much in my sleep and the clock plug come out of the wall. When I look out the window, my eye's hurting the sun so bright. But it not yet in the west.

So maybe it almost noon.

I sleep long. I don't know the time, but I know the day—16th of the month. Maybe I can get my $40 advance from Dadi. If I clean the lot by the video store I can make $8, then I don't have to bother Dadi till tomorrow, maybe the next day. I get paid early, Friday the 29th, because the first is on Sunday, so I don't want to wait too long to ask Dadi. The radio tells me it's 12:12. By now, most everyone else is up.

The smell from the bathroom is bad. Somebody throw up and don't clean up. My mouth taste bad, maybe I throw up. Can't remember. Got to clean it up anyway 'cause I owe the manager $20.

I strip down to my drawers. I throw jeans and shirt away the last time they get so wet with puke. I don't care Alicia see me like that. She'll see I'm ready for her. But she don't pass by and peek in. Just Jessie, the fat white boy always wear the same white shirt and tie. He almost slip on the wet floor. He should 'cause he too fat to tiptoe like that. I get out of there when he on the can; the sound as bad as the smell. It make me laugh when I'm not in there, near him.

After I dress I make the rounds past every door on the floor, listening and smelling to see who is up, who is alone, who cooking, smoking, who making love. Looking whose door is open enough to look in or lean against by accident. "Sorry to bother you, I trip on that lousy loose rug."

Robert's door is open all the way. He must have a new batch of wine he selling. He buy it by the jug, sell by the cup. I'm already into him for $12. That is why I got to see Dadi. Maybe Robert will roll me a smoke. Smokes are his hook. And you ain't leaving without smoking it right then. Meanwhile he'll pour himself wine, let me watch till he see my mouth opening, my tongue against my gums back and forth.

"Want a cup?" he ask.

"You know I can't pay. Why you ask?"

Then we argue, I say he making four times what he pay selling by the cup. I say he make interest off us, he say he making a profit "the good old American way."

"So what? Same difference," I tell him.

Then he ask me if I hear a lot of noise last night when the police arrest Amos. I say I don't remember anything about last night. I'm not going to tell Robert nothing, though I know all about it.

Amos Barber and I, we tight since we stay in the same rooming house, till they sell it. So I ain't telling Robert nothing. I leave Amos's room a minute before the cops come up to the third floor. They push me out of the way and shove the door open without knocking. Didn't take much. The locks in here real cheap; half don't work. Most of us have chains, too. Amos don't have his on. Then they take him out in cuffs. They cuff me too behind my back, push me down on the floor. Say they want to check my ID. I tell them I don't have no ID. Lucky for me Sgt. Romano come in ten minutes later. He tell the bull who hold me down to let me go unless I'm holding something. But he tell Romano what I say, that I don't have ID and maybe I was with Amos.

Romano say, "I said, let him go. That's Gato, Jesus Cárdenas, as harmless as a tomcat now."

I keep my mouth shut. Romano, he insult me, but he know me from way back, Latin Lord days. If he want, he could mess with me real bad.

I hear them talking. Someone who looked like Amos—six foot three, 240 pounds, black, mustache, shaved head—jump the liquor store owner twenty minutes ago. I know it ain't Amos. We be drinking beer for hours. I keep quiet; they not going to believe me anyway. They don't care they arrest the wrong guy, just they arrest somebody so they look good.

That's it for last night. Last I remember I'm dizzy. Thinking about it, I tell Robert, "Yeah, I'm good for a cup." It turn out to be three, maybe four.

"Hey, Gato, who you talking to?"

Muted voice. Alicia from down the hall. Maybe she think I have another woman. How can she be so jealous?

"What you want? I'm busy."

"What you want, baby?"

Lock unlatches, door creaks.

"Damn, Alicia, button your blouse; you know I'm broke."

"I thought you were busy."

"Can't you see I'm recording?"

"Where you get that from?"

"From my Dadi."

"Your Dadi? Who's your Dadi?"

"You never see him? Never mind who's my Dadi. I tell you I'm busy."

"Hey, it's turning. You mean it's recording what I'm saying?"

"Everything. You don't like it, leave."

"Can I say something into it?"

"You already saying something into it already, you just don't know it."

"OK, I'm Alicia Benitez, and Gato is my man."

"You crazy? Me and anyone else fool enough to buy your snatch."

"You're the only one I do free."

"Yeah, once in a blue moon, when you feeling sorry for yourself."

"Why you got to be so mean, Gato?"

"I tell you, don't tease me when I'm broke."

"Gato, why don't you turn that off and turn me on?"

WHO IS YOUR DADI?
GATO 2003

Everybody ask me, "Who is your Dadi?" or "Who are these white people you staying with?" Now I'm at the Cortez. "Who's that white guy always coming by your room?" Memo ask, Alicia ask, Amos ask and say, "Watch out. White folk always want something."

Amos was right about that, except Mami and Dadi seem different. Dadi get my check back when Social Security say I'm dead. Now he cash my check and don't take no cut. Mami let me stay in their house. She cook *habichuelas, arroz con gandules. Se hablan español.* They find me the room here, give me blankets, sheets, pots, pans. I'm with them for Thanksgiving. For *la Navidad* they give me this recorder. Maybe they're different 'cause they Greek, like Yianni the owner at Gus's Corner. Yianni, he let me eat even when I can't pay.

But living on the streets I watch my own back, *entiende?* Even when I first knew Dadi I wondered 'bout him. One time I work in his yard he ask me all kind of questions about Cuba. Then I see Fat Charlie, he live 'round the corner from Dadi. Charlie, he screw just 'bout everyone in the neighborhood one time or another. He ruin some people's places while he fix them, or he don't pay guys work for him. I work for him four days, never get paid.

He ask me, "What you doing at the Communist's house?"

"What's it to you? At least he pay me right away for working in his yard."

But Fat Charlie make me wonder 'bout Dadi when he ask me if I ever think I be better off in Cuba.

Couple of months later I'm waiting for Dadi to come home from work so he can pay me for cleaning leaves and stuff front and back of the building. This old guy, thick white hair, he's cleaning leaves from the sewers up and down the block. He come up and start talking to me. I see him before. He know I know Dadi. He tell me I do pretty good work and he tell me his name is Wilbur.

I tell him, "Just call me Gato."

"Cuban, hey?"

"How you know?"

"You work too hard to be a Puerto Rican, and you're too dark to be Mexican. My people, they're from Norway."

This guy liked to talk.

"We stopped in Cuba when I was in the navy. Good thing you got away from the Communists."

I make sure no one else can hear. "You know I appreciate the work he let me do for him," pointing at Dadi's house, "but is he all right? Fat Charlie say he's Communist."

"When's the last time that Pollock ever said something anyone could believe? George might be a do-gooder, but he's no pinko. You'd laugh if you saw him when this Indiana Baptist called him a Communist. He picked up that runt by the collar, slammed him against the wall. That whole crew of Bible beaters kept off the block for two months after that.

"No, only thing wrong with George is he don't know how to

do anything. Too much education. Hardly knows how to jump-start a car. Doesn't know a spark plug from a carburetor. Has a plumber in to change washers."

Wilbur sees Dadi coming and goes back to cleaning the gutters.

"See you been talking to the mayor of our street," Dadi says. "He been telling you war stories or going over the fine points of mowing grass?"

Wilbur yells over from two houses down, "Wouldn't hurt you to listen to experience once in a while." Then he goes over to the drain across the street.

Funny thing, since Wilbur die, Dadi clean the gutters on the block.

But 'specially before I let Dadi become my payee I try to find out about Dadi and Mami. Lady Love, I can't find her; she know Mami from the elections. First time I ever see Mami, Lady Love tell me then, "Don't mess with her; she's all right."

Radio, this Puerto Rican I see when I'm riding around with Dadi looking for places. I tell Dadi, "Pull over. I got to talk to someone." Really, I know Radio always have some beer in a bag, let me have a taste.

So Radio says, "George, I know him from Uptown. Black Panther."

"¿*Pantera Negra*? He's white like a marshmallow."

"Gato, there was a whole group of Anglos up there with their Panther newspapers, free breakfast program, legal program. Mostly they were cool, but they talk so much you have to tune them out, you know what I'm saying?" He take his bag and bottle back, take a long drink, looking right at Dadi. "George, he don't like people drinking around him."

"Tell me about it."

When I get back in the car, Dadi tell me, "Your friend look

familiar; can't place him, though. Who is he? Know him long?"

"I think he goes by 'Radio'; don't know why. I don't know him too long; seems all right."

"Why's that? Because he shares his bottle with you?"

"Hey Dadi, they got the special at Marta's today. Now I got my back pay, I treat you."

I got lucky, that change the subject from beer to food.

Before I got my back pay I went to borrow some money from Hector up at the projects. I don't like going there. I don't like the bus. And there's too many gangbangers and it smell like piss in those projects on Damen. But I need money bad and he probably help me again, 'cause he's from my hometown.

I ask Hector, "You ever see my Dadi before, you know that guy you see me talking to across from the park?"

"Yeah, I've seen him. Used to be around the projects here all the time when I was banging, maybe twenty years ago. Went around with magazines, newspapers. We thought he was Jehovah's Witness at first. He seemed to know Rudi, you know that little guy that ran the Snakeyes here for a while.

"I asked Rudi, 'You want me to chase the white dude?' Rudi says, 'That's the GED teacher.' Starts going off how he's going to get his GED, then go to college. He has to go to college because he wants to take the gang political.

"Yeah, Rudi got his GED. In Cook County. Took college classes too, doing five to eight in Joliet." Hector, he's laughing. Then his mood change. "My girlfriend took his GED classes; she's the one that got political. Campaigned for Washington, started some kind of tenant's rights group. Rumors were Mr. GED was trying to move on my girl. She swore there was nothing to it. He was just trying to help the community. After Washington got elected, someone else was teaching at the Boy's Club, and my girl got evicted."

"Hector, how 'bout just one hundred more? I got back pay coming now."

"Back pay? I thought you were dead," he said, laughing again.

"Your Mr. GED get me reinstated. That's why I want to know if you know him. Maybe he be my new payee."

"Hey, homey, if he can bring you back to life, why not? Sign me up for his classes."

One hundred dollars later I was back on the bus.

Someone else I have to ask. If I hang out by the Best Burger long enough, I can run into Sgt. Romano from Wood Street. He know I'm not banging no more so maybe I give him some information time to time. I'm no snitch or nothing, but I tell him stuff like, "Hey someone been rolling us guys sleeping in the park, you know, 'round the first of the month."

I have to know Dadi is no narc. I know Romano won't tell me straight up, but I'll know by what he say. Sure enough, second day I'm at Best Burger, Romano come in for his coffee and Doubler.

He come up to the booth. I got my feet up. "Hey, Gato, you look comfortable. You back on the dole?"

"What, you think I'm on easy street?"

"You're in here spending money."

"I borrow off the back pay I got coming."

"Good for you. Got anything for me?"

"You might want to keep your eye on the noodle factory; it seem every night the stack of pallets out back getting smaller."

"Come on, Gato, you know that's not even good for $2."

"No, no, I don't want no money. But I got someone I need to know about."

"OK, I'll help if I can."

"I don't want to talk here."

"In ten minutes I'll be on St. Paul, between Damen and Milwaukee. It's quiet there this time of day."

In the back of his squad, anyone seeing me would think he checking me out for something. So I ask, "You know George Demas?"

"Sure, used to work for the city, before Daley. Police Community Liaison."

"What's that, some kind of narc?"

"I wish. No, he was taking complaints against the police. Made things rough for us for a while. But once Washington died, it was over for Demas. His political career was dead. Why you want to know?"

"Just wondering; said he'd be my payee."

"Well, he's honest enough; too honest."

DEAREST NEPHEW
TÍA FELICITA 2003

Santiago de Cuba

February 24, 2003

Dearest Nephew,

Your letter brought joy to my heart and tears to my eyes. Imagine how I felt these past years, almost five now, since I last heard from you. I had no idea how well you were prospering. At times I supposed the worst, that something terrible had happened to you and this was why you did not write.

Instead I know now how successful you have become in your endeavors. Your waste management business, in partnership with your former lieutenant, seems to have really flourished. I never would have guessed that your company would have grown to cover so much territory, states and cities I have heard of from east to west, north to south. Ohio, Iowa, St. Paul, Milwaukee, Augusta, and of course Chicago. You seem to be always traveling from one place to another. No wonder your home is a hotel, the Cortez Arms in Chicago. Its name alone brings back memories of old *Habana* and its grand establishments.

Who would have known that you, who were merely his driver, would one day be so fortunate to have Lieutenant Dadier as your partner. His wide-ranging contacts from the military combined with your business acumen must be an unbeatable combination. Your strategy of letting smaller contracts lapse in order to capture the larger ones reminds me of the gambits my dearest Carlos employed on his way to becoming a chess champion. You certainly learned from a master.

These last several years have been lonely. It is as if the two of us, separated by more than geography, are all that remain of our family. It is so rare I hear from any of your siblings, and I do not think any of them are on speaking terms. Your dear mother could maintain the peace despite the political differences among your brothers and sisters. Of course, I could not. I was too sympathetic to the revolution.

Maritza's husband is too high an official, one of the corrupted, for her to have anything to do with the family. Miriam's order must keep her too busy for her to even write. Or perhaps she has forsaken all things worldly, including her family. You would think the Catholics would encourage contact with family, especially given the slender thread they must balance on here in Cuba. Juan keeps to himself, trying to avoid the rumors associated with his still being unmarried. You, like no one else, know it is too painful to talk of your brother, God bless his soul, who tried to join you in Chicago these many years ago now.

So the ten years since my Carlos died and the seven years since your mother passed have been unbearably lonely, even for a "Mother of the Revolution." Yes, I am still proud of that title bestowed upon me for my work with Carlos in the mountains. I only wish you had been able to be with us to see that the revolution was not about dogma but about helping people, bringing the basics to the *campesinos* who never knew anything but hard work and bitter poverty.

My fondest desire is to see you one last time after all these years. I know I am not long on this earth. Now that you are well established in business, perhaps you have the resources and contacts that would allow you to visit your lonely *tía*.

Please thank your employee, Jessie, for transcribing your letter. I felt important to receive a computer printed letter. I only wish you could have confided your thoughts to one of your Spanish-speaking workers. I do not get to use my English very often.

I love you as if you were still the young boy who lived with us off and on, the only son I ever knew.

Tu Tía Siempre,
Felicita

MY GREEK FAMILY
GATO 2003

Dadi, he's mad at me. Mami too. I screw up. I got to roll with it, lay low, try to keep away 'cause every time I see them they let me know they mad. Dadi, he come right out and say it.

"Who you think we are? We try to treat you nice, and look what you do."

"I know, I make a mistake," I say to him. "You know I respect you and Mami."

"You call how you act respect? You don't respect yourself; how are you going to respect anyone else?"

When he's mad like that, it don't work changing the subject. So I just look down so he can't see my eyes. Pretty soon he'll ask what I want so he can borrow me $40 from next month's check and he can be rid of me till the first.

Mami, she don't say nothing angry, but she ain't fixing me no chicken or *arroz con gandules* like she use to. Nick too, he answer the door, he just go back upstairs and tell Dadi I'm there. He don't ask, "How's everything?" or answer me when I test his Spanish.

Nick, he might be the maddest. I know I hurt his feelings. Too late, what can I do about it now? Coming to his school play all drunk, bringing Memo along, he's almost as high as me. But Nick, he don't say anything even though I embarrass him in front of his friends.

See, I be drinking and 'cause they be treating me good I start believing they are my family. My Greek family. I got nobody else. *Tía Felicita*, she's in Cuba. Now she know my address she write sometime, but who do I have here? Memo? Hector? Amos? They OK to hang with. Hector will help me in a jam, but that's not family. My own daughter only comes looking when she need something, and what can I give her?

Things be good with Mami and Dadi. They have me over for Thanksgiving and *la Navidad*; they call it *Christougena*. Have me over, even when their other friends visiting. They give me some warm clothes and the tape recorder. I stop by on a Sunday, and Dadi and I play chess. Most of the time I beat him. He good, but not as good as me.

So I'm at Nick's high school, best school in the city, Whitney Young, and I'm high, and I'm proud of my brother. He's got a big part in the play *Guys and Dolls*. So I tell them—the ticket takers, the candy sellers, people sitting next to me—Nick Demas, he's my brother. They look at me, think I'm crazy. Dadi and Mami, they don't sit anywhere near me, though I can feel their eyes burning holes in my neck. Even Memo, he sit a couple of seats away.

Next thing I know he's poking me, telling me put your feet down from the chair in front, wake up, everyone can hear you snore. I cuss at him, then I see where I'm at. On the stage, I think I see Nick glancing toward me. Maybe he's missing his lines.

It's a couple of months since then. I don't see them except when I get my money. I ain't doing much. It's cold, so I do my drinking inside, either at the bar where they sell bottles too, or just in my room, watching TV or tapes. I'm sleeping a lot, room is hot, makes me sleepy. All the ashes and bug spray for the *cucarachas* ain't doing me no good; they make me wheeze, and most of the time I don't have no inhaler.

Wait a minute, my computer is thinking. It's been six months since I'm in the hospital. I can check into the hospital for a couple of days. That be like stepping on a bunch of *cucarachas* at once. Get out of here for a few days. The hospital give me medicine, an inhaler, even help me get a medical card. I can call Dadi from the hospital. Maybe he forget I act like a jerk. 'Cause I'm sick, he and Mami visit.

I can get the fat boy, Jessie, to call the ambulance. He see me coughing and spraying myself on the stairs. I'll leave my door open. Usually he come by around six thirty every night; don't know where he's coming from. He'll see me on the floor, wheezing, unable to get up. I'll hardly be able to say his name. When I'm out of the hospital I can get him to type another letter to *Tía Felicita*. It's too late for today, so I have to wait for tomorrow.

Least I still have some dollars. Robert can sell me something to drink, give me a few smokes to get me through the day tomorrow.

All this thinking making me tired.

CITIZEN CÁRDENAS
GEORGE 2003

Perhaps seeing Gato in a hospital gown for the first time rattled Alexia and me. How thin he was, wearing that flimsy, cotton, light-blue, diamond-patterned gown. It barely reached his knees and it covered so little that it made his features stand out: the angular lines of his face, his unsymmetrical cheekbones, the yellowed teeth, the few that there were.

Through the slits of the gown we could see his chest. Electrodes were attached, monitoring his heart and lungs, and a four-inch scar ran diagonally below his right ribs. How vulnerable Gato was, like that other scantily clad, gaunt, face-drawn-in-pain Jesus on the cross of my mother's favorite icon. Gato was no God, not even a fallen angel, but compassion required that we put behind us the anger we harbored from his "high school" performance.

Gato needed help, more than we could provide. I knew enough about the system to know that he would never get food stamps, medical benefits, or low-income housing if he didn't have ID. It wasn't easy getting Social Security to admit their mistake and reinstate Gato's benefits. But they wouldn't give him a new Social Security card without a birth certificate and a photo ID. Getting a birth certificate from Cuba wasn't going to happen. Getting a state of Illinois ID would be tough without the birth certificate or some other official document.

Two government sources, the Immigration and Naturalization Service and the US Army, seemed to be starting points. Gato said he served in Vietnam and during his stint became a US citizen. What better identification could there be than a copy of his naturalization papers?

After Gato was out of the hospital, I invited him over on a Sunday afternoon to play chess. Delaying the prospect of a third loss, I asked, "What do you think, Gato, should we send away for your papers? I printed out an application for a replacement copy from the computer."

"If you say so; you know what is best. What they want to know?"

"The usual: name, birthplace, birth date, something called an 'A' number, and $55."

"You know I don't got that kind of money."

"Mami and I will cover it."

"I don't want to trouble you. You already do so much for me."

"Hey, I'm not giving you $55 to drink away."

Sitting at the kitchen table, with the application and pen next to the wooden chess board, between my moves, I reviewed his story. "What years were you in the army? Sixty-seven to '69? You became a citizen toward the end of your active duty?"

With each question he'd nod and make his move. "What you trying to do? You think you can beat me if you distract me? I don't think so."

"You know what an 'A' number is?"

Without hesitation he rattled off his: "A-459-08-762. I got I-94 too." I wasn't surprised, given Gato's way with numbers, "the computer in my brain" as he would put it. But I was thrown when he hesitated in answering my next question.

"You said your birthday was July 26? 1946?"

"You better put down 1954. There was some kind of mix-up; they might have the wrong year."

Bureaucracies do make mistakes. But why wouldn't he get them to correct their mistake? I let it go.

The next day I mailed the form to the Naturalization and Immigration Service. I knew it would be a waiting game; how long was anyone's guess. There had been articles in the newspapers about backlogs at the government's immigration agency. But I also wondered what would come back.

Six weeks later, I came home from work one day and, as usual, sifted through the three households' worth of mail tossed by the mailman in the first-floor hallway. Amid the advertising circulars, catalogs, bills, and credit card offers was a large manila envelope with a government franking mark. Before I could even get to the second-floor landing I ripped it open, only to see our $55 check stapled to a form letter.

The 5 ½ by 8 ½ half-sheet explained that the fee for naturalization papers was now $145 payable to the Department of Homeland Security. Fifty-five dollars I would put up for Gato. One hundred forty-five was another story, especially since something about Gato's behavior those days was making us reluctant again to help him. There were no more Sunday social visits. He only showed up on payday or when he needed an advance.

Plan B was the army. I downloaded the application and instructions for release of military records from the army website. When I saw there were no fees required, I wished this had been Plan

A. The form asked for the usual information: name, Social Security number, date of birth, place of birth, and information regarding his active service: branch and dates of service, status (officer or enlisted), and service number. Unlike with the "A" number, Gato's "computer" froze as if it were a bug-laden software product. The "A" number had flowed out right away. Why not the army number? I wondered. At least it wasn't required. The army also allowed the papers to be released to a third party. That would be me, approved with Gato's signature, Jesus Cárdenas, written carefully, though a bit shakily. I listed my contact information, including e-mail address and phone number.

A big surprise was that within a week, a representative from the army's archive station called on the phone telling me they could not locate any records for Jesus Cárdenas. Did I have the name, Social Security number, and birth date right? Was there any possibility of getting the service ID number? I explained the possible mix-up, that his birth date might be listed as 1946 or 1954. I told her I'd try again to get the ID number.

Next time I saw Gato I confronted him.

"So far the army cannot find anything on you. Let's try again. What was your military ID number?"

Silence. Just that sullen look I'd been getting for two months.

"OK. Let's review what you do remember."

"They just don't want to give you my papers."

"Why would that be?"

"'Cause of my discharge, maybe. You know, mental discharge. Same reason I'm on SSI disability: hallucinations."

This didn't make sense. But just then Gato had given us the reason nothing made sense.

When I called back the archive official, I couldn't give her anything new. She told me discharge status would not affect the release of his records. She'd keep trying, there was another database she could probe, but she didn't offer much hope. "Our systems are pretty good; I would have found it by now."

In the database circles I traveled, I heard the same thing. Unlike many government agencies, the US Army's computer systems were A-1.

Plan B was now a bust. I was more reluctant than ever to fork over $145. But though my wallet was resistant, I was more curious than ever. Who was this cat? Was there ever a Citizen Cárdenas?

WHO'S HE THINK HE IS?
GATO 2004

Finally I'm by myself. I let Memo stay in my room. Hey, I owe him; he let me off that money I owe from when I'm "dead." And now it's not like I'm getting nothing. This month's money's already gone and it's just the 12th. So Memo's buying the food, buying the beer and smokes. Sometimes he give me a few dollars if I'm going out and he's just going to sleep or watch television. Anyway, he's helping me till his money run out.

I'm so mad at Dadi I don't even want to ask for my advance. That's why I'm glad Memo is gone for the rest of the day. He went out to some suburb to see his Mami. Berwyn? Cicero? I don't care, just so long as he not here. I can't think when he's here. He don't say that much. I do most of the talking. Someone's in the room, I'm talking. Hey, no one's in the room, I'm still talking into the machine. I hope Dadi hear this someday, hear just how mad I am.

Who's he think he is anyway, looking into my life? He just my payee, send the rent in every month, but it's my money. It's OK just the way it is. What do I need ID for? The police? Some no-good outfit want to see it? My friends don't ask me for ID. The liquor store, they don't ask me for ID; they can see I'm as old as an antique.

Without ID I can be whoever I need to be. Need the ambulance to the hospital, I'm Juan Morales. Police stop me, I'm Antonio Rodriguez, live over on Humboldt, whatever number pop out from my computer.

He's poking around so much I can lose the little I got. Just because once he got Social Security to put me back on, he think he can get me stuff from welfare? Link card, medical card, low-rent housing? I don't mind those things; I got them coming. But you get them, there's always strings and more strings. He's right, the system is screwy. But he think he can fix it. Smart as he is, he's a fool. Don't he know people like me never get nothing? No, all we got is nothing.

And he giving it to me. "When were you in the service? When you become a citizen? What base were you at? They got your birthday mixed up? You don't know your service number?" Nagging and nagging me. By the time he's done they probably take my check away, say I'm some kinda cheat. Why they want us to come in the first place if they not going to take care of us? Just to make Castro look bad? Anyway, he always gets the last laugh on the United States.

I got to get Dadi to cool it. He's making me nervous. Wait, I got to find my bottle.

Noises, footsteps, sound of things falling. Useless ashtray, now it all over my pillow. Dadi even say I got to clean up this place. When's he think I got time to clean up?

Slurping sounds. Burp. Almost out, good thing Memo give me five dollars. Wait, I hear someone coming down the hall.

Door opening.

"Amos. Where you been? Want a taste?"

"Yeah, I need something." *Pause.*

"That's good. I was down at 26th and Cal. They finally dropped that charge."

"From that time someone jumped the owner of the liquor store?"

"That's the one. Arab never showed up. Guess he ain't going to make waves, you know, 9-11 and all that. That's OK by me. I walk. But you know what time it is, I was with you that night.

"Hey Amos, you got minutes on your phone? I gotta call someone."

"Tell you what, I got to use the can. You call whoever while I'm in there. Lucky me, it's clean as a whistle. Looks like you been paying off some debt."

"I'll pay you when I get my check."

"Forget about it, *amigo*. Let's just say today's my day, might as well be yours, too."

Toilet flushing.

"I hope I remember her number. 773-555-9045.

"Excuse me, I'm not sure I have the right number . . . What, you recognize my voice? . . . I know it's been long time . . . I never want to bother you . . . You always have my utmost respect . . . No, I still got my check . . . Something else I need your help . . . Maybe I could get someone to give me a ride . . . Cortez Arms . . . Marshfield . . . Today? . . . Okay, about an hour . . . Still driving a Buick, right? . . . Don't I know my lady? . . . I'll be waiting . . . Latin Love."

Toilet flushing again.

"Got yourself a date?"

"Business."

"With a woman? You need me to spot you?"

"Business, just business."

"Got it, none of my business."

"No disrespect. I got to keep this quiet."

"Say no more. You just give your business a big hug, tell her, like I always did, 'Ain't no one else but Lady Love'; she'll know just who's representing."

"Latin Love."

"Brother Love."

LADY LOVE
ALEXIA 2004

It was a typical Sunday afternoon, like countless others for George and me over the last twenty years: lunch out after church, shopping at the Jewel, gathering the groceries on the stoop for the trek up three flights. But the usual was interrupted by a familiar, though at first unidentifiable, southern-tinged voice, "Hey girl, some of those bags for me?"

I saw the big boat of a car before I saw the face behind the wheel. The old Buick identified the voice and the driver, Arianna Lopez. "It's about time you showed up; you know how many times I drove around the block?" It had been years since we'd last seen Arianna. Incredibly, her hair was still blonde, no telltale dark roots, the golden-wheat color still real. Though double parked, she got out of the car, revealing a somewhat smaller figure than I remembered. She was still overweight, just not as overweight. Her eyes, drawn from rest-shortened nights but blue as ever, hinted at her once-famous beauty.

"Arianna, I thought I'd never see you again; you look great. You better have time for some coffee."

"I do if he'll park the car for me." She grimaced a bit as she tossed the keys at George, nearly hitting him in the face. She never spoke directly to George. It was a command, despite the conditional language. Arianna never liked George much.

"Surgery, again, on my knee, almost a year ago," she answered to my unasked question about her cane-aided limp. "You still up on the third floor? It's about time you moved down to the first, isn't it?" Again a command, suggesting her regular visits would be resuming. "Tell him, if he still wants to get some, those stairs will make his dick limp." Same Arianna.

I drip-brewed some Bustelo coffee while Arianna slowly made it up the stairs, sitting on the second-floor landing bench for five minutes, occasionally taking hits from an inhaler. "Nice dining set; I like these chairs. Saw the old table in the alley. What's the neighborhood come to? Nobody grabbed that table soon as you put it there?"

When I told her teenagers took three of the four unattached legs, making the rest of the table useless, she smiled. "At least some things never change; better than a baseball bat those dining-table legs." No question, the sultanness of swat had done plenty of swinging, and it wasn't baseballs that were soft when she was done. "Why didn't he leave the legs on? He still doesn't get the 'free market'; probably still reading Marx." Glancing away from the Che Guevara poster above the bookcase, she timed this last remark perfectly to George's stride at the top stair with the last of the groceries.

George kept right on walking into the kitchen, stopping to set the bags down, open the fridge, and swig on some juice. Quietly he sorted cans and boxes for the pantry; meats, produce, and dairy for the refrigerator. He settled himself in his office, adjacent to the dining room, and began clicking around the Internet. George didn't like Arianna any more than she liked him, so he situated himself where he could hear every word, every word she intended him to hear.

We updated each other. Arianna's daughter Rita was now living in Racine, Wisconsin. Rita's twins, Sol and Belle, who were raised more, than less, by Arianna, were living again with Rita and attending community college. One was working as a hairdresser; the other was thinking about going to culinary school. Our Nick, three years younger than the girls, was a senior in high school, on tenterhooks, waiting to hear where he had been accepted to college. My work, her health problems were constants, not because they connected us, but because they were each our constants. What really connected us was the neighborhood.

Arianna and I had first met in 1987 at a Harold Washington campaign office on Division somewhere near California. It was a long, wide storefront, divided front and back by a makeshift wall with a cheap wooden door in the middle. Both sides of the door fulfilled the cliché for smoke-filled rooms of political lore, in this case serving as the campaign hub for the predominantly Hispanic 26th and 31st Wards and ten precincts of the 32nd. People were constantly coming and going, picking up buttons, posters, literature, and for the serious, poll sheets. Some just hung around talking, because it was easier than walking the precincts.

The cross-section of campaign volunteers reflected the mosaic of the community I grew up in: a salad-like mix that tossed more and more in the fifties and sixties. Poles, hillbillies, Puerto Ricans, Italians, Mexicans, Blacks, even a smattering of Greeks like us, populated the wards of Westtown and Humboldt Park. What surprised me was the half-dozen machine-types mixed in with the eighty of us who were on hand for the ten a.m. Saturday kickoff and training session when it started at eleven fifteen.

Hanging close to the donuts and weak coffee was the heavy-set blonde I later learned was Arianna Lopez. After several double takes, I realized she was an election judge in my precinct, the 51st of the 32ⁿᵈ Ward. Was she trying to get a city job, or was she a spy? And what about the Colangelo brothers? Didn't the Washington staffers know these guys were fired for being Streets and San no-shows? The firing was one of Jayne Byrne's last-minute "reforms." The Colangelos must not have believed Harold when he said he was going to bury the patronage system.

Billy Rosario, 31ˢᵗ Ward Washington coordinator and a former aldermanic candidate who nearly toppled the legendary Tom Keane with 17 percent of the vote, revealed the secrets of the poll sheet: zeros, plusses, and minuses penciled next to voters' names. His message: elections are won by bringing in the voters you identified as supporters during the campaign, the plusses on the voter lists. On Election Day you had to bring them in, even if you had to drag them or babysit for them while they voted.

George Demas talked next about voter registration. In 1983, calling cold from a list of possible supporters, George nearly convinced me to support Harold Washington. "It's not just about the man; it's the plan. We registered 200,000 people to vote before the governor's election last fall. That's how Adlai Stevenson, III came within five thousand votes. Those were anti-Reagan votes, and they'll become anti-Byrne votes in this election." His anti-Reagan rap struck a chord with me, but he knew me as a feminist. Eventually I did vote for Jayne Byrne, Chicago's first woman mayor, in the democratic primary, but felt I was missing something by not being part of the Washington movement. After Washington's victory he'd call me from time to time, inviting me to community events or Washington political rallies. During one call about the 1986 special aldermanic elections, the conversation became flirtatious. Moments after hanging up, he called me again, to ask me on a date.

The number of people in the backroom dwindled as everyone received their assignments. Finally, almost as a question, he called,

"Arianna Lopez, Alexia Stone."

"Sorry you came up last, Alexia. I was just going by ward and precinct, 32–51, no higher than that here." He paused and winked his eye. "I'd keep you longer if I could."

"Honey, you better watch out for that one," Arianna drawled as we stepped out of the office. Pointing at a '72 Buick parked in front of a hydrant, she offered me a ride. "That's my car." The braggado started as she ripped the ticket from the windshield. "I have connections; never worry about tickets." Eventually her nonstop bluster gave way and revealed more substance. "I noticed you're not like most of the yuppies moving in." I hadn't noticed she noticed. "You don't call the cops soon as someone sits on your steps. Didn't move out Herb and Betty or raise their rent when you bought the place." But apparently she didn't know that George and I were involved romantically . . . or did she? "Had him up to your place yet?" I was getting angry, but her laugh started me laughing.

"Who are you, J. Edgar Hoover in drag?"

"No, I'm just Lady Love. I know everything 'cause I have to, and I know every teenager for blocks around. They talk, I listen. Information is power, honey."

Indeed, as we walked the neighborhood, I found out what an encyclopedia she was. She knew without the poll sheet who lived in most buildings. Quite often she knew who the plusses were before we talked to them. I insisted that we talk to everyone who would answer the door, despite Arianna's admonitions, "Don't bother with that one; precinct captain's cousin," or "You'll never get them out to vote; Jehovah's Witness."

After awhile I'd follow her advice. Then there were the buildings where she'd lay back, keeping out of sight, knowing not everyone in the neighborhood liked her.

It seemed some in the neighborhood had information on Arianna. One family I knew pretty well saw her leaning against her car down the block. "You're not with her, are you? If Washington is backed by the gangs, you won't get our votes." I assured the Millers I had never seen that woman leaning on that car before, which of course was literally true—I merely had seen her driving the car. Now I had bigger concerns about my precinct partner than whether she was trying to get a city job. I had to find out, was Arianna associated with a gang? If she was, my liberal tendencies would be tested.

On the next block came another clue in the form of a slender, dark-skinned Hispanic, mustached and wearing a fedora, sauntering down the stairs of a once-Victorian mansion turned rooming house. Seeing Arianna, he thumped his hand, forefinger and thumb forming an L, twice against the heart side of his chest. "*Señorita Luv*, the pleasure *está mío*. And who's your *amiga bonita*?"

"Gato, don't be flirting with my friend Alexia. We're here on business. We're going to make sure everyone here gets registered to vote for Harold."

Was that thumping the Latin Lord sign? I tried to hide my nervousness by getting to our business. I started reading the list of voters at 1372 N. Hoyne, but Arianna stopped me before I could finish reading the first name, "Aguirre, Domingo."

"Let me see that list. Gato, you're registered already. Tell you what, Alexia, you call it quits for the day. I'll cover this place with Gato," commanded Arianna. For the moment I was happy to comply. I just wanted to go home, drink some wine, and think about whether I was getting myself into a stew that I'd regret.

Seventeen years later I was thinking about that moment when Lady Love crossed the dining room to get closer to a photo hanging slightly crooked on the wall above the radiator. "What's he doing with Nick? Picture looks recent."

"Oh, George is Jesus's payee, has been for about a year and a half now. I took that shot when he stayed with us for a while."

"Jesus Cárdenas, I'll be. Last I heard, Gato was dead."

TURNING THE TAPES
LADY LOVE 2004

Toilet flushing, water running, whispering.

"Hope I'm working this thing right. I pressed the red button; its turning. Hell, if it doesn't pick up through my purse, no sweat to me. I should have told Gato I wouldn't tape my friend Alexia. But he says, '*Señora Love*, I got to find out if they messing with me.'

"Go figure. Sounds like they're the only ones helping Gato. Screw it, here goes."

Doorknob turns, footsteps.

"Alexia, you have a lot more pictures on the wall since last I was up here."

"Time doesn't stand still, Arianna."

"I like these shots of the neighborhood. Glad someone took pictures before they tore it all down."

"I've missed a lot. Sometimes without those pictures it's hard to remember what was where."

"You sure captured Nick growing up, too. I wish I had more of Rita and her kids."

"I could probably dig up a few. God knows, there were more than a few birthday parties when we were all together."

"Hey, is that who I think it is with Nick? Picture looks recent."

"Oh, George is Jesus's SSI payee. He's been getting his check and paying his rent for about a year and a half now. I took that shot when he stayed with us for a while."

"Jesus Cárdenas, I'll be. Last I heard, Gato was dead."

"According to Social Security he was, except it was his payee who died, not Jesus. George straightened that mess out then got stuck being his payee. Lately George has been trying to get his official documents so he can get his ID. Jesus can be a handful."

"Well he always was a character. Quite the ladies' man, too. I bet he flatters you no end."

"Calls us Mami and Dadi. He does compliment my cooking."

"That's Gato."

"Arianna, how well do you know Jesus, and how'd he get the name Gato? I remember we ran into him during the Washington campaign, over by the rooming house on Hoyne. He greeted you as 'Señora Luv.' That was the first time I heard your title."

"Haven't seen him in years, but back in the day of the Latin Lords he was Carlos's number one driver for quite a while. He'd come up to the apartment, eat with us. They'd play chess together. Carlos said he'd sneak his pieces up on you like an alley cat. Guess that's why he started calling him Gato."

"Chess? He plays chess with George, too."

"Bet you he kicks your ass most of the time, doesn't he, George? I know you're listening. Speaking of kicking ass, you should have heard them going on all night after they came back from that Ali-Foreman fight in Africa. 'Rumble in the Jungle' they called it."

"They went to Africa?"

"George, you are one dumb cookie. They saw it at the Congress Theater, like anyone else who knew what time it was. Guess you couldn't afford the ticket."

"How did Carlos meet Jesus?"

"I'm a little fuzzy on that, Alexia. They were both in Vietnam about the same time. Maybe they met at County Jail, waiting for some charges to come to trial. Could have been one, could have been the other. Maybe both. Carlos never told me exactly; he believed in the 'need to know' rule."

"Vietnam? How come the army never heard of Jesus Cárdenas?"

"George, Arianna and I are having this conversation. If you want to join in, come out of your hole in the wall office and you won't have to shout."

"She comes in my house and insults me. I'm not shutting up."

"How would I know why the army never heard of Gato? They lost the war, probably lost half their records. I seem to remember some draft dodgers like you burning up all kind of military records."

"You know that war didn't make any sense."

"Yeah, well, guys like Carlos and Gato didn't have much choice. It was jail or the jungle. What was it for you—college or Canada?"

"I would have gone to jail if they called my number. And I'll tell you another number that didn't come up, either. Jesus's immigration number when we tried to get his citizenship papers."

"Well, Gato voted. Made sure of it myself in '87. Matter of fact, he was proud to vote, seeing as your buddy Fidel isn't too keen on elections."

"All of a sudden you're Miss Red, White, and Blue. Next you'll be telling me that gangs are a time-honored American tradition."

"You're damn straight. No group ever got ahead without them, even the Greeks."

"Alexia, I'm out of here. Call me on my cell when she's gone."

Silence interrupted by heavy feet on stairs, door slamming.

More silence, then a wisp of laughter giving way to a loud uproar.

"Arianna, you know I'm going to be hearing about this for a week of Sundays."

"He never could take a tease." *More laughing.*

"You're not exactly subtle."

"Serves him right, getting mixed up with someone like Gato. What's he think he's going to do, reform him?"

"What do you mean reform him? He's not still with the Latin Lords, is he? Wait a second, I thought you said you hadn't seen him in years?"

"Sister, I'll bullshit George, but not you. When I said I heard Gato was dead, what I meant to say was that I heard he was such a drunk, such a *borracho*, he might as well be dead. No I haven't seen him, probably since the early nineties. Carlos was already in State-ville by then. Something happened to Gato and he lost his nerve. It happens to some of the brothers in the family. Once I moved out of the neighborhood I lost touch with a lot of folk. Then every once in a while I run into someone, hear about this one, that one. That's how I heard about Gato."

"You want me to say hello for you?"

"Sure, give him a kiss for me. Just don't give him my number. I don't want to have to change it again."

"What if he says he'd like to see you?"

"Tell him I'm a Pentecostal now; he won't ask again."

"You're not, are you?"

More laughter.

"I better go or I'll bust a gut. Pentecostal? If he ain't ready for reform, you think I am?"

"Arianna, let's not go another ten years."

"Honey, I don't have another ten."

Steps on stairs, labored breathing. Door opening and closing. Car passes.

Car door opening and closing. Ignition, engine revving and quieting.

"Well, I'm glad that's over with. Something's wrong when you're bugging one friend for another."

Car horn blows twice, playfully.

"Hey buddy, can't you see I'm pulling out?

"Another suburban construction worker. Why they working on a Sunday for, anyway?"

Radio running through stations.

"Wait a second."

Music playing in the background.

"Oh yes, they're playing 'The Great Pretender.' The Platters. No, they don't make songs like they used to."

Music again in the background.

Horn blares angrily.

"Hey, asshole, look before you pull out; this ain't the suburbs, you tourist."

Music ends. The announcer proclaims, "'The Great Pretender,' one of the greatest oldies of all time. Classic R&B by the Platters."

"If ever there was a pretender, it's Gato now. He sure is in a lonely world of make believe. Hey, that's his problem. All I can say is he better be looking for me. I'm not going up in that dive. He's not in front, I'm booking. OK, there he is. I'll get him. I'll just leave this recorder on, see how he likes being taped."

Sound of door opening.

"If it ain't the great pretender. Get in; I don't have all day."

"*Señora Luv,* my pleasure."

"Cut the crap. I got the tape, just like you wanted. I'm not sure what good it's going to do you. Like you asked, I steered the

72

conversation around to you; easy enough with your picture on their dining room wall."

"You mention I fight in Vietnam?"

"Said you were a vet, maybe met Carlos there. I didn't pussy-foot around, told them you were Carlos's driver in the '70s, even mentioned that Muhammad Ali fight you guys went to and never stopped talking about."

"'Rumble in the Jungle.' The Congress—that's the place to watch a fight."

"George wasn't quite buying the story, not with Immigration and the army coming back with nothing. You can listen yourself. That's why I made the tape, ain't it?"

"*Señora Luv*, now I owe you even more. How can I pay you back?"

"First of all, I don't want to hear from Alexia how you ripped them off or somehow got them in trouble. She's my kind of people."

"Mami, she has my utmost respect. I never hurt her."

"Well, watch out; there's more than one way to hurt someone, but maybe you drink too much to know that anymore."

"I can't help it; I drink."

"I don't have time to argue that. Like you'll hear when you listen to the tape, I told Alexia you're not ready to change; probably never will be."

"*Señora*, I have all this pressure, never have enough money, food."

"Gato, you forget who you're talking to? You think I'm a shrink? I've heard it all before. And I've seen people with worse jones than you lick it."

"But . . ."

"But never mind. As far as George goes, you know it, he knows it, I don't have much use for him. But you do. I'll give him this much, he knows how to work the bureaucracy. I guess it takes a bullshitter to figure out the BS. You know that too. Let him help you. Maybe he can get your papers."

"OK, but he better not mess up my check."

"He got your check back before, he's not going to let them take it away."

Sound of car door opening.

"Hold on, don't you want to see the latest pictures of the girls?"

"Of course. *Qué bonitas.* You do a good job raisin' them."

"What else a grandmother going to do when everybody else got problems? Now where you going? I'm still not done with you yet."

"Yes, *Señora,* something else I can do for you?"

"You remember Cuatro, don't you?"

"¡*Por supuesto*! I see him just before I move to the Cortez. End of 2002."

"Must have been when he was out on bail."

"We don't talk. I just pass him on the street driving around with Dadi, looking for rooms."

"Well, he was in Stateville with Carlos until just last month. Now he's staying at my place, but his schedule doesn't agree with mine. I love him, he's a brother, but he stays up most of the night as if he was still in the joint. I'm thinking, you guys used to run together, why not you let him stay with you till he has his own place? He's got some money, you know."

"*Señora,* my room is very small, room for only one bed, and Memo, he's already crashing with me."

"So you may all have to share one bed. From what I remember, Memo was always inclined that way."

"He sleeping on the floor. You know I like women."

"Easy, Gato; no disrespect. I'm going to send Cuatro to see

you. You work it out or not. It's up to you."

"*Gracias, Señora.* Anything else?"

"You're so eager to go. Don't you want your tape?"

"I forget."

Pause, some rustling sounds.

"Here."

"What, it still running?"

"Guess I forgot to shut if off when I left Alexia's. Well now you got it, friends bugging friends. And one more thing: lose my number."

ADMISSION ESSAY
MEMO 1972

Editor's note: In the *Prologue* and in a few other chapters, Jesus's friend Memo is mentioned. On occasion they seem to share a room, although as Jesus made clear to Lady Love in *Turning the Tapes*, Memo slept on the floor. You might recall Jesus bringing Memo along with him to see Nick in a school play at Whitney Young in 2003 (*My Greek Family*). When Jesus introduced Memo to me, I commented later to George that he looked vaguely familiar. But with Jesus's antics that night, I soon stopped wondering about Memo's identity. Recently, however, while doing a bit of spring cleaning, I found a box filled with student essays I collected while teaching English at *Casa de Westtown* in the early '70s. Taking a break from my clutter reduction tasks, I started paging through the essays, trying to remember the faces that went with the names, occasionally reading a poem or short topic assignment. As soon as I saw the name Mamerto Rodriguez, it hit me—Memo. I hadn't recognized him a year ago because, like me, he had aged. More so, life on the streets had taken its toll. Perhaps he recognized me, but if he did he didn't say anything.

Mamerto had been a promising GED student with a way with words. I encouraged him to apply to the University of Illinois Circle campus, where I also taught. If Mamerto could pass the GED he would be accepted under UIC's open admission program still in effect at the time. I told him I would work on his application with him and review and type his admission essay. A week later he handed me the essay, telling me it wasn't done and asking me to tell him if he was on the right track. On the way home from school that day I read it on the bus. Its honesty and detail took me by surprise. I wasn't fazed by his writing style, but I knew it needed substantial editing. The material was too open and frank for a 1972 college admissions essay. That very night I typed it up, only correcting misspelled words. I wanted the decisions on what to cut and how to revise to be Mamerto's, not mine.

Two days later, a Wednesday, Mamerto did not show up to class. Neither did he attend on Friday or again the next Monday. In fact, I didn't see Mamerto again, until Jesus introduced us more than twenty years later at Whitney Young. Mamerto's unfinished, unedited essay follows. Perhaps now that our lives have crossed again, he can tell me the rest of his story.

Alexia Demas
May 2004

My name is Memo Rodriguez. Memo is short for Mamerto. I was named for my grandfather but no one ever called me that. My people are originally from Texas but I was born here in Chicago in 1953. My father came here a few years before that and got a job at one of the tanneries along the Chicago River. Then he sent for my mother and my older sister and brother. I was the first of six more children born in Chicago.

For many years we moved from one too small apartment to another in the area near Pulaski Park. Some people think that all of the Mexicans living in that neighborhood are illegal. But we were Chicanos, not only legal, but US citizens. In fact, my people were US citizens before the Polish came to this country and that neighborhood from the late 1800s up till the depression. A lot of big names in Chicago politics like Rostenkowski, Gabinski, and Jorzak came for the same reason my father did, to work in the tanneries and foundries along the river.

They built up the neighborhood and the Catholic churches and schools. They got into politics and trades and businesses and started moving up and out along Milwaukee Avenue all the way out to the far part of the city and the suburbs. After World War II there were jobs. At the worst places, like the tanneries, people like my father came up from southern Texas to take those jobs.

I think because our fathers and mothers were Catholic and worked in the same factories that the Polish families had started out in we were tolerated. Not accepted, tolerated. We could attend the Church, but when the mass changed from Latin it went to Polish and English, not Spanish. Same with the Catholic school where English and Polish were taught. The Polish continued to move out but hung on to their buildings and rented them to second generation Mexicans and more and more to hillbillies and illegals.

But as I got older I never felt accepted. Perhaps it was because I was scrawny and not much good in sports and not good at all in a fight. And in that neighborhood there were always fights. Because of this they called me sissy. Sometimes even my brother Eddie would say, "What are you some kind of a sissy?" At that age 9, 10, 11 in the early '60s we weren't thinking sexually. Sissy was a boy who acted like a girl.

And the more they teased me, the more I did act like a girl. I was shy and I liked to dance. At the class parties, I was just about the only boy who danced. I'd sneak peeks at my sister's teenage magazines. I'd read about the movie stars and the men like Frankie Avalon, Bobby Daren, and of course Elvis the most. Unlike most of the boys, I was a good student at the Catholic school, some called me Sister Jadwiga's class pet.

When I became a teenager I got pimples and body hair, especially around my privates and because my grades were good for 9th grade I got into Lane Tech. Eddie had graduated the year before. He was a star on the baseball team. I made friends, sort of, with a couple of guys in my homeroom and my biology class. Johnny Jessup was from Uptown and his family was from Kentucky. Aaron Stein was Jewish and lived in Albany Park. His hair was really curly and his nose a little hooked and his green eyes really sparkled. I didn't know then that I was attracted to him.

My main problem in school was PE. They pushed hygiene in health class and they expected us to take showers after gym. I wasn't worried about someone seeing my hairy privates but about getting hard. One day two guys from the football team started laughing and pointing at me. "Look he's getting a hard-on." That was the first time I heard the words faggot and *maricón*. A couple of days later I was jumped after school by the same guys. I didn't dare tell anyone. I told my parents my black eye was from an elbow I got playing basketball. But they seemed to see the changes in me.

Mama would ask me, "*¿Es todo bien, mi hijo?*" My father just said less and less to me. Eddie stopped letting me tag along with his friends to movies, ballgames and especially the pool hall. He'd say, "You're too young to hang around with us." Maria my sister must have felt sorry for me, so she invited me to a couple of her friends' parties.

I started acting sick a lot so I wouldn't have to go to school but Mama stopped believing that I was sick. Then I played hooky. That's how I met Gabe at a Vienna hot dog place a couple of blocks from school. I was trying not to draw any attention in there sitting at the counter along the wall with my back to everyone else. Maybe he had seen me in the stands at the school baseball games or waiting outside the locker door for Eddie after the games. He sat at the stool next to mine as I tried to look the other way.

"You're Eddie Rodriguez's brother, right?"

Was he really talking to me? The guy who when he came to the plate I was always anxious and wanting him to get a big hit.

He didn't wait for me to answer. "Eddie was the best shortstop our team ever had. Hard to fill his shoes."

"You're telling me?" I managed to say.

"One motion: field the ball, fire to first. Smooth. You ever play ball?"

"Do I look like I ever played anything but seven to nine playground league?"

He laughed, not at me like Eddie might, but in a way inviting me to laugh too.

I did a Marlon Brando imitation. "I could have been an All-Star. The coach, he just didn't believe in me."

Now Gabe was busting a gut and soon I was too.

From then on we'd look for each other at that hot dog joint. After awhile we'd make dates like, "When should we cut school next?" Since it was winter and Gabe didn't have practice we'd meet almost every day after school.

But I wondered, Why does Gabe have anything to do with me? Everything Gabe was, I was not. Gabe was tall, athletic looking with wavy, reddish-brown hair, unusual for a Puerto Rican. His complexion was smooth, his voice deep, with only a slight accent. The previous spring he was the leading hitter on the varsity team as a freshman.

I had a lot of firsts with Gabe. My first beer, my first marijuana, my first blow jobs, both ways, my first kiss, my first love, my first heartbreak. Whatever it was we had was over by spring. The start of his ball season, the end of mine. When we had been seeing each other I never minded his displays down the hall with girls on each arm. Now it hurt, so I played hooky more and more and almost flunked ninth grade. The school gave me one semester probation. Get back on track or I'd be out of Lane and into Wells.

It was the summer of 1968. What a crazy year. Scenes from Vietnam were on the news every night. Around the time Gabe was giving me the cold shoulder the West Side was on fire after Martin Luther King was killed. Students in France rioted. Then Bobby Kennedy got killed. One day in August Aaron called me up. Said he and Johnny were going down to Grant Park. Did I want to protest the war? I didn't know anything about protesting but I was afraid Eddie might get drafted and I wanted to see Aaron.

We agreed to meet at the Armitage "L" stop. It was early afternoon when we made our way into the park east of Michigan and Adams and headed south through the park toward Balbo Avenue where the largest group of protestors gathered. Even though there were a lot of police down there it seemed like a big hippie party. Aaron saw some girls he knew in a group of about eight, so we walked over. Everyone was wearing red bandanas and smoking Panama Red. They didn't seem to care that there were pigs all around. A few hits later neither did I.

I don't know how much time went by then the mood suddenly changed. People with armbands started coming through alerting the crowd, now three times more packed than when we first arrived.

"Get ready, the pigs are coming."

"Stay with your affinity groups."

"Put damp cloths over your nose and mouth, they'll be tear gassing us."

I was really getting into the chants, "1,2,3,4 we don't want your fucking war. Hey, hey LBJ, how many kids you kill today?"

Between the chants I heard a few words here and there from dueling bull horns.

". . . unlawful assembly . . ."

"The whole world is watching."

". . . last chance . . ."

"The whole world is watching."

". . . you will be arrested . . ."

"The whole world is watching."

I couldn't see what was happening unless I jumped straight up and caught a glimpse of a line of light blue riot helmets. The next moments are a jumble of memories. *Pop. Pop.* Clouds of grey smoke. The crowd moving at first back toward the lake, then people running every which way. I could see night sticks coming down on heads and backs. A pig pushed Johnny down and raised his club. Not thinking, I grabbed the cop from behind, twisting him enough for Johnny to get up. The pig tripped and we ran and ran. My eyes were burning from the pungent gas so we kept running toward the lake and toward the Art Institute. Aaron was yelling to us from an entrance to the parking garage below the park. We ducked down the stairs not thinking it was probably a dumb thing to do. But there were no police near the stairway we went down.

We crouched behind cars and scooted from one to the next heading as far south as we could go and changed levels more than a few times. Sometimes we just sat to let the time go by. It was dark when we went upstairs near Jackson. Flashing lights broke the constant sodium-vapor light. Sirens and chants seemed to be coming from a few blocks south of where we were. We looked at each other.

We didn't need to speak to know we all had enough. We made it to the Ravenswood "L" and then sat apart from each other in case the police might think we were a group of protesters. Before Armitage, Aaron came by and said he knew a hippie house near the Belmont stop we could go and watch the news on TV. We all wanted to know whether they would show the police cracking heads.

BARBECUE
ALEXIA 2004

Was it a coincidence that Mamerto's life and mine crisscrossed again after a span of thirty-odd years through such an improbable third party as Jesus Cárdenas? Some may ponder the cosmic nature of coincidences, but I was just plain curious. What had happened to Mamerto since he handed me that amazing essay and then disappeared? The promising writer of then seemed a hopeless write-off now. Memorial Day was approaching and might provide a perfect opportunity to find out over barbecued chicken and shrimp. George hesitated as usual, figuring he'd have to spend his time with Jesus and face the moral dilemma of offering him a beer or not while I was catching up with Mamerto. Of course he was right. Then again, I countered, he'd be able to show off his grilling techniques and perhaps win a game of chess or two.

George was already in the yard getting the fire started when Jesus rang the bell at three, exactly the time we suggested in the note we left under his door at the Cortez Arms. Mamerto was a few steps behind on the stoop, his head bowed, slightly swaying.

"Hello, Mamerto, or would you rather I called you Memo?"

With a question mark on his face, Jesus turned back toward Memo. "What, you know her too?"

"Miss Stone," Mamerto said to me.

"It's Demas now, but call me Alexia," I said, but wondered to myself about the "too" of Jesus's question.

"Hey Mami, where's Dadi?"

"He's in the yard waiting for you. He can use your help setting up the table and chairs. The chess set is already down there."

As Jesus swaggered toward the gate at the side of the building, I had to wonder. He had next to nothing; nothing actually, but he still had that "I'm a bad-ass" walk. Mamerto started to follow him.

"Memo, how about giving me a hand?"

As Mamerto followed me up the stairs, I heard an unevenness in his step. His eyes were red, his face puffy, still showing signs of youthful acne. But he also seemed more muscular than when I knew him as one of my students.

Once in the apartment he asked if he could use the washroom. From the kitchen I could hear him washing his hands.

"Miss Demas, I didn't think you recognized me."

"I didn't last year. But a few weeks ago I found something of yours while going through old papers. Do you remember the essay you wrote before you stopped coming to class?"

"That's a long time ago."

"You were a good writer. You ever write now?"

"Sometimes I write a poem or a song, but I always lose them. You know I don't exactly have my own place."

"Well, it's good of Jesus to let you stay with him."

"Gato's a friend, but it's not free, and I don't have a regular check like he does."

"How do you support yourself?"

"Sometimes I work at the tire shop, or I might wash dishes for a while at a restaurant till I get fed up with the way they treat me. Over the years I've done a lot of different things."

"Ever peel shrimp?"

"You kidding? I'm a pro. I went to cooking school. Did short order for a few years."

As Mamerto kept talking I pulled the bag of uncooked jumbo shrimp from the fridge, then set him up with a sharp knife and colander by the sink. He knew what he was doing all right.

"Wow, one motion to slice the back of the shrimp and pull out the vein. Smooth."

"Hey, that's like I wrote about my brother's fielding all those years ago."

"So you do remember that essay."

"You know Gus's Corner? I worked there till he had to hire his cousin just over from Greece. Hey Alexia, you're Greek, right? George too?"

"Yes, we are." He was already rinsing the twenty or so shrimp.

"Don't tell me. Your marinade is going to be olive oil, lemon, oregano, salt, pepper."

"Already made. Next up, coleslaw. Are you up for some chopping?"

"Bring it on."

In two minutes the entire head of cabbage was perfectly sliced and diced for a Puerto Rican–style coleslaw.

"OK, you've earned a rest. I have something for you to look at." From my desk I retrieved his essay and handed it to him. "Take your time."

He sat down at the table where he had chopped the cabbage. First he just thumbed through the pages. He paused on the last and seemed to be reading the end first. He closed his eyes, cradled his forehead in hands, then pushed back his neck-length grey-streaked black hair, paged backward, and began reading from the start. As I cleaned up from the food preparation I caught a glimpse of a smile, then moisture at eye's edge moments later.

As he read, I tried to stay busy gathering plates, cups, utensils, napkins, and a tablecloth into a basket for easy carrying down the stairs. When he finished, I hoped he would break the ice. But instead, the sound of footsteps on the back steps and a dog's woof broke the silence. The porch door swung open, revealing our two strays—Jesus, still swaggering, and Domino, our border collie, panting and wagging his tail.

"Mami, what's taking you so long? The fire is hot. What you think, we waiting for the pizza man?"

"Well, we were waiting for you to help us carry all the food and supplies downstairs. We only have four hands between us here."

"Your wish is my command."

"Jesus, you're no genie, but you can take the basket with the plates and everything. And this baking pan with the chicken. The chicken will take the longest. We'll bring down the shrimp, coleslaw, and lemonade."

"How long the chicken take, enough for Dadi and me to play another game of chess?"

"You'll have time for at least one game. We'll be down in a bit."

As Jesus retreated down the stairs with Domino at his heals, Mamerto and I smiled at each other. "Gato and I go back quite awhile. Of course it's different now than back in the '80s."

"How so?"

"We were riding high reaping the benefits of our business. But we didn't have much to do with each other then, except business. He was part of the wholesale operation. You could say I was more on the retail end."

"You mean drugs?"

"Let's just say there are different kinds of markets. I had a few gay bars where I'd make the rounds with the product supplied by Jesus's group."

"Latin Lords? You were with them too?"

"No. Like I said, they were the suppliers. Because of my 'persuasion,' I was tolerated, not accepted. Actually, if it weren't for Gato, I might not even be alive. Most of the gang was made up of a bunch of macho types, with a bite worse than their bluster.

"There was a gay bar on Armitage west of Kimball. Usually we'd stay inside because we didn't want any trouble with anyone. Well, one summer night the air conditioning wasn't working so a few of us went outside to see if we could catch a breeze." He paused, perhaps feeling the heat of that night. "You have some of that lemonade?"

"Of course. I should have offered it sooner," I said. "So this was in the '80s?"

"Can't say for sure. But I remember Jane Byrne was mayor."

After drinking half the glass, he got up and walked restlessly around the kitchen. He told his story, not just with words but with his movements. "A convertible pulls up with three gangbangers in it. I went toward the bangers as they got out of the car, giving cover to my friends as they scurried back toward the club door, 'Anything I can do for you?' I said.

"'You can suck me off, *maricón*'. This guy was slick. It's night but he's wearing sunglasses, pressed slacks, silk shirt, gold chains.

"'And while you're taking care of *mi amigo*, you can take me in your ass,' the heavy one threatened. My friends were inside now, but I knew no one would call the police. Why bother? The bangers would be gone and the bar would be raided. So it was just going to be me against the three of them.

"'Tell you what. Come inside the club and I'll give your skinny friend a hand job at the same time.' Now I was the one with the bluster.

"The skinny one, in a thick accent, said, 'Faggot, you got balls. Now let me see what you carrying.'"

"I figured that's what they really wanted, so I gave them my little patterned bag, hung around my neck with its long purple string. The night was young so I only had about $40 in cash. More valuable was what I had in the inside of my slacks.

"The slick one wasn't satisfied. 'Where's your stash, queenie?'

"'OK, OK, handsome. Let's see what I have inside my panties.' His mouth dropped as I unbuttoned my pants.

"The skinny one stepped forward to take what I pulled out— six little white paper packets. The bruiser moved in. 'You're looking for more than something up your ass, you deal in our territory.'

"'I'm dealing in your territory? I do my business inside. So our club is your territory, honey?' I didn't know where these words were coming from. Remember, I was the kid no good in a fight.

"Lucky for me, Gato, who you may have guessed was the skinny one, stepped in front of me. He was small, but his body language alone stopped *El Gordo*. '*Hombre*, use your brain one time. I do the talking now.' Turning to me, he asked, 'You got as much as you need?'

"'I could use more; they're all looking for some blow. Here and the other bars.'

"'No names, but where you get it now?'

"'Not in Chicago. Let's just say I have friends in Milwaukee.'

"'That's a long way. We could do some business.'"

"So that's how you met Jesus?" I asked. "You know, you're quite the storyteller, Mamerto."

"That's no story, Alexia. That's how it went down."

"I'm sorry. I don't doubt you. I liked the way you told your story."

For a minute neither of us talked. "Mamerto, do you know how to type? I have an old typewriter I could give you; it's a portable. I'd like to see you write down more of your experiences."

"Would you believe I went to business school for about six months in the '90s? Can you give me some paper too? I'll give it a try, but I'm not promising much."

Mamerto walked out to the back porch and looked out the window. "They're still playing chess. I think I'll go down and check them out. Got something for me to carry down?"

"Here, take the bowl with the shrimp, and this big bottle of lemonade. I'll be down in a minute with a few other things."

I hadn't eaten a thing yet, but already this was the best barbecue we'd ever had. I was hungry for more.

CHECKMATE
GEORGE 2004

My luck. Just as I finish mowing the lawn and raking up the cut grass, the dogs and I hear the clanking of the front gate being opened at the front of the gangway. Domino and Bruno race each other to see who it is. I brace to see what kind of condition Gato will be in before our barbecue even begins.

"Dadi, I get that," he offers, whisking the yard bag from my hand, then sauntering with it back to the garbage cans on the opposite side of our back fence. "Dadi, why don't you wait till I get here? I don't cut the grass good enough?" Loosely translated: if I had waited to let him mow the grass, I would have felt obliged to give him five bucks for his efforts.

"I wanted to cut it before you arrived so we'd have time for chess while the fire's getting hot and the food's cooking."

"You know I'm going to kick your ass."

"You might get lucky."

"What you and Mami cooking?"

"Chicken, shrimp, and corn. Alexia is making coleslaw. Where's Memo?"

"Oh, he went upstairs with Mami. She say she need a hand."

"And I can use one too."

In barely five minutes we set up the tables and chairs, but Gato was moving like it had been five hours. "Hey Dadi, what you got to drink?"

"Alexia's fresh-squeezed lemonade. She has it upstairs. Can you go up and get it?"

"Lemonade. What, no beer?"

Of course he saw me raise my brow as I tried to look away from him.

"You know I respect Mami, don't want me drinking."

"Mami? What about me?"

"You thirsty too? Here ..." He pulls a quart bottle from a deep cargo pocket, well past the knee of his baggy denim shorts.

Now I'm looking right at him, my lips pursed, trying to contain my anger. The afternoon is still early. He knocks down a long hit of the Miller brew, wipes his mouth with his forearm, smiling wickedly at me as if to ask, "This between you and me, right?"

Once the fire was lit, we set up the pieces of the glass chess set he bought for me at a yard sale and gave me the previous Fathers' Day. Usually I need a warm-up game, and that day was no exception. On my sixth move I made a careless mistake, starting an exchange that left me a Rook and a Knight down. I resigned and got up to check the fire.

It was hot, so I asked Gato to go up and get the chicken. The bone-in breasts and thighs I figured would take a good forty minutes on the Weber. Enough time for us to have at least one more game.

While Gato was upstairs, Nick rode up to the back gate on his mountain bike. He was in the chess club at school and volunteered on his own to record our next game. "Algebraic or traditional notation?"

"Traditional, of course. I know, the algebraic is less ambiguous, but the traditional method gives the moves from each player's perspective. No translation necessary."

"If you say so."

Gato and Domino returned from upstairs. He exchanged greetings with Nick. "You staying out of trouble?"

"Trying to," said the usually taciturn Nick.

After placing the wet cherrywood chips on the coals, I aligned the chicken pieces on the side of the grill without the coals directly underneath. Cooked with the cover on, the chicken would wind up with a sweet, smoky taste. That done, I sat down for our next game.

I was White for the second game. As I contemplated a Queen's Pawn opening, Gato took another long hit on his beer. I opened, unusually, King's Bishop's Pawn to the 4th rank, with Gato quickly responding King's Pawn to King 3. But his accompanying verbal move was more surprising.

"Memo says he knows you."

"Sure, we met last year at Nick's school play." I played my King's Pawn to K4.

"No, way before that. In Milwaukee." He played King's Bishop to Q3.

As I searched my memory, I scanned the young board. No one like Memo came to mind, but Queen's Pawn to Q3 looked good, protecting two pawns with one move. "Can't place him." I didn't let on that I had lived in Milwaukee before moving down to Chicago.

His King's Knight to Bishop 3 threatened my Pawn. He had a plan I'd have to figure out, but the verbal game continued as well. "You ever work on ships?"

Had I ever mentioned to Gato my days as a stevedore in Milwaukee? "You mean the navy? No way." I shored up my exposed

King's Pawn, moving my Queen's Knight to Bishop 3.

"Memo says he load ships same time you did in Milwaukee," he countered, pinning my Knight with his Black Bishop. With each move he lined up his arsenal and weakened my defense.

"Easy for him to say, if you told him I worked there." I had no choice but to bring my King's Knight out to King 2 to defend my Queen's Knight.

"How can I tell him what I don't know? I thought you from Chicago all your life." He castled.

The two games, chess and chatter, continued, cat and mouse. I thought I was developing a strong position in the center of the board, especially after an exchange of pieces there left me up a Bishop. But in haste my twentieth move proved rather shaky. Gato took advantage and opened a hole in my defense, taking a Knight and checking my King. It was a move I should have anticipated. "It look like he know Mami too."

20 White Q-Kt5?

"Nothing new there. He was her student thirty years ago."
I tried bravely to use my Queen's Pawn to block the Check and
threaten his Queen.

The game was tight. His advantage was positional, our pieces
were even, but it was getting harder to concentrate on the chess.
When he moved his Queen away from my Pawn, he threatened
both a Rook and my White Bishop. Instead of interposing my Bishop between his Queen and my Rook I moved it two ranks farther.
He pounced on my Rook.

I tried to slow down the usually rapid pace of our games, but
by the twenty-eighth move a serious exchange of pieces seemed in-
evitable. By the thirty-third move seven pieces were taken, including
both Queens and one of his Rooks. I was down only a Knight at that
point, with the board as follows, when Memo came down the back
stairs carrying some things for our meal.

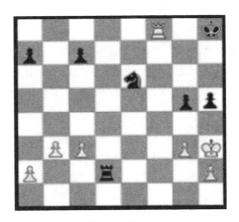

After 33 White RxR

I looked at him (though not too hard, as we nodded hello to each other). But still I could not place him. He said nothing at first, but approached the table where we were playing. "Who's winning?"

"Who you think?" boasted Gato.

"Not so fast. I'm not out of this one yet," I offered.

"You ask him yet?" Memo says to Gato.

"Oh he asked me, something about loading ships in Milwaukee."

"Well, you remind me of a guy I used to work with up there. I was a longshoreman for several years there in the '70s."

"You don't strike me the type."

Up until this point I continued to play, somewhat absent-mindedly, even as Gato checked me on the thirty-fourth and thirty-fifth moves. After Gato's thirty-sixth move, an endgame Pawn advance to King's Rook 4, I was dumbstruck by Memo's move.

"What's the type, Mr. Demas, or can I call you 'Just George?' Seems there were all types working there: Blacks, hippies, Filipinos, a Greek or two, a few women, even a Mexican gay guy. Queen Danny would remember me, would he ever."

Gato was visibly impatient now that the conversation was between Memo and me. "Excuse me, we still playing chess?"

"You should talk, Gato. You're the one who started talking about Memo, matter of fact as soon as the game started." But I did start to ponder my next move even as I pondered this latest turn of events. No doubt Memo had worked at the Port of Milwaukee while I did. He knew my nickname, knew my gang mate Danny Stevens, who made no attempt to hide his feminine side. As I pretended to concentrate on the game, I made such a questionable move that Gato's path to Checkmate was as clear cut as Memo's.

37 White R–B8+??
Black to Checkmate in 4

Then it hit me: Hot Rod. I'd never known him as Mamerto or Memo, just Hot Rod, short for Rodriguez, of course. He wasn't in our gang, because he was about twelve or thirteen guys down the seniority list. Once or twice, during the year of the wildcat strike, he was a fill-in jeep driver in our hold. We didn't talk, but he and Danny sure used to put on a show for us.

"Just testing you, Hot Rod," I said, waving my hand, not having to wait for a high-five.

Nick and Gato played the next game of chess as I started paying attention to the chicken. Memo brought a chair over next to the grill.

"How long you last at the docks?" I asked Memo. "You might remember, I left in '73, took a job on the assembly line at American Motors."

"A couple years after that," Memo answered. "I started supplementing my income when things got slow down there. Before I knew it I was making more selling weed than at the Port. Remember the lead man, Paul Simmons?"

"Old black guy, tall, maybe six-six? Yeah, he sure was easy going, great to work for."

"Yeah, that's him. He'd been smoking reefer for thirty years. He hooked me up with some sources in the Black community. He never wanted a cut. I think he just thought the world was a better place when people were mellow, like him."

"What about Queen Danny?" I asked. "I lost touch with him once I left the docks."

"Would you believe he joined the navy?"

"Why the hell would he enlist?"

"For one thing, there's no shortage of lonely guys in the navy, especially when you're on a nuclear sub, like he was for months at a time."

"Well I always liked him, in spite of his persuasion."

"Are you sure it wasn't because of his persuasion? How about me, do you like me?" he said as he flashed me a flirting smile just like Danny would to everyone on the docks, longshoremen and ships' crews alike.

HE AIN'T GOT MY BACK
GATO 2004

That barbecue too spicy. My stomach burn bad, real bad. Pretty soon I have the hot shits. So I have to leave. And I leave without Memo. Why I bring him anyway? Just 'cause Mami say to bring him don't mean I have to. This guy, he know them longer than me. He know them longer they know each other. How that figure? That's like me beating Bobby Fisher.

Now Mami and Dadi they got their new poor boy. They gonna help him, forget about me? That *maricón*? And what they think? I'm like him 'cause I charge him to sleep on my floor? Forget him. I'll get someone else in the room. Lady Love say Cuatro need a place to crash. But that's been two checks since she told me.

Maybe me leaving not so good an idea. Who know what Memo tell them, I'm not there? If he tell them the time he find me at Humboldt Park, I kill him. It's different for him. He like men. I do it, I need the money. Plus, I don't take it. I only give it.

I remember, he see me standing behind that guy. He wait till I'm done and I'm walking away. "Gato," he call from behind some

99

bushes near the buffalo statues. I don't recognize him. "Gato, it's Memo."

It's years since I see him, not sure how many. He's heavier, not looking too good. I guess I'm not looking too good either. Did he see me?

"Memo, what? You out?" I hear he did time for cocaine.

"Yeah, I'm out awhile now. You surprise me, seeing you in our part of the park."

"What's it to you?"

Memo start to laugh. "Hey, you're the one who once accuse me of dealing in your territory. From the looks of us, neither of has anything. So do what you got to do, just be careful."

"No one messing with me, including you, unless you want this knife up your ass."

He flip some rubbers at me. "These will do you more good than that knife. Haven't you heard of AIDS?"

"I ain't no faggot."

"I saw what I saw, but I don't care. You know what I like from the day you met me. By the way, you can get AIDS from the ladies, too. You helped me back then, maybe saved my life. I'm just trying to return the favor."

"Hey, where you staying?"

"I have a place on California, now that I'm working. What about you?"

"I'm in the park two, three months, since they sell the rooming house on Hoyne."

"Damn. You've been staying there forever. I know you know Gus's Corner. I'm doing short order there. Come by before seven if you need a meal."

"In the morning? That's kind of . . ."

"Gato, don't give me that bull. You think I haven't been in your shoes? You sleep in the park, you're up early with the sun if the wet grass don't wake you first."

I stop at Gus's enough. Not too much; wear out my welcome. They not too busy. Memo, come and sit with me. They got a good breakfast, eggs, potatoes, bacon. I sweep up the parking lot. So Memo and I get to know each other again.

Different than when we dealing. I got nothing on him. He supplying me with food, sometime he lend me money. When it start getting cold he says I can stay at his place, as long he don't have no boyfriend staying the night. He never try anything with me. He don't ask, but I give him money when I have it, after I get my check.

Mac Wilson, my payee, get my check each month. I go over to the West Side Y and get my cash from him. We drink away a big part of it, first of the month. Be drunk silly, crash there too, and other places. For a while a lady lets me stay at her place. Two hundred a month for a closet. Just room for a mattress and the little TV Dadi give me. No way I mess with her. Too fat. Anyway, she sleep with her German shepherd; he don't let no one touch her.

Then the next winter Memo no longer at Gus's. Yianni don't say why or where he go. Probably don't know. I ask around; no one knows. Next spring and summer, I look in Humboldt Park, ask people; no one knows. I'm sleeping most of the time in Wicker Park, three or four of us. More than a few *Cubanos* live in the senior building 'cross the street. I don't know how, they ain't that old. They pay low rent, still they want some dollars when it rains, especially that *gusano* Salvador. Same one ripped me off when he my payee and I get my big check for back pay.

Then all of sudden Memo, he's back. He ain't saying where he's at when he gone. First he has some stuff he's selling. Maybe he in Milwaukee again. He's doing some of it again, crack I think. When that runs out he's hustling junk like me, fixing tires. He don't have no check like me, but my check don't last half the month. Even now with Dadi it don't last.

Both of us would be over in that part of Humboldt Park when we had to. But ever since that first day he saw me there, I protect myself. Some others, they had the AIDS and they die, like he say. Most from the needles. Lucky the alcohol's enough for me. I'm glad he's back; now I owe him. So I watch his back. He talk good, but he can't fight.

Memo go with me to Mac's when we find out he's dead. Dead almost three weeks. Mac paid the Y by the week. He don't have nobody, so they just clean out his room. What? He's holding my ID, holding it till I pay him back my $40 advance. Memo go with me, too, to the Currency where Mac picked up the check. It's gone. Gloria say by law they have to send it back, or they can't cash nobody's check. Memo go with me to Social Security, keep me from punching the security guard when they tell me I needed ID to get my check.

Memo go with me the whole time I'm dead. He'd even tell everyone in the park, "Look at Gato. He's dead." He's watching when I run across the street telling Dadi and Mami I'm dead. He always watch Dadi from a distance. Now I know why. When he tell me he know Dadi from long ago, he said, "You tell him, I'll kill you. I'll tell you when you can tell him."

Now everybody know everybody. But he better not tell everything. I don't care. I love him like my brother. He talk, I still kill him.

Wait, I think I hear someone talking in the hall.

Knocking at the door.

"Who's there?"

"Open up. It's me."

"Open it yourself; it ain't locked."

"I can't. I don't have a free hand."

Door creaking open, then shutting, lock latching.

"What's that?"

"A typewriter. Ms. Demas gave it to me. Says I should type up some of my stories and poems."

"I don't got room for that. I'm not sure I got room for you, Mamerto."

"You got your recorder, now I got my typewriter, Gato. Excuse me, Jesus."

"You hear about what happen at the park?"

"No, I came straight back here."

"Just on the news. They say they knife someone in Wicker Park."

"You think it was Victor, talking crazy about someone he shouldn't talk about?"

"Word get out, that's what happens. More than one way to stab some in the back. *¿Entiende*, Memo?"

"I get it, Gato. You think I'm talking too much to your Dadi and Mami. I talk about me. I didn't say anything about you, except you're my oldest friend."

"Keep it that way. You see, I still know how to use a knife. And if you don't know what I'm talking about, just rewind my tape and listen."

FREEDOM OF INFORMATION
GEORGE 2004

Now that we had discovered all the connections between Memo, Alexia, and me, Gato's identity bugged me more and more. For some reason that I couldn't quite figure out, I was more inclined to help Gato obtain the ID that could be key to his long-term survival. A lawyer friend recommended a not-for-profit agency, *Familias Unidas*, which provided services to immigrants.

When Gato came to pick up his cash for July, I suggested a visit. "This is our best bet, Gato. Immigration must have some record of you."

"Last time we get nothing."

"But I was shooting in the dark. The lawyers at *Familias Unidas* are experts."

"Lawyers, I got no money to pay lawyers."

"This is not-for-profit, strictly donations for their services. I'll take care of it."

"You know I appreciate what you and Mami do for me. You do too much already."

"Look, Gato, you get your ID straightened out, you could get into subsidized housing."

"Do I look like a senior citizen?"

"Subsidized isn't just for the elderly. It's for low income and disabled, too. But you have to have ID."

"How much the low rent?"

"Thirty percent of your income. That's about $200 per month, less than half what you pay at that dump the Cortez Arms."

He seemed to be doing the math.

"That place getting bad. Everybody doing crack in there."

"Including you?"

"What? I told you I don't do drugs, just drink."

Lucky for me, *Familias Unidas* was open by appointment on Saturdays. I could take him without having to miss work. Unluckily, by noon on the agreed-upon Saturday, Gato had already been drinking. "One morning, you couldn't wait? You better be on your best behavior," I told him even though he didn't seem too far gone. Our appointment was for one p.m., and Alexia wasn't too happy that Gato's problems were taking up another Saturday afternoon.

We arrived fifteen minutes early for our appointment. Already on the way north to Albany Park, where *Familias Unidas* was headquartered, Gato was talking about how hungry he was. When he saw the taco place across from *Familias Unidas*, he raised the ante.

"Dadi, let me buy you a burrito."

"You don't need to buy me anything. Besides, Mami and I had a late breakfast. Save your money."

"How come you never let me treat you?"

"Gato, you know I have a lot more money than you have."

"Next time you try to buy me lunch, forget it."

"What about that time on Milwaukee Avenue? I let you buy me a Cuban sandwich."

"What's that, two years ago when I get my back pay?"

"OK. I tell you what. You buy some tacos or a burrito and get two coffees, one for you, one for me. I think we both can use some."

"You think I'm drunk?"

"I didn't say that. We just need to be on our toes when talking to the lawyer."

He ate his steak tacos before my coffee was cool enough to sip. We carried our cups across Lawrence Avenue as I scoped out the storefront office with the words "*Familias Unidas*" curving in bold red letters and "Immigrant Services" in black right underneath. The sun reflected off the windows so I couldn't see in. But once I stepped through the door I felt comfortable, reminded of my days as a community organizer and GED teacher.

Flyers in English and Spanish for ESL and GED classes, employment counseling, and a cooperative child care program were tacked on the 4x8 cork bulletin board. Handwritten 3x5 Help Wanted, For Sale, and For Rent cards filled a smaller *Noticias* section of the board. Spanish magazines littered the table by a water cooler. On the other side of the cooler was a two-foot stack of *La Raza*, a weekly published in Chicago.

All the people coming and going reminded me of the campaign offices I worked from in the '80s, except no one was smoking until Gato lit up the half-smoked butt he found outside. When I pointed to the *No Se Permite Fumar* sign, he took a long hit, walked slowly to the door, took another hit, opened the door, flipped the cigarette through it, and then blew his smoke inside the office. I smoldered.

During the ten minutes we waited, Gato paced the office, flirted with the receptionist, and knocked some magazines from the lobby table. He spilled his coffee within minutes of sitting down for our meeting with the staff attorney, Mel Franklin.

Franklin was an unassuming man with thinning blond hair. I had a hunch that he was once a priest or had studied to be one because of his quiet walk and soft voice. That thought became stronger when I saw the pictures on the wall behind his desk: one of Pope John Paul II flanked by larger ones of two disciples of liberation theology, Salvador's Bishop Oscar Romero and the Sandinista, Father Miguel D'Escoto.

I tried to explain to Franklin our earlier efforts at obtaining citizenship papers for Gato. He scanned through copies of documents I had sent to the immigration service and the "no record of a Jesus Cárdenas" replies. But Franklin wanted to talk directly to Jesus. "Mr. Cárdenas, do you speak English?" Franklin waited a few seconds for Gato to answer. "*Sr. Cárdenas, ¿Entiende Inglés, habla usted Inglés?*"

Again Gato did not answer. I jumped in. "Jesus, Mr. Franklin wants to know if you speak English." He didn't respond to me either. "Gato!"

Jarred, he grumbled, "I'm speaking English." Then glaring at Franklin, he asked, "*¿Hablas Español?*"

"I speak some Spanish, Mr. Cárdenas, but if you don't understand English, we have an interpreter."

Trying to talk just to me, Gato says, "What? He say I need an interpreter?"

I gave my answer to Franklin, "I think we'll be OK."

With the language issue behind us, Franklin interviewed his prospective client. When and where did Jesus come into the United States? When was he naturalized? When did he serve in the army? What was his immigration number? Where and when was he born? Gato rattled off his "A" number, but as it had been with me, he hesitated at his birth date. First he said July 26, 1946, then, "Some of my papers had a mistake; they say 1954 instead of 1946."

Franklin's ill-at-ease use of the computer reinforced my thought that the law was not his first calling. While he fidgeted with entering information, printing forms, and making copies, Gato got up, strutted around the room, and pretended to look at the books and journals lining the walls. A younger, red-bearded, curly-haired man sitting at one of the other two desks in the room became a magnet for Gato's curiosity.

"¿Hablas Español?"

"Seguro. Me llamo Guillermo O'Reilly. Estoy el traductor."

"Hablas Español muy bien. Me llamo Jesus Mercedes Cárdenas, pero mi amigos me llaman Gato. ¿Eres Mexicano?"

"Medio y medio Irlandés."

Their conversation continued in Spanish beyond the pace and vocabulary I could understand until Franklin returned from the copy machine.

"OK, I have a few papers I need you to sign. This one is a form saying that I can represent you, pro bono, free of charge. And this one is a Department of Homeland Security Freedom of Information request.

Gato was up out of his chair, back at the interpreter's desk. The only words of his I could make out were "boner," "maricón," and "terrorista." I think those were the only words Franklin picked up as well. He seemed to blush. I must have turned red as well.

I was losing it. "Gato, sit down here. Everyone is trying to help you, and you're playing games."

Franklin quietly tried to regain control. "Mr. Cárdenas, Homeland Security is the new department that oversees the Immigration Service. No one is accusing you of doing anything wrong. I'm not promising you results, but I cannot do anything without your consent."

I looked the papers over. "Jesus, everything here looks fine. Just standard legal papers. Sign and we can get going." He took the papers and carefully signed the spots where I pointed.

Talking to me, the lawyer summed up where we were at. "With such scant information, this is our best hope. But don't expect a quick response. Under this administration, I'd be surprised if we heard anything sooner than nine months."

On the street outside the office, Gato had his own summary. "I don't like that guy. He more like a priest than a lawyer. I only do this for you." He didn't say another word all the way home.

NEIGHBORHOOD STUPOR
MEMO 2004

Editor's note: Found in our mailbox, neatly typed.

Alexia Demas
August 2004

Bingham

Ron Bingham, blond hair hanging,
Three-day face growth, cultivated bicep look,
Jaw jutting, mouth agape,
Saying nothing of consequence,
College-grey t-shirt, not graduated,
Bottom of the rung trading-floor runner.
Ron Bingham's variety,
Ignorant of Wicker Park's former self,
Red-lined, poor,
More Puerto Rican than anybody else,
More Black than White,
More Polish than Irish, Jewish, German.

Ron unaware a neighborhood could have soul,
Having grown up in Almwood Hills,
Each subsequent division with bigger houses,
More garages.

Occasionally Ron would overhear an old-timer,
Talk summers past when people sat on stoops,
Slept in hammocks on back porches and roofs
Because no one had air, not central, not window units,
Not even burnished overhead fans attached
Where gas-lit chandeliers once ruled the night.
Ron and his fifteen clones adjacent didn't know
Their townhomes stood where absentee-owned
Two and three flats became abandoned
Then burned in an arson-for-profit scheme
Killing two homeless men.

Ron, dribbling text messages,
Grooving to his randomly shuffled play list,
He didn't listen to old-timer noise,
Unpreferred to heart-pounding amplified
Street parties, fests, and tastes
That attracted his kind to Wicker Park
In the first place,
Six years, six months, or sixty seconds ago.

But Ron Bingham was ready to fight
Someone like me looking at him wrong,
Asking for some change
Until someone like me steps toward him,
Unafraid, knife drawn perhaps.

Whitehead

Agnes Whitehead, blue-patterned bandana,
Holding back self-named hair,
Twenty years past prime,
Ever trying to be trim,
Jazzercycling, low-fat, high-fiber,
Yoga meditations,
Never quite losing fifteen extra pounds
Separating size 8 from size 10.
Half-frame glasses pinching once-freckled nose,
Attachment beads curling against puffy cheeks.

Agnes Whitehead's self-satisfied band
Counted the overvalued Victorian market,
Capital gain reductions and exclusions,
Rolled-over IRAs,
Doubled rents on garden apartments,
Washers and dryers,
Remuddled wallboard,
Dropped ceilings,
Something smelling not quite right.

Tenants like Ron Bingham,
Tripled and quadrupled up,
Rotating in and out before leases expired.
Knowing all about the neighborhood founders,
1843 to 1923,
But nothing of the community floundering
Until urban Columbuses
Rediscovered Wicker Park, late '70s,
Landmarking, gentrifying,

Whitewashing history
Past, present, future.
At least she's got jobs,
Odd ones for me and my kind.

Wroblanski
Stanislaw Wroblanski, balding pallet,
Pale blue shirt unbuttoned,
Showing near bald chest and stomach,
Walking stiffly with cane
That threatened kids of color '60s, '70s, '80s.
Not much use for yuppies either
Excepting they got us Spics out.

Stanislaw Wroblanski's clan,
Most gone north and west,
Avondale to Mt. Prospect,
Couldn't stand the neighborhood changing,
Black and Brown,
Falling values now bubble high,

Heart sunk for never cashing in.
Stanislaw yet waiting
For that perfect selling time
While bitterly blaming himself,
Parish preaching "Love of stranger" priests
Sweetheart dealing, Solidarity shouting union chiefs,
And garbage can rewarding, ward-healing cheats.
Wroblanski left his junk in the alley,
Shards for us to treasure.

Demas

Alexia Demas, olive-skin, jet-black hair,
Few strands silvering,
Thick eyebrows expressive
In Greek, Spanish, parochial school Polish,
Lips parted to listen.
Living in the now,
Always near her Eden,

Alexia Demas, accepting and changing the neighborhood,
Active teaching, school councilling,
Park advising, underdog campaigning,
Children mothering.
Ever true but now dismayed
As aldermen sell out,
And rents pierce neighbors' hearts.

Alexia Demas, her kind,
Rainbowing the neighborhood,
Color aware not blind,
Seeing the greater sum,
But not seeing the gentritide not ebbing.
While inertia held the poor in dwindling place,
Unable to leave this location, location, location.

Alexia saw me, listened to me,
Still sees and hears me,
Even if I don't hear myself.

Rodriguez

Memo Rodriguez, older than my years,
Self-abused, slovenly overweight,
Under-combed, shaved, and bathed,
At best in a few-day wait for the next fix,
Now off rehab,
Living halfway,
Transitioning to training,
Job readiness failures to comply.

Memo Rodriguez, my type slides,
Bums along downhill
From highs never high enough,
Consorts low and wide,
Using up scant goodwill too soon.
Not accepted,
No longer even tolerated,
Just ignored, invisible
Styrofoam cup in my cellophane skin.

In this stupor,
It happens upon me, unconvincingly,
Words alone will make me lucid.

HE'S MY MAN
ALICIA 2004

Hello, I'm Alicia Benitez. I told Gato I want to say something into his recorder without him listening. So he let me take this recorder to my little room down the hall on the second floor of the Cortez Arms. I want to give you an example why Gato is my man, why I love him, even though most of the time he's got to pay me, just like everyone else.

A week ago was the first of the month, usually a pretty good day for someone in my line of work. The guys who get their monthly checks usually want to have a nice time while they can still afford it.

That afternoon, I'm turning the corner from Ashland onto Cortez. Just then I see Gato coming out of our yellow brick building. He's wearing his three-quarter leather coat, still unbuttoned, and his brown wool cap. As he approaches I can see he's got that first-of-the-month glow. Must have had a good breakfast and a few drinks. He's walking, slightly favoring one side, not 'cause he's hurting but because he's cool. I remember everything about that day as if it just happened.

"Green Eyes," he calls to me, smiling.

"Gato, how you feeling?"

"I'm feeling good, real good. This going to be *una día especial.*"

"You want to party all night with me?"

"You mean for $80 I can get two hours? I only got the $40."

"Gato, let's not fight. You know I have to pay the rent too. Let me see what I can do. I'll make my other appointments late. You will be my first."

"You come by early, I'll have something *especial* for you."

"You're always special, Gato." Maybe if he listens to this tape he'll believe me when I say that.

When I come to his room about seven thirty that evening I can hear him singing "Bésame Mucho." He really has a sweet voice. You wouldn't think it, hearing him talk. Spanish or English. I think it's his missing teeth that makes him hard to understand to some people. Not me, of course. But when he sings . . .

As I knock gently, I smell something cooking. He's all quiet now. Probably listening at the door.

"Gato, it's me, Alicia."

"You alone?"

"What you think, baby?"

He opens the door, pokes his head out, then glances quickly both ways to make sure.

"Come in, come in. Got to be careful."

"Not with me, I hope."

"No, no, you're cool. Too much shit going on here."

"Cool? I thought you said I was hot?"

What was hot was the chicken and rice bubbling on the stove. I couldn't believe it. The stove was so clean. The pots, usually two or three piled up, with boil-over marks into the burners, were stacked on the shelf above the refrigerator, it too unusually white.

I enter easily into the room. For once no garbage and alley finds lay here and there. I see the rug, its oriental colors swept bright. The bed was made, the sheets look washed. A *Feliz Navidad* decoration hangs in an arc from the top of the window. I wonder, Am I on the right floor, or is this Amos's room exactly above Gato's?"

"You like what you see?" he says, breaking into a wide smile, lightly blinking his right eye.

"Gato, you do this for me?"

"You're the one. Hungry?"

Everything about him is making me wet. I lean in to kiss him, my hand resting where his loose, tan trousers bulged.

He turns a little away from me to push the play button on his recorder and I hear his voice singing "Bésame Mucho" and I feel the tenderness in his voice as if he were singing only to me, sadly, as if it were the last time.

He gathers me into his arms for a slow dance, on our feet, and then on the bed. The creaking springs ever more frequent and more intense replace Gato's soulful voice.

Afterward we lay next to each other and share cigarettes, though I beg him not to smoke. "You're killing yourself. Gato, please don't smoke."

Suddenly he clasps his left hand over my mouth and holds his right forefinger to his lips. I nod and he lets go and tiptoes naked to the door, listening with his right ear, right hand on the lock latch.

Three heavy knocks shake more than the door.

"Gato, open up. It's Max. I need your rent."

Gato stays silent.

"Gato, I know you're in there. I heard you screwing."

More silence.

"Ten seconds I'm coming in, and I'm not counting."

He comes back to the bed. I'm under the covers, but he whispers, "Damn it, where's my pants?"

I hand him the towel he gave me to wipe up. "Wrap this around you. I whisper back."

"All right, Max. I'm coming now."

"Open the door now, I'm not your bitch."

"Screw you, I don't got to let you in."

"Time's up, wetback. Get away from the door."

But Gato doesn't open up; he's leaning against the door. Max is twice his size, but the door's not budging, not because it's a good lock, but because Gato is so strong.

I hear Max grunting, pushing on the door. "You don't pay your rent, it's my room."

"My Dadi always send the check."

"Your Dadi? He's late with the check."

"He has five days to pay his rent," I shout.

"Quiet, Alicia."

"We got rights. Gato, he can't bust in; he's got to take you to court."

"So it's you in there, Green Eyes. I told you I don't want you screwing that diseased faggot."

"You don't own me, you sick bastard."

All of a sudden, Gato opens the door wide, and Max falls in, flat on his face. Without hesitating, Gato kicks him in the side two times and spits on him, all the time holding the towel closed to his waist.

The ruckus attracts the others from the floor: Robert, Jessie, Dalia. Then Horace Figueroa, Max's goon, pushes his way in and reaches down to pick up Max. Horace is too dumb to whisper, so we all hear, "Police down in the lobby, that Sergeant Romano."

"You won't be so lucky next time, you snitch. You know what's best for you, you'll get your ass out of here by New Year."

On their way out, Horace pushes the chicken and rice off the stove onto the floor and licks his fingers clean. "Not bad. Plenty for the cockroaches now."

Gato slams the door shut and I notice his right foot is bleeding, his face deflated. He sits on the bed and is quiet as I dampen some napkins and wipe clean the gash on his big toe.

We're both naked. I try to make him feel good, but he pushes away my hand and pounds his fist into the mattress. He mutters, "Dadi not going to believe me. He going to say it's my fault. What am I going to do?"

The tear forming at his eye bares much more of him than the fallen towel.

HAIKU DREAMS
MEMO 2004

Editor's note: Arriving home after meeting with a potential client, I was the first in our building to sort through the day's mail. Being the Christmas season, the catalogues and circulars outnumbered and obscured the cards I looked forward to all the way home on the "L." That day there were four. Postmarks and address stickers were the clues to what I'd find inside the envelopes. C. Williams, Oak Park, Illinois: the annual family snapshot of Carol and Jack, children Tim, Edie, Jimmy, and Jill; Demas Family, Elk Grove, Illinois: not-so-close cousins, not the really desired card from closer cousins in Makria, Greece; Mark Stanford Insurance Associates, Chicago, Illinois: Thank you for your business, have a prosperous New Year; Milwaukee, Wisconsin, no return address: the obvious choice to open and read on the way up the stairs. Inside was a card with a jolly Santa. Before I could read the greetings, a sheet of folded white paper slipped to the second-floor landing. I opened it and saw typewritten verses. Then I spotted the farewell, "Your friend, Memo," scrawled inside the card, underneath a penciled message.

The greetings and Haiku poems I leave for you to ponder.

Merry Christmas, *Feliz Navidad, Kala Christougena.*

Alexia Demas

December 20, 2004

Alexia,

Feliz Navidad. It seems I am always writing things for you to read without giving you much of a chance to respond.

I had to leave town. Gato was getting a little weird to be around, even for me. The weather was getting cold, so this was no time to be out on the streets. I'm staying with an old friend in Milwaukee, but I'm not sure how long I'll be able to stay here. Not many of my old crowd are still around, but I'm making the rounds with those who are.

Tell George that Queen Danny sends his love. He's not doing as well as I hoped. It seems there may be a limit to how long one can keep taking the HIV cocktail.

Have George tell Gato to keep cool at the Cortez Arms. That pig Caldwell will try to trick, goad, and screw as many people out of there as he can. He knows his days are numbered before the city shuts him down. If Gato can stick it out, he can play the situation and walk out of there without paying three or four months' rent.

Tell Nick I've been listening to the bouzouki CDs he gave me. I don't understand the words, but I can hear why they call it the Greek Blues.

Alexia, perhaps one day we will not be like ships passing in the night. For now I hope my words sustain our bond.

Your friend,

Memo

Haiku Dreams
Profound dreams erupt
From the middle of my soul
And leave me awake

Dreams leaking from an
Alternative universe
Surprise and delight

Nightmares slap my face
Dispirit, disarm, expose
Myself to Myself

Nodding off rescues
Disembodied sleepwalking
Half-awake dream state

Waking much confused
Discombobulated, whew
It's only a dream

Continuous dreams
Into the morning sunlight
From thoughts at bedtime

Absent all night dreams
Imitate my sorry ass
Beat down, lonely fate.

Dreams now forgotten
Sleep all invigorating
Day to night to day.

CORTEZ CRACK
GATO 2005

Excuse me, talking low. Things real messed up here at the Cortez. Never know who's listening. I don't know Dadi believe me or not, but they gonna shut this place down. The police and inspectors here every day, poking around. The owner, Max Caldwell, he don't care. Everybody say he want to make a condominium conversation.

Max, he here every day now. Use to see him only once a week, collecting rents. First he'll stop by Randy's. Randy, he deal crack. He always got stuff after Max visit. You add two plus two. Usually I stay away. I ain't getting hooked. I drink. Why not? I tell Dadi I don't have to drink, I ain't no alcoholic.

When Max is done with Randy, he be doing one whore or other. Alicia, Dalia, if he's really high he might do the he-she, Roberta. They say he giving them free rent. No one is paying any rent anyway. How he going to evict anyone? They gonna close the place.

Wait a minute.

Creaking floor noise. Two minutes go by, few more floor noises. Lock unlatches, different creak, door opening.

"OK, assholes, I know you listening."

Door creaks shut, lock latches.

Caldwell's people are spying. They asking about Dadi, who he is. Is he a lawyer? They ask what did Sgt. Romano want. How they know Romano stop me over by the liquor store? I tell them, "How I know what he want; I don't talk to him." Hope they didn't see him slip me twenty. Snitching on Caldwell ain't like ratting a friend. Caldwell, he an asshole. Run this place down looking to cash in. I hope they catch him with the crack.

I don't think Dadi believe what I tell him about Caldwell. Maybe I tell him too many stories last few years. Now he get that priest to send for my citizenship papers. Lucky so far nothing come back. He says he want to help me get ID. OK, I need ID, but I don't need him snooping.

You never know who's listening at the door. All my people, they say, "Hey Gato, open up, it's me, Memo," something like that. These people from the city they knock, don't say nothing. Twenty minutes later I poke my head out, they all over me like flies. Asking me, do I know anything about the dope dealing 'cause they trying to close the building. What, they think I'm crazy? Caldwell an asshole, but they shut the Cortez I'm out on the street.

No, they tell me. They'll help me find a place. That I'll get $500 rental assistance.

They don't tell you what you got to do to get it. No, they working with Caldwell. He using the city to make his money. He don't make no money on rent. He not making money on drugs or pimping. He make money turning this place condo.

The *puta* Dalia, she trying to get me hooked on crack. She get me hot, she get half naked, then she pull it out. Tell me only $10 more. She already got my $40, I might not get what I pay for if I don't give her what she wants. I push her naked ass out and slam the door. I clean my own rifle.

Now the fat boy, Jessie, he want me to go to legal aid with him. He say the lawyers will help us. Help themselves to our money. That boy from Wisconsin, what he know?

Dadi, sometime I think he from Wisconsin too. He say take the city money. Go to their hotel, go into their program, you need to stop drinking anyway. He say I could get six months free rent. Maybe he still work for the city, even though Romano say not for years. Maybe he is a narc. Maybe he working with Caldwell. Maybe that's how he get me the room two years ago. He going to make money selling the condos with his partner Caldwell.

See how they got my head spinning? They got me blaming Dadi. He and Mami only ones helping me, and they got me believing lies about them. I don't know what to do, but I ain't praying no more. Where that get me, shouting, "*Aleluya, el Señor*" and putting $10 bills in their buckets?

Knocking at the door. Quiet. Eighteen and a half minutes of background noise. An occasional car horn. Floorboards creaking as someone walks past. Breathing.

I have to pretend no one is here. Probably the asshole Caldwell. I ain't moving unless they take me to court. I got rights. I may look stupid, but I got rights. They think I don't 'cause they look at me like I'm an illegal Mexican. They should know I'm a *Cubano*.

Knocking at the door.

"Jesus, you in there? It's George, Gato. It's your Dadi."

"Wait a minute." *Long pause.* I got to hide the recorder so I can tape what Dadi says.

"You got someone in there with you? I don't have all day."

Lock unlatches.

"Who you talking to, or were you talking in your sleep?"

126

"You see anybody in here? You want to look under the bed? All you see is cockroaches."

"What a mess. You might clean up once in a while. I see you haven't used those garbage bags I gave you."

"Well, I not been feeling so good."

"No wonder, you're going to get sick if you eat from dirty dishes. What is it this time, your stomach, breathing, or just drinking too much?"

"My lungs, I have trouble breathing."

"Probably been smoking someone else's shorties."

"You know I can't pay for cigarettes."

"You can't afford to smoke; it's killing you."

"Hey Dadi, what you hear about the building? You see that article in the newspaper?"

"I talked to Sgt. Romano."

"What you talk to him for? You think I'm selling that stuff?"

"You gave me his number, remember?"

"Oh, yeah. Guess I didn't think you call him."

"Well, Romano says the city is taking Caldwell to court on the 14th. Tuesday. Think you can get a few other tenants to go down there? I'll drive."

"That fat boy, Jessie, he say he want to go. Maybe Robert, maybe Amos."

"You guys don't go, you won't have a chance. They'll order this building closed in a minute."

"Dadi, you think I can get some money from the city, or they just say that?"

"I don't know, probably some strings attached."

"You mean chains?"

"Hey, you can always go back to Cuba."

"Man, you crazy."

"Easy, Gato; just joking. When's the last time you see the people from the city?"

"They were here before. But I didn't open the door."

"Next time they come, you call me. I want to talk to them myself. See what they're talking about. In the meantime, talk to your guys about Tuesday. If I don't hear from you, I'll stop by on Monday."

"Dadi, I need some money to call you and to talk them into going to court."

"You mean you'll need to talk to them over something to drink. It's going to come from next month's check."

"OK, I'm not paying no more rent here."

"You may need to, if you want the money from the city."

"You don't know? No one paying rent no more."

"What's that? No one's paying rent? Good, I'll get you all thrown out of here."

"Who said you can come in, Caldwell?"

"You don't want me in here, keep your mouth and your door shut. Who's this, Gato? Your Dadi?"

"George Demas, I've been wanting to talk to you."

"Well, don't be stirring up the tenants here if you know what's good for you, Dadi Demas."

"You don't scare me. Seems like you're the one in trouble, Caldwell, according to Sgt. Romano."

"So you've been talking to that pig too, just like your little snitch."

Crash, bottle breaking. Scuffling.

"Come on, Gato, come and get me."

"Gato, he has a gun. Put the bottle down. I'll take care of this; you're going to make things worse."

"He ain't talking to me like that. I'm a man."

"Such a man, needs his Dadi to break things up."

"Caldwell, get out of here. I'll calm him down. I'll talk to you later."

"Yeah, Demas, you do that and then get off my property. I got nothing to say to you."

Door slams.

"Dadi, I got to defend myself. I'm a man." *Wheezing, sound of spray aspirator.*

"You just got to hang in here a little longer, take care of yourself. Let's see what happens in court, see what the city's going to come up with. They have to give you something if they're going to vacate the building."

"Dadi, I respect you, but believe me, I'm not getting nothing from the city. You think I got something when they close the rooming house? Same thing. We never got nothing."

"We'll see. I got to go now. Promise me you'll keep cool."

"What about the money?"

"Thirty's all I got, and it's coming from your check."

"You coming Monday? What time?"

"I'll come around noon, unless you call me, tell me the city people are here."

"OK. Say hi to Mami and Nick."

"OK. See you."

Door opens and closes. Latch closing. Silence.

Good, the tape still running. They can't set me up. I'll sue them.

BUILDING COURT
GEORGE 2005

According to the tenants at the Cortez Arms, Max Caldwell knew exactly what he was doing. He wanted the city to shut his building down, and by letting prostitution and crack dealing to operate freely, he had the ticket. He didn't mind the thousands in fines that would come because what he really wanted to do was to quickly turn his building into nine or more condominiums that he'd sell for about $200,000 apiece. But evicting sixty to seventy tenants would take months, perhaps a year. The city, responding to complaints from gentrifying residents pressuring the alderman, could close it in a month or two by taking him to Building Court.

Building Court is different than Housing Court where landlords go to evict tenants who aren't paying rent. It's not really a court, but the city's Administrative Hearing Department's Building Division, where the city seeks action against the owner for code violations. Adopted in 1996, the Municipal Code's provision on "Drug and Gang Houses, Houses of Prostitution, and Other Disorderly Houses" outlines measures the city can take to "abate" criminal activities in buildings such as the Cortez Arms. When owners like Max Caldwell do not take action themselves, the city can vacate the premises. In extreme cases they can take receivership of the property. Fines can range to $500 a day for each violation.

Gato told me no one was paying rent anymore and that city officials were going around the building and telling tenants the city would give them $500 toward their next apartment. I was out of work at the time, but I was more nervous about Gato having a place to live than about me finding another job. For the last few months he'd been acting strange, even volatile. Like the day when he was about to take a broken bottle to Caldwell. What would happen if they closed down the Cortez? The last thing we wanted was to have him as a house guest again. But that wasn't the only reason I felt compelled to help. Something had propelled Gato into our lives, and the connections Alexia and I had to his friend Memo were almost unbelievable.

On the day before Building Court hearing, I stopped by the Cortez Arms as I had promised Gato. When I arrived, a Department of Human Service (DHS) outreach team was on site. A beefy guy, the kind you usually see on Election Day passing voting cards for machine candidates, was the first one I ran into. His White Sox cap and "da Bears" way of talking suggested "Soutside" Italian.

"You live here?" he asked me.

"Just visiting. Who are you?"

"I'm with DHS," he said as he thrust his card at me. I eyed it curiously, noticing his name, Ray Parmello. "Who you visiting?"

"One of the tenants. I'm his SSI payee. So what's going down?" I asked.

"There's a hearing tomorrow. The city's got a strong case against the owner, Caldwell."

"What do you think will happen?"

"They'll close the place. The yuppie neighbors are all over the alderman."

"What about the tenants?"

"They'll get about three weeks to get out," said Parmello.

"I thought they get thirty days in an eviction?"

"This ain't no eviction. This will be a vacate order. The hearing officer could close it tomorrow if the violations were bad enough to make it dangerous. You know, gas leaks, bad electricity."

"Anything to this $500 relocation money?"

"Depends. They got to be on our list as legitimate tenants. And they got to sign up."

"And you help them find a new place."

"We ain't going to hold their hands. We give them a list. It's up to them to check out the places," Parmello said as he checked the time on his watch and started down the hall.

I called to him to wait up. "One more thing. What do you have to do to sign up?"

"It's all on this," he said, thrusting a two-side printed sheet toward me.

"You have one in Spanish too?"

Parmello dug around in his aluminum clipboard box. "Must have run out."

I quickly scanned the sheet, my eyes zeroing in on the line I knew would be there: Picture ID such as driver's license or state of Illinois ID required.

I lowered my voice. "My guy is Jesus Cárdenas, 214. Is he eligible?"

Now Parmello was scanning his sheet. "Yup. Finally caught up with him this morning as he went into his room. Never would open the door for me, or any of us. Seemed a little suspicious."

"You could say that. He's been through a lot. A few years ago another place he was living in was sold. He was homeless on and off for a couple of years. Then in 2002 Social Security cut him off, claiming he was dead. It was his payee who died. I helped him get back on. That's how I became his payee."

"You ain't telling me anything I ain't heard before." Again he checked the time and started away.

"Hey, does DHS ever help anyone get ID?"

"I told you we don't hold hands. He need ID, he can go down to the State of Illinois Building just like everyone else."

"Easy for you to say. He doesn't have any identification. No Social Security card, no immigration card, no birth certificate, and he can't exactly call Cuba to get one."

"You say he's an immigrant? There's a caseworker at our Westside office who might know something about that. Name is Gabriela Hernandez. The number of the office is on that sheet I gave you."

With that, Parmello glanced at his watch, this time pointing his chubby finger at the dial. I looked at mine. It was noon. "Got another building to get to," and he hurried down the steps to the lobby and out the door. My guess was the building he had to get to was a local taco and burrito shack.

I headed up to Gato's room where, to my surprise, I found his door open. Jessie, the heavy-set Wisconsinite, was standing outside while Gato's friend Amos was inside sitting next to him on the cluttered bed. Another tenant, Robert, ambled toward the room, wearing his tan terry cloth bathrobe and flip flops. His belly threatened to push open the loosely tied robe and reveal, let's just say, everything about Robert.

"Dadi, you say 'get some people to go to court.' Here they are. I think you already met Amos and Robert."

"Hello, Mr. Demas," said Amos. Robert nodded and belched his robe a little looser.

"That's Jessie, he going tomorrow," Gato said.

"The Legal Aid lawyer says I better go, Mr. Demas." Jessie's voice was unexpectedly high and somewhat nasal.

"Please, you guys, just call me George."

"Just George, Mr. Demas? That's not right; you're Jesus's father."

"He ain't God, Fat Boy. Just shut up and listen to what he has to say," Robert commanded as he pulled his belt robe tighter.

"Mr. Demas, I mean George, what do you think our chances are in court?" Amos wondered.

"Remember, this isn't your case; its Caldwell's."

"Yeah, but if he loses, we lose," Robert said. "Just like the electrician's union complaining to OSHA. The officials weren't out of work; we were."

"Robert, you gonna listen to my Dadi or you gonna do all the talking? You gonna blame the union again? When you lose your job? Twenty years ago?"

I tried to cool things. "Easy, Gato, that's what they want, everyone fighting each other."

"All due respect, Mr. Demas, George, who is they?"

"The city, Amos. You think they really want to pay everyone $500 to move out of here?"

"Mayor Daley, he's full of crap, just like his old man, that bastard. I got no use for any politician. You some kind of politician, Demas?"

"Robert, I haven't been in politics since Washington was mayor."

"He was the worst of all, that . . ."

Amos was off the bed. "You better watch how you talk about Harold, at least around me. Best mayor we ever had, in my book."

Again I was refereeing. "For now let's agree to keep politics out of it, OK?"

"That's easy, I don't even vote," said Jessie.

"Dadi, what you think we should do?"

"Jessie is right. If no tenants show up, you're going to get screwed. You need to speak up and say you need more time to find another place or they'll push you out in a couple of weeks."

"You ask me, they won't let us say a word," belched the robed one.

"Who's asking you, Robert?" Amos spat back.

"Maybe they won't let you speak, but you sure won't be heard if you're not there. What do you have to lose? It's not like you guys have busy schedules. I'll give you all a ride."

"Dadi, you know I go with you. Amos, you with us? You, Robert?"

"I'll see," Amos Replied. "I was supposed to visit my auntie tomorrow. She's in the hospital way south."

"Well, I ain't going with just Gato and the fat boy. They ain't talking for me," said Robert.

"Robert, you've been staying at the Cortez for twenty years. No one better to represent the group than you," I said.

"We'll see. You come by my room in the morning. If I'm going, the door'll be open."

The next morning I arrived at the Cortez Arms an hour and a half before the eleven a.m. hearing time. I knocked first at Gato's door, normally, then harder. I tried yelling through the door, "Gato, you in there? Gato, its Dadi." I waited. Again I rapped on the door, again I called. I heard some stirring. "Gato, open up, it's Dadi."

The wooden door opened two inches. His eyes were red and he was naked except for a towel wound around his waist, his nappy, greying hair standing up, making him look like Don King. Groggily, all he said was, "Wha?"

"You remember we have court today?"

"What time is it?" By then it was 9:45.

He was waking up. "Can you be ready in fifteen, twenty minutes?"

"Yeah, I get ready," and he shut the door.

Halfway down the hall was Robert's room. I lightly rapped on the open door. From his chair he could see it was me. "Come in, Demas."

I'd been in his room once before, dragged there by Gato, looking for a smoke. It was more than twice the size of Gato's room with a small closet on one side, a small toilet on the other. Robert sat in a wide, threadbare, overstuffed fifties arm chair a few shades darker, or dirtier, than his usual attire. Once again his robe was open a bit, and from my angle I could see a sailor's tattoo on his chest. He motioned me to sit, or should I say sink, in a chair similar to and across from his.

As he rolled a cigarette and sealed it with his tongue, I took in the room. Tidy actually, a couple of shelves he'd hung on the walls, one with a hard hat and a tool belt, another with cigar boxes piled on top of each other. Some pots hung on hooks above the stove. Next to it was a white enamel table, extensions lowered on both sides. On the wall, above and to the left of Robert's throne, was a framed *Chicago Tribune* front page. The lead story and picture: "Sears Tragedy Worst of High-rise Fatalities."

"I worked there for two years, '71 to '73. I knew a couple of those guys." He took a drag on his cigarette, let it out slowly. "Could have been me." He must have noticed me fidgeting, so he changed the subject.

"Believe it or not, I'm going to miss this place. It's a dump, but it's the only one I know. He reached down to the left of his chair and pulled up a gallon jug of cheap white wine, a half dozen small Dixie cups atop it. "Want a cup? On the house." As he downed one himself, I declined and figured it was the 400 percent profit margin he made selling cups of wine to a ready-made market that he'd miss the most.

"Heard anything from Amos?"

"That good for nothing? Yeah, he stopped by on the way out. I knew we couldn't count on him. But I got one better than him who'll come with us. You know John Welch?" The name didn't ring a bell. "You pass him by almost every time you walk in downstairs." My face must have curled like a question mark. "You know, the old guy with the straw-colored beard."

I thought, The bearded one? The first human face I associated with the Cortez Arms. "How long has he lived here?"

"Only thirty-seven years," he chuckled. "And he knows everything that's been going on around here and ain't afraid to say it."

Right then Jessie poked his head in the door, nearly dropping some papers he was carrying. "Hello, Mr. Demas. We still going to court?"

"Yes we are. What you got there?"

"Petitions. I got thirty-eight signatures."

"What's it say?"

"It says we need two months to find new homes. It asks that we not be thrown out on the street in the middle of the winter."

"Lot of good that'll do us. But thanks for trying, Fat Boy."

Next Gato came strutting into the room. He cleaned up nice for court but glanced at Robert, who once again grabbed left for his jug of wine.

"Don't you think it's a little early for that?" I asked.

"One little cup just to wake me up."

I wasn't going to argue; this was his turf. There was no money exchanged, but I had the feeling Robert kept his books in his head.

The round over, I suggested that we head out. Downstairs, John was waiting for us. Sizing up the lot of them, I realized it was going to be a tight squeeze in our Saturn station wagon. The old man would have to sit in front. Not only was he large, but he moved stiffly. The problem was, as Robert would put it, Fat Boy. But Gato and Robert sucked it in, and I managed on the second try to shut the door. Luckily we could get to the court on Superior Street in about fifteen minutes.

Like many public buildings, the Administrative Hearing Building looked like it was built in the '30s, with its cheap art deco effects adorning the long, two-story greystone. At the entrance's metal detectors John hesitated. No wonder, the contents of two of perhaps fifteen pockets made heads turn. From one he pulled an expensive-looking watch fob and a gold money clip thick with bills. The other had a four-inch knife. The security guard promised he could get it back upon leaving the court.

We walked through thick black metal doors and then a long, wide granite hallway until we found room 1014 and entered. A narrow hall led us past some small rooms to a larger hearing room with wooden benches. We sat down and sat and sat and sat while a parade of cases proceeded before Administrative Hearing Officer Andrew Ryan. Gato became restless, said he was hungry, and borrowed four dollars from me to buy something from a roach coach parked across the street from the court building.

No sooner had Gato stepped out then John recognized the city attorney assigned to Caldwell's case standing just inside the entrance of 1014. John had seen him before at the Cortez Arms. He whispered to Robert, Robert whispered to me, I whispered to Jessie, asking him to get Gato from outside. We approached the official, a thin, neatly dressed man in his early thirties. Recognizing John, he motioned us into one of the conference rooms. Stepping into the hall, I saw that Jessie and Gato were stuck in the security line again.

The city attorney was another Ryan, in this case William. He told us they had six counts against Caldwell, and that at fourteen days the fines could reach up to $42,000. But Caldwell, in order to cut his losses in half, had agreed to a vacate date in two weeks. Ryan also said that each of the tenants whose rent was paid through the end of the year 2004 would be getting $500 directly from Caldwell. Ryan showed us the list. John, Robert, and Jessie were on it. The name Jesus Cárdenas was not.

I had been quiet until then. "I pay his rent every month, and I have the cancelled checks to prove it."

Now in the room with us, Gato's pacing told me he was agitated. I said to him, "I'll take care of this."

Jessie brought out his petitions from a pocket inside his jacket. "What about all of these tenants? They don't get anything either?" he protested.

The door opened. It was Caldwell's lawyer, Erich Salten. I had heard the name and his reputation, well-connected in political circles. Behind him was Ray Parmello. I brushed past Salten to Parmello.

"I thought you said Jesus Cárdenas was on your list."

He had upgraded his aluminum box to a leather binder from which he pulled a paper that he handed to Ryan. "I see you are right, Mr . . . What did you say your name was?"

"Demas, George Demas. So Mr. Cárdenas will get his relocation allowance?"

"It seems he will," said Ryan.

Salten, much heavier and taller than Ryan, leaned over to whisper in the younger man's ear.

"The hearing officer is ready to hear the case."

Jessie tailed after Ryan. "What about our petitions? We can't be out in two weeks; we need two months. Give us until spring."

Reluctantly, Attorney Ryan took the petitions as he approached the paneled partition behind which Hearing Officer Ryan sat elevated above everyone else, including the five of us standing at the third row of benches.

The hearing officer, bald and wearing black-rimmed glasses but no robe, took the documents the city attorney handed him and glanced through the papers. "Defendant stipulates to six violations and a fine of $21,000 plus relocation allowances totaling $5500 dollars, based upon a date to vacate of February 21, 2005. Is that correct, Mr. Ryan? Mr. Salten?"

"Yes, your honor," Salten muttered.

"Your honor, there is a twelfth tenant, according to DHS," said Attorney Ryan.

"His name?"

"Jesus Cárdenas. And the tenants here and by petition have requested an extra week, requesting additional time to find lodging because it is the middle of the month."

"Mr. Salten?"

"We'll pay the extra $500 relocation. If the city wants another week, that will not affect us." Clearly Caldwell would not have to pay more than the new total of $27,000.

"Next case."

Outside we walked to the car. Gato was brooding. "That asshole try to mess with me again, I'll kill him."

"Take the money and shut up, Gato," Robert told him.

"Is there anything else we can do, Mr. Demas?" Jessie asked.

For the first time John Welch said something. "Young man, you did good. Now just find yourself another place to live." This was advice I knew Gato and I had to heed.

After retrieving his knife from the security desk, John told us he'd get home by himself. Perhaps he was going to check out some rooms himself, or maybe he just didn't want to squeeze into the Saturn again.

HOSPITAL CALL
GEORGE 2005

When the phone or doorbell rang at dinnertime, Gato was among the usual suspects. He knew we'd all be home by six fifteen. He knew not to ask before the 7th of the month to borrow against next month's check. He also knew that $40 once a month was our limit. On his own, he figured that before the 20th we'd want a story. The earlier in the month, the wilder his story would be.

But every few months the intrusion was not about money. He'd call us from the hospital. His asthma was not getting any better. Add a cold, flu, bronchitis, or stress to the mix, and his gasps for breath might signal someone to call for an ambulance. Never was it clear how he wound up in the hospital; something was always amiss in the story.

Our attempt to enroll Gato in a substance abuse rehab program soon after the Cortez Arms was vacated illustrates the point. Three days into the month-long, first phase of the in-residence Pullman House program, he called us from the hospital. He'd had an asthma attack. The program had called for an ambulance, and he was brought to Cook County Hospital. We visited the next afternoon.

Hospital gowns always revealed how small and gaunt Gato was. The circular patches that hooked him to vital sign monitors seemed bigger than their two inches. Alexia asked, "Jesus, what happened?"

"I can't breathe. Mami, I can't breathe." To me, his direct address seemed an attempt to gain greater sympathy than he deserved. To me, he was breathing just fine. "Dadi, please talk to the doctor. He won't tell me what's wrong."

The doctor was nowhere to be found. The nurse at the floor's station wouldn't page the doctor or provide any information. "You're not listed as next-of-kin, sir. The patient has not signed a release authorizing you to receive information. HIPAA regulations." She sounded more like a lawyer than a nurse. Being in the healthcare industry I knew about the protections of the Health Insurance Privacy and Portability Act. But here at County Hospital I recognized just another excuse to underserve the patients. Ever so clear because she refused to budge from her seat to bring a release form to Gato.

We left knowing as little as we did when we arrived. By the next day the picture became clearer. Another call, this time at eight a.m. "Dadi, I need to pick up my medicine. I need a ride."

"From where?"

"From the program, Pull . . . Pullman House."

"Slow down. When did you leave the hospital?"

"Yesterday, just after you and Mami visit me."

"Didn't they give you any medicine?"

"The line too long. It close before I got there."

"What about Pullman House? Can't they take you back to the hospital?"

"They say the van's not working."

"So what makes you think I have the time to take you? I'm waiting to hear back about a job interview. You always think I can turn on a dime for you."

"Please, Dadi, don't be cruel. You know I respect you. I do everything you say. I go to the program, but I get sick. The pharmacy, they say come back at ten a.m."

"OK, but I'm coming right away. Be ready in fifteen minutes."

At Cook County, two lines were already stretching forty feet from the door of the dispensary. Inside, every bench was filled, more so counting the children on their mother's laps. I asked a couple of people which line was which but got two different answers. Gato asked someone he seemed to know who seemed to know and snuck in behind him. No one complained, perhaps knowing they'd be there all day no matter what. But I wasn't going to be there all day. I had a job to find and some promising leads, none of them at Cook County.

I tried to leave. "Dadi, how I get back to the program?"

"That's for you to figure out. Take a bus, call Pullman House." I gave him two dollars and he looked at me as if I had picked his pocket.

"I have to eat too. I'll be here all day."

I just wanted to get out of there. In my wallet was a ten and a twenty. "Ten dollars more, that's all I have. Now I have nothing for lunch." If he could exaggerate, so could I.

That night I tried to reach him at Pullman House. Once again I was given the third degree. "What's your relationship to Jesus Cárdenas? Actually, it doesn't matter who you are, you're not on our list. You will have to call the office in the morning," said the receptionist, obviously fully trained, examined, and certified in the wiles of HIPAACRACY.

"Can I speak to Mr. Deacon? I met him at Mr. Cárdenas's intake interview. Surely he will put me through to Jesus."

By the time I reached Deacon two days later, Gato was long gone. "Wait a minute, let me get his record," Deacon said. I waited seemingly forever, listening to some pretty dreadful Muzak. Finally, throat-clearing sounds announced Deacon's return. "OK. It says right here he checked out to go to Cook County to pick up meds on Wednesday, 8:55 a.m. Then he called for a ride back at 4:20 p.m. And next it says he was discharged from the program at 9:15 this morning. Hold on." And hold on I did to the tune of more Muzak. Deacon again cleared his throat. "Al Bland was on duty Wednesday evening. The five p.m. Cook County van returned eight passengers. He says none of them was Cárdenas. Our rules are pretty strict: you don't sleep here, you're out." Deacon was preachin'. "See, this isn't no jail here. Doors are always open. You can leave anytime you want. You have to want to stay. You have to want to come back."

I got the feeling that guys like Deacon and Bland, working the program now, had once been in the program. They knew that beating a habit wasn't a straight line. You might not make it the first time, the second, or the third.

Fuming, I called Alexia at work. "He's gone. Kicked out of the program, and now he's AWOL, missing, who knows where."

"You think something happened to him?"

"Yeah, something happened. He took that money I gave him in the hospital, took his buddy from the line, and found the nearest liquor store. That's what happened."

"Well, there's nothing we can do now."

For the next three days we couldn't do anything, as far as Gato was concerned. And then he was at our door again, true to form, at six thirty p.m. I'd have felt better had the bell been a food delivery, ringing our top bell thinking it was the first floor, or a Green Force canvasser raising the money that paid his stipend and saved the rainforests.

"Dadi, I found an apartment. Kedzie and Division, $425 a month." He acted as if it was two and a half years earlier when he was resurrected from death by the bureaucracy and we were on a mission to find him an apartment, as if our last encounter in the hospital was last year and not last week, that the Pullman House was a rich coffee blend and not a substance abuse rehab facility serving the weakest instant coffee this side of the equator. "I need my rent money from not paying rent the last two months."

"What about rehab? If you'd stayed in the program, the city would have paid your rent for six months," I said, shaking my head.

"That place was like jail. I need my freedom."

I couldn't argue with someone relishing the freedom that comes with a $550 monthly check and an alcohol dependency he could not admit. But cash was out of the question. I insisted we go to the Currency Exchange to get a money order for the $850 he'd need for a month's rent and security deposit, made out to B&S Management, Inc.

Three or four times again in the two years Gato stayed in the studio on Kedzie we'd get a call from him at one hospital or another: St. Mary's, Swedish American, St. Elizabeth's. Once he used a false name, another time the police brought him wheezing and drunk to the hospital rather than the station house. Always within a day or two he would be enjoying his freedom again.

SHRINK RAP
ARTURO GUZMAN 1981

Editor's note: It was so many months since Gato and I had seen the lawyer Mel Franklin at *Familias Unidas* that I put it out of my mind. Gato was in his new apartment. Our relationship was on autopilot. On the first of the month I'd cash his check, get a money order to cover his rent, send it off to the building management company, and wait for Gato to ring our bell in the evening. We'd chat a little, but I'd just want to get him off our front stoop as fast as I could. He just wanted to get his cash as fast as he could. The fifteenth of the month came around and he'd be ringing the doorbell again, looking for his $40 advance against his next month's check. This was our rhythm.

It was a bit strange to get the call from Franklin at about eight p.m. on a weekday evening. Then again, Franklin himself was a bit strange. Did he have a life apart from *Familias Unidas*? It didn't seem so. In his quiet voice he told me he'd received a response to the Freedom of Information request on behalf of Jesus Cárdenas. According to Franklin, the results were not anything like what Mr. Cárdenas had suggested. There was no record of citizenship and no record of political asylum granted. Mr. Cárdenas was a Cuban refugee who had arrived on the shores of Florida as part of the Mariel Flotilla of 1980. Franklin was noncommittal as to what his status was. "My guess is that Cárdenas has what Immigration and Naturalization calls 'Parole Status,' meaning if he gets into trouble, they could deport him back to Cuba. Best I could do in this case is to make sure he has an up-to-date parole card."

Did I want to come to the office to pick up the papers? When I hesitated he offered to send the papers to me. In return he asked me to send a donation of twenty dollars to *Familias Unidas* to cover postage and copying.

A week passed before the package, a thick manila envelope, arrived by mail. A cover letter from Franklin outlined the contents of the envelope and again requested a donation.

Alexia more than once had suggested that Gato was a Mariel refugee. He was a slacker in America. How could he have been anything else, or worse, in Cuba? I wanted to believe Gato's story. I wanted to see after all these years, since coming here as he claimed in 1961, after all the hardships that left him disabled, dirt poor, and off and on homeless, whether his views of the United States and of Cuba might have changed because of his experiences.

Now the papers were staring me in the face. The picture of Gato that came across, especially in the psychiatrists' evaluations, gave credence to the lore that Fidel Castro had emptied his jails and mental institutions of the "undesirables" of Cuban society.

CITIZEN CÁRDENAS

I'll let you read for yourself Dr. Arturo Guzman's evaluation.

George Demas,
July 2005

Jesus Cárdenas Beltran   Arturo Guzman, M.D.
A-459-08-762   2/24/81
RSD

PRESENTING PROBLEM:
The patient is a 27 year old mulatto male,
who left Cuba about 11½ months ago, and was
transferred immediately from Key West to Fort
Chafee, Arkansas. He stated that he had been in
prison for three months for going AWOL from the
Cuban Army. The sentence was two months but was
extended because he assaulted another prisoner.
The patient says that he has an older brother in
Detroit, Michigan but has had no communication
with him for over three years.

    At present, the patient feels well. His
health is good. He sleeps and eats well. He
denies weight loss but appears gaunt. He claims
that he is not nervous and is not taking regular
medications. His only other contact with the
hospital here was in January when he received a
serious laceration in a knife fight. The patient
said he was provoked by a remark challenging
his manhood. Jesus was married at Fort Smith to
another Cuban refugee about five months ago. His

wife was pregnant at the time of their marriage. At some point after his marriage he was offered a sponsorship in Louisville, KY but decided to stay in camp because his wife would not be able to join him until after the birth of their child. He has now been told that "he could not be sponsored again because of the altercation involving knives." Earlier this month, his wife said that she wanted a divorce because he beat her. The patient claims that he has never hit a woman, let alone a pregnant woman.

PAST HISTORY: The patient was born on 7/26/54 in Guantanamo in the province of Oriente. He was the youngest of five children. His parents are alive in Cuba but they separated when he was six. He thinks their separation had something to do with the Cuban Revolution. After the separation he lived with his mother but also spent time with an aunt in Santiago de Cuba. He went to school until the ninth grade. He can read and write, and denied problems at school. He quit in order to work, eventually as a construction worker, which he did for 8-9 years. During this time he had a common law wife for three years. Together they had a daughter. After three years he left his wife and moved to Havana where he worked for 2-3 years as a cook in a hotel until he was drafted into the army. After one year in the army during a shooting range practice the patient froze to a machine gun with live bullets and began shooting indiscriminately about the range. As a result of this incident, the patient was evaluated at a military psychiatric hospital and treated with Meprobamate and was also injected with one shot of Chlorpromazine, which made him very weak, according to the patient. He was treated for two months. About one month after discharge the patient went AWOL. Eventually he was arrested but released and brought to Mariel for emigration to the United States.

MENTAL STATUS: Patient is hyperverbal, likeable, oriented to time, place, and person. Abstract ideation and calculations are all within normal limits. Attention span and concentration within normal limits. He denies suicidal ideation at this time. Mood is elevated, affect inappropriate. Patient complains of insomnia, epigastric tenderness, with increased psychomotor activity, jitteriness, tension, heart pounding, dizziness, polyuria, occasional lumps felt in the throat, constant worry, hypervigilant because of violence in the camp. He denies thought broadcasts, insertion, and withdrawal. Patient at times appeared to be consciously withholding information.

CLINICAL IMPRESSION: Based on the information available from the patient, since his records are not available at this time, is to rule out generalized anxiety disorder and antisocial personality.

<u>PLACEMENT RECOMMENDATION:</u> Patient should be seen by a psychiatric service here at Ft. Chafee and psychopharmacologic treatment provided for patient's symptomatology and complete medical examination, including GI workup, to exclude organic illness and afterward, as indicated, patient should be placed in a semi-structured environment with educational and vocational program as the patient can learn the necessary skills to adapt to a new society, to which he should be gradually exposed.

A. Guzman, M.D.

PLEASE BELIEVE ME
GATO 2005

So what? I don't care Dadi listen to this tape someday. I'm screwed.

The papers come back from immigration. They say what I think they say. Jesus Cárdenas come to the United States in 1980. Jesus Cárdenas come with all those other losers Castro throw out of his prisons and mental hospitals, the tiefs and the *maricóns* he put on boats at Mariel.

Jesus Cárdenas screw-up at the camp in Arkansas. He get in fights, get arrested, knock up a girl so he got to marry her. Jesus Cárdenas is crazy, say two or three doctors, what you call psi . . . psi . . . psi . . . chi . . . a . . . trist.

So now I'm drinking all the time since Dadi show me the papers when I went to pick up my money.

So what he think of me now? He think I'm a liar. He think I'm no good. He probably not going to be my payee no more.

He don't believe me I came in 1961 or that I was in Vietnam or I'm a citizen. He don't believe I went back to Cuba when my mother die in 1979 and then Castro put me in jail. This one I make up, but how he know that?

Why should he believe me with what the papers say? He don't believe me before that from the other time nothing come back from immigration, nothing come back from the army. But nothing is different than something.

Now he won't believe nothing I say, like why my rent go down. Or no one, not even Memo, living with me. He won't believe I have a daughter from Racine.

Only thing he believe is that I'm a no-good drunk. He think I have to drink every day. OK, I have to drink. I feel this way, no one want me, no one believe me.

Now he won't believe I don't got nothing two days after I get my check. He won't believe I lost most of my money in a taxi. He'll say, "Why you taking a taxi anyway, you think you are rich?" He won't believe me. Worse, he won't lend me money. Too early in the month.

I don't know what I'm going to do.

Knocking at the door. Silence. More knocking at the door.

"Gato, it's Memo. I know you are in there."

"Go away. I'm not talking to nobody."

"Wait, I need something in there."

"Come back later, when you got something for me."

"You broke already?"

Door opens and shuts.

"Broke as can be."

"What happened in here? This place is a mess. How am I going to find my stash? You have the bed overturned and all the clothes from the closet on the floor. Dresser drawers emptied all over the place. I know you didn't find my stuff . . . or did you?"

"What? I don't know what you talking about."

"You're too drunk to even know where to look."

Rummaging noises.

"Here it is. See what you missed in this box of macaroni? This isn't any cheese in here. It just looks like a packet of cheese."

"You think you sell it today?"

"I might. Don't worry. If I get some takers, I'll give you something for letting me keep it here, especially since you didn't know it was here."

"I appreciate. You want some beer?"

"You know I'm trying to stay clean."

"You seen Mami lately?"

"Been awhile, why?"

"Nothing."

"Gato, you say nothing like it something."

"The papers come back from the immigration lawyer. Dadi, I can tell, he's mad. Maybe Mami put in a good word for me."

"And you want me to talk to her?"

"You the one she really like, Memo. She do it for you."

"Yeah, but what can I tell her?"

"Did I sound like I was just off the boat when I met you?"

"You sounded like just another macho man."

"You should talk, *maricón.*"

"You sure you want me talking to Ms. Demas for you? You might not like what I say any more than what those papers say."

"What, you turning on me too?"

"Easy, Gato. Why don't you get some sleep. I'll go sell my stuff, we talk about what I can say over some *mixta* at Marta's, when your head isn't spinning. My treat, OK?"

Door opens and closes.

"That *maricón.* He going to treat me? He going . . ." *Voice trails off.*

Silence for several minutes. Sound of something dropping to the floor. Silence for several more minutes until the tape stops.

TATTOO DÉJÀ VU
GEORGE 2005

It had been almost a week since Gato's immigration papers had arrived from the lawyer when I showed them to him. His initial response was hard to read. More defiant then silent.

"It says you came to the United States in 1980."

"That's when I come back."

"Come back?" My eyebrows furrowed.

He didn't answer, acting like he was still reading the pages.

"It says you were born in 1954. You couldn't have come here in a boat in 1961 if you were just seven then."

"I told you before, they mix it up, they put down the wrong year."

"And you were married?"

"I already told you I have a daughter, Marisol."

"I thought you said her name was Maribel."

"What? You don't hear me right."

"Mami heard the same thing."

He shifted the gears a bit. "You know I'm going to visit her in Racine."

"How will you get there?" I asked.

"I pay a friend twenty dollars. He drive me."

"OK, that's your business."

We left it at that. It was clear he did not want to talk about the immigration papers or his daughter. He had his first-of-the-month money and was ready to spend it.

About a week later on one of those hot and humid Chicago days that slows your walk and quickens your temper, I zigzagged home from the "L" stop on Damen through baby buggies and parents, dogs and walkers, sweaty joggers and teenage gaggles. Across from the park I heard the voice I didn't want to hear.

"Dadi, Dadi."

As I turned to see him running a bit haltingly across the street, I imagined his state, having been in the park all day long with his crew, some among them still having enough money to buy whatever brew or bottom-of-the-line liquor they preferred.

It was a déjà vu moment, like the time he ran across the street shouting to Alexia and me, "I'm dead, I'm dead."

"Make it quick, Gato. I've got things to do tonight." He wasn't in a hurry, but he was out of breath, so I moved the conversation along. "You look like you are limping. What happened?"

With effort he bent down to push up his light grey jeans, uncovering three-inch-wide gauze wrapped several times around his shin.

"I was in accident. On my bike. Car almost hit me. I go into a parked one."

"Who bandaged your leg?"

"Hospital, St. Mary's. They take X-ray, nothing broken."

"You're lucky. What about your bicycle?"

"Iss no good, all bent up. Now I got another one. Dadi, you think you can spare something for me? I'm as broke as my bike."

"Why is it my problem? Did I tell you to buy a new bike or pay someone to take you to Racine?"

"Don't be cruel."

"You come by on the 15ᵗʰ. In the meantime, try to make a few bucks. Or did you forget how to hustle?"

I started walking again and didn't look back. But when I turned the corner onto our street, another familiar face was walking toward me, Memo Rodriguez. We exchanged greetings and hand slaps as we might have back in the day when we loaded and unloaded ships in the early '70s on the Milwaukee docks.

"Just George."

"Hot Rod. You coming from my place?"

"Yeah, I ran into Miss Demas at Walgreens. She invited me over for some lemonade. Sure hit the spot."

"I'm sure it did. You in a hurry?"

"I'm late. I was supposed to meet someone."

"If it's Gato, he's at the park."

"No way. He's not my type," he said, punctuating his sentence with a wink.

"Well, have fun."

The lemonade did sound good, especially as the temperature rose at least ten degrees between the first and the third floor. Inside the apartment the overhead fan whirled at top speed, its effort only once in a while felt as a slight breeze.

"I'm home," I announced. "I just ran into your friend."

Alexia came out of her office. "My friend? I thought he was yours, too."

I borrowed Memo's words, "He's not my type. So what did you and your former student talk about?"

"He showed me a couple of his poems. One was about Jesus; actually it was pretty good."

"And did this masterpiece shed any light on our *amigo Cubano?*"

"Actually it deepened the mystery. Not directly, but there's a duality to the poem, a reflection of Jesus's vivid imagination versus his stark reality. The imagery flips dark to colorful and back between lines, sometimes within lines. It starts and ends with the tattoo on his arm, *el gato negro*. Did you ever notice the small banner with the year 1979 at the bottom of the tattoo? Read these lines. I memorized them so I could write them down for you."

Gato's yellow eyes burning fiercely, gleaming black coat's sheen blue,
Brown Afro-Cuban skin absorbing gold banner 1979 greeting me
Like a hot new tattoo.

I wasn't too impressed with the poetry. I was more concerned with Memo's actions and attitude. I wondered why hadn't he left the poem here and what his reaction to the immigration papers was.

"He said he wasn't sure he was done with the poem. I had to tell him about the immigration papers because he never heard anything about them. Likewise with the Mariel boatlift. But he said he knew Gato when that tattoo was fresh, back in 1979. The tattoo was a gift from one of the Latin Lords to celebrate Gato's promotion."

"How come, whenever questions come up about Gato, one of his cronies comes around to back up his story? First it was Arianna, excuse me, 'Lady Love,' with her cock and bull about the 'Rumble in the Jungle.' Now it's his sometimes roommate Hot Rod Memo and his lyric tattoo poem."

"What's with you? Bad day at work, or is it just the heat?"

"First, I have to battle the yuppie crowds just to make it two blocks from the 'L,' then Gato accosts me, looking for money as usual, then Memo and his bull. And you think he's the next Pulitzer Prize winner."

"Don't take your bad day out on me."

"I thought we were in this together. One day you're telling me I give in to Gato too much, and the next day you're cooking *arroz con gandules* for him or believing his stories."

"Me? Look at you. You read something on a piece of paper and it's God's truth, like that doctor's report from the camp in Arkansas. Everything in it is based on what Jesus told the doctor, and he even admitted Jesus wasn't exactly forthcoming in their sessions. How do you know Jesus wasn't feeding the shrink stories? You believe that he went berserk on a Cuban Army shooting range and lived to tell about it?"

"You have a point there," I said, retreating.

"Look, I know Jesus is no saint. But he has his good side."

"And what side would that be, Alexia?"

"The side with that sexy tattoo, naturally. OK, he's a liar, but to paraphrase Truman, 'He's our liar.' Like it or not, he's become part of our lives."

"Too much so."

"Don't you think I also feel that way at times? I've told you, George, let him find another payee."

"Well, if I knew from the beginning that he was one of the Mariel worms, I'd never have given him the time of day," George said.

"I tried to warn you," Alexia said, when she could have said, "I told you so."

"Well, it's there in black and white now."

Alexia reminded me about the fifteen blank pages and that the naturalization cover letter said right up front that some information cannot be divulged. Yet the usual confidential health or legal information was covered in the pages.

"I've thought about that," I replied. "Not today, but I have. In my wildest thoughts I'm thinking, 'He's sent back to Cuba on a secret CIA mission. He's an army veteran, yes, a gangbanger too, but that's what makes him tough enough to go back into Cuba.'"

"Who's hallucinating now, George?"

"Well, do you have another explanation for the missing pages?"

GATO AND HIS DAUGHTER
ALEXIA 2005

I had a feeling I'd be hearing from Memerto. Jesus's immigration papers had arrived and, as I expected, they revealed that he was a Mariel refuge. I always thought the story about his coming here as a teenager had as many holes as the boat on which he said he arrived. He was no heroic refugee who had the spunk to leave Cuba on his own, but someone thrown out of Cuba by Castro as a "parasite." The Cuban dictator saw an opportunity to get rid of his misfits and make headaches for the United States at the same time.

I don't know how many aspirin the United States took because of Castro's scheme, but George and I downed our share once we acquired the migraine known as Jesus Cárdenas. There were times he would put on the charm, but more often he'd find a way to pound at us, wear away at our nerves, until he accomplished some advantage, usually perceptible more to him than to us. That's why I expected the visit from Memerto, as an emissary from Jesus trying to smooth over the damage done by the immigration papers.

What I hadn't expected was the "appearance" of Gato's daughter in our lives. This series of events turned out to be a vivid example of Jesus's tenacity in the face of resistance. Last May, Jesus, having already received his $40 advance from George, shows up at our doorstep a mere two days later. Gushing with pride, as if he had been her ever-present father as she'd grown up, he tells us his daughter from Racine, Wisconsin, is in Chicago and enrolled at the Culinary School of Illinois. This was the first time that he ever mentioned being a father. I pondered this new facet of Jesus, without realizing it was a hook, until he said he had to buy her a birthday present. The glance between George and me acknowledged that we both smelled the same rat, an attempt to get a second advance against his check. I knew how to call his bluff. From a closet I retrieved an unopened Easter basket of soaps and lotions, a perfect re-gift.

Jesus was so thankful. "Maribel will appreciate this gift from you very much. I tell her all about my Mami and Dadi. But she ask me for something you don't have, some kind of Sunny Walker to play CDs."

I suggested we could pick up one for her. "We bought one for Nick, so we know just where to get a good deal."

"What? You give her something else?"

"No, you'll have to pay for it out of your next check," cautioned George.

"Her birthday tomorrow. You pick it up tonight?"

"Wait a second, Gato," George responded with a bit of irritation. "I've told you before we're not going to jump every time you need something."

"I'm sorry, I don't mean no disrespect. I owe you everything. I appreciate everything you do. I go myself."

"You mean you'll go yourself if we give you the money."

"I pay you from my check."

George's tightening body language prompted me to change

the subject. "Jesus, we'd like to meet Maribel. How about you bring her for dinner on Sunday?"

"She go back to Racine for Saturday and Sunday."

How convenient, I thought, but I was not going to let him off the hook. "When you see her tomorrow, tell her we'd like her to come with you for dinner some evening. Ask her what night would work for her."

"She working nights at a restaurant."

"Well, you ask her. We really would like to meet her."

Now George was changing the subject. "Where is Maribel staying?"

"Her uncle's, my wife's brother."

"Your wife? Aren't you divorced?"

"Dadi, you know divorce too expensive."

"Anyway, like Alexia said, we'd like to meet your daughter— our granddaughter."

A smile broke into a nod down and to Jesus's left, then shaking slowly into a wide grin and laugh. He took the basket of soaps. "So I can borrow $30 for the walk, erh, Walkman?"

Later I asked George why he gave in to Jesus. All he could say was, "Maybe he really does have a daughter."

Then one evening in July, after Mamerto had shown me his Tatoo poem, Jesus came to our door, later than usual, at about eight p.m. Extremely agitated, he was out of breath as if he had been running.

"Mami," he caught his breath. "Mami, my daughter," he caught his breath again. "Marisol in trouble." His hand was on his chest.

"Sit down." I said, pointing to the slatted folding chair on our front porch. He sat, took his inhaler from his pants pocket, and sprayed it once into his mouth.

"He says his daughter is in trouble," I told George, by then down the stairs as well. "Start at the beginning, Jesus. What happened to your daughter?"

"Remember I tell you she live with her uncle?"

"Yes, I think you said they live in Logan Square," George answered.

"Yeah, but he no good. He make her go out with his friend. He's forty years old."

"Did she go?" George asked.

"She think she has to or she can't stay there no more."

"OK, did something happen?" George asked.

"The man take 'vantage of Marisol. I find the man, I kill him."

"Oh no, is she OK? Did she report this to the police?" I asked.

"When did this happen?" George wanted to know.

"That's not all. Tonight the man show up at her work. He go right into the kitchen and say she got to go with him now."

I glanced at George, telling him to ease off his staccato questioning.

After a breather, Jesus continued, "She say she started yelling at him and throwing things at him, then she hit him with a frying pan and he fall down. She hurt him real bad."

"So where is she now?" I asked.

"First she was at the police. They let her go. Now she at my place. She want to go home to Racine, but she don't have money." At this point he was looking at his feet. His expression said he didn't have any either.

After he left with the $40 she needed to get to Racine, I asked George, "Did he call her Marisol? I thought her name was Maribel." Whatever his daughter's name was, it would be a long time before he mentioned her again.

DEAREST NEPHEW 2
TÍA FELICITA

Santiago de Cuba
September 11, 2005

Dearest Nephew,

After all these months, you don't know what a relief it was to get a letter from you. Now it seems you were too busy preparing to move to your own home after that unfortunate burglary at the Cortez Arms. I'm sure you will be much happier and secure in your new building overlooking Humboldt Park. It sounds magnificent. You must have taken great pains to furnish the expansive space of your new residence. From what you tell me Humboldt Park is one of Chicago's oldest parks and has quite an interesting history.

But you did not speak of anything I wrote in my letters to you. Were not my letters forwarded to you? Strange if they weren't. The Cuban post office, though they might steam open letters from abroad, is meticulous in making sure they make it to their intended party. Isn't this true for the US post office as well?

How unfortunate that you lost all of your documents in the burglary. I have made inquiries into obtaining a copy of your birth certificate as you asked. My old comrade, I'll call him A.H., in the Ministry of Records in Guantanamo gave me the forms to fill out and information on the fees required, one-hundred eight dollars, US. It wasn't long ago that an acquaintance like A.H. would have simply provided me with the papers you need. But the recent campaign against favoritism keeps all of the bureaucrats looking over their shoulder. I have enclosed the form. From everything you've told me I'm sure the fee will be insignificant for you.

I have nothing new to tell you of Maritza, Miriam, and Juan. It seems they don't want anything to do with your mother's only sister. But I do have news, obtained in a roundabout way, of your father.

My friend at the ministry verified to me that your records were on file at the Guantanamo office. While looking over them, he recognized your father's name and recalled recently reencountering him at the Hospital General Saturnino Lora in Santiago. Your father is in a ward for the chronically ill, where the wife of A.H. was also assigned. Your father's lungs are diseased from his many years of smoking Vegas Robaina Cigarettes. I imagine you remember those are the non-filter variety. His prognosis is not good.

I could not bring myself to visit him for what he did to your dear, departed mother. I know you too hold him responsible for the breakup of your family, but perhaps you can find it in your heart to write him. The address of the hospital is: Carretera Central, Santiago de Cuba, Cuba.

Now I must tell you my news, and this is difficult for me to tell and I'm sure for you to hear. I too am in deteriorating health. I have been diagnosed with lymphoma, a type of cancer. For too many years I sensed something wrong, but I was afraid to visit even the neighborhood health center. Here I am, the wife of a doctor, and yet I would not put my life into another's hands, until the pain became more than I could bear. I am sorry to burden you with this news.

I am resigned to my fate. I have lived a long and good life. I married my love and closest comrade, and together we had more than 40 years together. We served the people during the birth of the Revolution, providing healthcare, teaching those who could not to read. But we also grew old and perhaps stale with the Revolution and its leaders.

The world is much different than it was at the time of the Revolution. We have each seen and experienced many changes, you in North America, I here in Cuba. Who would have predicted the fall of the Soviet Union? We here did not see it as the fall of Socialism. We *Cubanos* knew they were using us, no matter what the official line. And four years ago this day our hearts were with the people of your adopted country, no matter the stance of the two governments.

Please thank your friend Memo for typing your letter in Spanish. Also tell him I enjoyed his dream poems and look forward to the one he is writing about you. He says he is still working on it.

I do not believe we will ever see each other again. But I will hold you in my heart until my end.

Tu Tía Siempre,
Felicita

RAZING CANE
GEORGE 2006

Gato's request was ridiculous. Shortly after he received the letter from his *Tía Felicita*, he visited Alexia at about eleven in the morning, knowing that I would not be home. According to Alexia, he was pretty drunk and pretty pitiful, practically crying, lamenting, "Why me, why me, why am I all alone?"

Alexia was facing a work deadline and when this was the case, at times like these, she'd call me at the office, telling me, "I don't have time for him and his interruptions. You have to tell him to leave me alone during the day." When she called this time, the conversation was very different.

What changed her mind this time was the letter. She told me how she turned her back on Gato to go back up our stairs when he pleaded, "Mami, please look at this letter from *mi tía*." Until this point, we hadn't heard of *Tía Felicita*, let alone seen any of her letters.

Alexia read the letter, handwritten in beautiful Catholic school script, as best she could in Spanish. On the phone Alexia described to me the roller coaster of the letter, its comedic description of Gato's studio as his "expansive residence," leading up to her revelation of her deteriorating health, and thoughts exposing some of her political consciousness.

Despite her pending deadline and Gato's drunken self-pity, Alexia opened her heart to him as she was apt to do. She invited him upstairs and offered him freshly cooked red lentil soup. As the nourishment countered the liquor and loathing, Gato became more lucid. He talked of his aunt, how he had spent summers with her and her husband. It was the husband, a doctor, who taught him chess. But before long his lucidity turned to absurdity.

"Mami, I have an idea. Mami, I want you and Dadi to visit my aunt, maybe even my father in Cuba."

Alexia could not believe what he was proposing. "Do you have any idea how much it would cost just to get there?"

"I know. I found out from Hector; he from my town. It cost $700. Don't worry, I pay."

No wonder he didn't want me home. I couldn't have held my laughter the way Alexia claimed she did. That night we didn't have to, and we didn't. "Let's see, he'll work three months straight at the tire shop. On a good day he'll make $32, drink and eat $20 of that, and pay a cab $6 to get home," I calculated. "Maybe that will pay the bus fare from Havana to Santiago."

"No, he's going to collect it all in cans that he'll have to haul to the recycling station," Alexia countered. "Except they closed the one on North Avenue, so he'll have to pay a friend to drive him to another recycling lot. With what he has left over, we'll be able to afford a cab to the airport."

But there was reason to Gato's madness. He knew we were Greek and liked to travel to Greece to spend time with family there. He also knew my sympathies toward Cuba. We had our discussions, playing chess in the yard, sipping lemonade.

"So Gato, you ever think you'd be better off in Cuba?"

"What, you crazy?"

"Well, you're not doing so well here. You live on barely $600 a month, you're homeless every time they sell the building where you live."

"I have my freedom."

"Some freedom, being broke three weeks every month."

"That's my fault. I spend what I don't need to."

"In Cuba, you'd have free healthcare."

"I don't pay nothing here."

"Yeah, that's because taxpayers like us are footing the bill." But my argument went over his head.

"I go back, Castro put me in jail."

"Why do you say that?" I asked.

He didn't have to answer. The look on his face said it all. It was I who didn't know what he was talking about.

But what Gato didn't know was that I had been to Cuba in 1970, as a member of the *Venceremos* Brigade. I was in the second contingent of the brigade, made up of North Americans who broke the ban on travel to Cuba, not as tourists but as participants in the historic sugar cane harvest, or *Zafra*, of 1970. We were mostly young, college-age kids, open to the ideas of socialism, having soured on the US system because of the war in Vietnam and the racism exposed by the Civil Rights and Black Power movements of the '50s and '60s. I fit that description, but my Greek heritage gave me another reason.

At the very time the Vietnam War was at its height, a right-wing military junta seized power in the birthplace of democracy. The dictatorship of the generals was backed by the United States. The letters my father received from his village in the mountains of Arcadia stopped coming. Papa hoped his relatives were just being cautious, but he remembered the letters had stopped during World

War II, when German and Italian forces occupied Greece, and for a few years afterward when Greece imploded into a bloody civil war between Communists and the British-backed government. In the fifties, the letters resumed but weren't frequent. Family members had died resisting the Germans, in the famine created by the Nazis, and on both sides of the Civil War.

By the time I became interested in this history, my father and I weren't talking much. I remember a conversation we had sometime during my freshman year of college. I told him, "Socialism seems like a better system than we have with our meaningless materialism."

Papa shook his head. "Sounds good in the book. Too bad you no can ask you dead cousins about it." And then he walked away, sat in our worn armchair, and buried his head in his Greek language weekly, signaling the world to leave him alone.

When I left the University of Wisconsin-Milwaukee in 1968 without a degree, again he wasn't too happy. "Why you no stay in school? You want to wind up like me, a cook in someone else's restaurant? You could become a doctor, instead you go to work at a factory." Soon after that encounter, he died.

When I heard about the *Venceremos* Brigade from activists I knew at the university, I applied. I think they accepted me because they liked my "working class" background and my essay, which included references to the military regime in Greece. As our departure for Cuba approached, I gave my notice at Brice Foundry and promised to write to some of my coworkers.

Gato's idea that Alexia and I travel to Cuba prompted me to think back to my days there and to dig up and read a copy of the letter I sent to the "Brothers at Brice Foundry" about my experiences. I began to wonder whether I would talk myself into returning to Cuba on behalf of Gato.

Brigada Venceremos
Aguacate, Cuba
March 20, 1970

To my Brothers at Brice Foundry,

My impressions of Cuba are changing every day and so much is happening that if I tried to write about everything it would be more like a book. So I'll try to give you a few of my thoughts—especially about working in Cuba.

I am seeing Cuba as the people here see it—with a machete in hand and a mass of sugar cane in front of me, to the right and to the left. The *Venceremos* Brigade is no pleasure trip. We came to Cuba to work, to cut cane, to participate in the *Zafra*, the harvest of 10 million tons. Fidel (Castro), everyone calls him Fidel as if they knew him personally, says it better than I can.

> This leads us to the conviction that work is the most important thing in this Revolution, that the duty of the worker is the most sacred duty of the Revolution, and that to be called a worker is to have the most honorable title in this society. It is the worker who creates the wealth, the bread for all. Our society has become more and more a society of workers, a society of those who produce, a society in which there are fewer parasites.[1]

I can't believe it. I was a pretty lazy dude at BF (who isn't), but here I work harder every day. And let me tell you, the work is hard as hell. Although I've never worked the welding line or a

---

[1]From a speech given by Fidel Castro to a rally in Havana on April 19, 1962, commemorating the first anniversary of the victory over the US-backed invasion at the Bay of Pigs.

punch press eight hours a day, I'm sure it is harder and hotter.

Like I said, the cane is all around you 12 to 15 feet high, kind of like bamboo. Grab one or two in the middle with your left hand, swipe it with your machete above where you are holding it. Damn it, one cut, but the other only went halfway through. Cut again, turn the stalks down, cut off the green leafy tops and toss them to the pile a few feet away. Clear away the straw from dried-out leaves that is everywhere at your feet. Bend down to cut the cane close to the ground. Sometimes you have to hit and hit and curse and hit to cut through the stalks. Pick it up, toss it, grab the next cane to cut. Now it is coming directly at you at a 30 degree angle, almost striking you in the gut, impossible to get to the root. But never do I ask, "What am I killing myself for?"

Cuba, like the cane, is all around us. Life to the fullest, whether it is the constant chopping sound of the machetes hitting cane or the conga drums heard nightly. The Cuban people have an amazing drive to make their country and their Revolution a model for the rest of the underdeveloped world. Even now it is late Saturday night, and off in the distance, when the conga drums are soft, you can hear the tractors and the spider-like cane-hauling machines doing their work. Tomorrow, on Sunday, volunteer cane-cutters will be in the fields, factory workers, bank tellers, and teachers will be in the fields, while the *macheteros* who cut cane six days a weeks will be running the sugar mills, which run 24 hours a day, 7 days a week.

Can you get the idea that Cuba is a country dedicated to work? The national hero is the best *machatero*. Movies are about working people. The Communist Party of Cuba is made up of the most outstanding workers, elected by their fellow workers. More and more it is the ordinary people, the workers, who are running the society—who else in a society where no individuals make huge profits off the sweat of others, while the children of these same people breaking their backs are starving?

How things differ with what we read in the newspapers where we are told that workers labor with a gun at their back, rather than in their own hands. How different from the tales of constant indoctrination. The people of Cuba can never be indoctrinated as long as the speeches they hear and newspapers they read tell of their own accomplishments that they know of firsthand.

In finishing this letter, I'll tell of an experience I had in the fields yesterday. My cutting partner, instead of being another North American, was a Cuban student. Although only about 5'7", Omar is a very fast and smooth cutter, and a cat who really knows where things are at. I had never cut faster myself than I did trying to keep up with him. And as I thought, what can he be thinking to make him work so hard, I started singing to myself a song I first heard on the boat to Cuba.

Cuba qué linda es Cuba . . .
Cuba how beautiful is Cuba . . .

Power to the People,
George Demas

HOOK, LINE, AND CYNIC
GEORGE 2006

Yes, I took the bait, impressionable as I was when I was in Cuba. On my return I remained enthusiastic until reality set in. An early blow was when my friend at the docks, Queen Danny, started bashing queer-bashing Cuba. Later in the '70s, socialism and communism bashed themselves with the excesses of the Chinese cultural revolution, and more so with the millions of Cambodians killed by the Khmer Rouge. Then Solidarity, which came forward as an anti-communist, yet working-class social movement, was repressed by the Poland's Workers' State.

Increasingly let down with socialism and communism, I moved to Chicago in the late '70s. I became involved with a group in Uptown, a community with many residents who were from Appalachia and had little choice but to move north to find work in the cities after so many coal mines shut down after World War II. In Chicago, many settled in the Old Town area, but urban renewal replaced the tenements with Carl Sandburg Village. Though gentrification was not a common word in those days, it was becoming a reality.

At the same time, communities across Chicago were organizing themselves around various issues—police brutality, affordable housing, immigrant rights, welfare rights. A common theme was the displacement of poor people from the valuable real estate they lived on in neighborhoods close to the Loop or along the transit lines heading downtown.

In 1979, Jane Byrne was elected mayor as a reformer but soon showed her true colors by lining up with the old Daley machine she ran against. She put a notorious, shady real-estate developer as head of the Chicago Housing Authority to oversee public housing, she removed African Americans from the Board of Education, and proposed a 1992 World's Fair for Chicago.

By 1982 the community forces had become political. Volunteers, including me, registered 200,000 new voters at unemployment and welfare offices across the city. This effort was key in pushing a reluctant Harold Washington, who beat the machine when he was elected to Congress, to run for and become Chicago's first African American mayor in 1983.

After Washington's victory, election fever was in the air. Instead of community struggles, all eyes were on the battle between Washington and his twenty-one allies in the city council and the twenty-nine alderman aligned with the two Eddies: Ed Vrdolyak and Ed Burke. A local comedian called the city government standoff "Council Wars," with opposing armies headed by Harold Skytalker and Darth Vrdolyak. Community activists more and more saw the solution in ousting the politicians, starting with Democratic Committeeman elections in 1984. In late 1985 a federal court ruled that Chicago's aldermanic map, drawn in 1982, violated the Voting Rights Act by denying African American and Hispanic American communities fair representation in the city council.

With the smell of political victory in the air, the community-based movement that elected Washington drew to it disgruntled city workers looking to change loyalties. Others just wanted to get a city job for the first time. So-called progressive aldermen looked to beef up their political organizations by pressing the mayor's administration for jobs and complained of narrow "Black Nationalism" when enough jobs didn't materialize.

Even the pure at heart began to think, "Why shouldn't I get a job? Better someone active in the community for a long time like me than a Johnny-come-lately." And so when Washington gained four additional votes through the special elections, his own tie-breaking vote in the council allowed him to exercise political power in the city. Less than a year later, Washington won a second term as mayor, and I got my job as a community-police liaison serving the 13th Police District. For the first time in a long time I had a steady income, a decent one at that, and enough to give me the nerve to propose to Alexia. She accepted.

Neither of us had much in the way of family nearby, and it was the second marriage for each of us. So with a small group of friends and my son Marty, we were married the weekend after Independence Day, 1987. We made our home in the building Alexia bought a decade earlier, on a block very different than it is now. Within three months, Chicago was shocked when Washington died soon after suffering a massive heart attack in his city hall office.

Almost immediately, remnants of the old Vrdolyak twenty-nine plotted to divide the Washington forces. They nominated an African American alderman, Eugene Sawyer, to be mayor. He eventually won, with twenty-nine mostly white old-guard aldermen backing him over the progressive candidate, Alderman Tim Evans. Sawyer's election proved to be the stepping-stone for the return of the Democratic machine. Richard M. Daley was elected in 1989, assuming the office his father held for twenty-one years. Even more "progressives" backed Daley this time.

Early on during my community-police liaison job, I realized it was not going to be a place to bring about change. Sure, I was able to advocate on behalf of residents harassed or brutalized by police. Occasionally I had modest results, but the bureaucracy was a constant obstacle. Within months of Washington's death, I was let go, and a cousin of the local alderman took my job.

By this time, Alexia and I had something else to keep us busy: Nick was born late spring, 1988. We baptized Nick at St. Gerasimos Greek Orthodox Church. It was natural that we gravitated back to the Greek Church in our second marriages, but first for each of us to another Greek. Initially we attended services only at Easter and Christmas, but when Nick was old enough, we started attending regularly. Then we started taking Greek classes, forty years after each of us walked away from the classes our parents forced us to take on Saturdays. In general, our interest in all things Greek grew and grew. We each read several books by Nikos Kazantzakis, not just the standard *Zorba the Greek*. Local author Harry Mark Petrakis became another favorite of ours.

But the book that had the biggest impact was Nicholas Gage's *Eleni*, the true story of a village woman in Northern Greece trying to protect her children during World War II and the Greek Civil War. Other books portrayed how inept the Greek Communists were. Some said the government could have been theirs, if during the Fascist occupation they had fought the Nazis more than they had attacked the non-communist resistance. But Gage tells his mother's story by telling the story of his own search for her killer. In doing so he exposes the incredible brutality of the Communists and their heinous *Paidomazoma*, the forcible taking of young children from their families to live in the socialist "havens" of neighboring Bulgaria and Albania. Eleni arranged the escape of four of her children from her village in the midst of a fierce battle zone of the Civil

War. The children made it to safer areas of Greece and eventually to the United States where her husband had already settled. Eleni wasn't so fortunate. She was killed by a firing squad.

I had had enough of all kinds of politics. Socialism, communism, local progressive politics. Instead I was a family man, an active member of the church, and eventually found work using my computer skills, enabling me to provide and tithe. I realized that what had attracted me to socialist and to community movements was their quest for justice for the common people, similar to the Christian principle that the "last shall be first." But these movements, once in power, at best turned their backs on the people and at worst brutalized them. Divorced from these movements, I was frustrated that I was becoming divorced as well from the common people, especially as our community became gentrified. Until, that is, Jesus Cárdenas came running across the street yelling, "Dadi, Mami, I'm dead, I'm dead."

SANTIAGO DREAMING
MEMO 2006

Student of dreams that I am, I remember vividly the waking dream Gato told to me right around the time he concocted the idea that the Demases should visit his *Tía Felicita* in Cuba.

I was crashing at his studio on Kedzie, near Division, the same one *Tía Felicita* referred to as his "expansive residence." Calling that 12' x 16' room, with a closet turned toilet, a studio is laughable enough.

It was a summer Saturday night with one of those brief, humidity-breaking storms that drove me to Gato's door at about ten thirty or so. Traffic was flooding *La Division* as people poured from the park and sidewalks into their cars to ditch the rain. Earlier, the first nonviolent shower had reminded me of the lyric from *Guys and Dolls* about the smell of wet sidewalks after an early morning rain. But lightning flashes separated by shorter and shorter spans were signs I could not ignore.

Luck was polite as a lady that night as Gato was home and alert enough to open the door, if not to close the window, where

181

water had already splattered the floor where I usually slept, or tried to. Sleeping was always difficult in a Gato Cárdenas room, smelling of smoke, stale beer, spoiling food, and early in the month, hetero sex. It could not have been earlier than two thirty that I fell asleep. By then the first round of bars would have emptied and most of that loud after-bar talk on the street below would have quieted enough for me to doze off.

Sometime in the midst of my own dream, a jumble of screeches, darkness, and flashes of light were punctuated by Johnny Robinson reprimanding, "Memo, baby, I told you to stay out of that subway." Smothering me with his embrace, amid the plastic canopies covering endless hangers of shirts, suits, trousers, and blouses conveyed through the back section of his near Cabrini Green dry cleaning establishment, I was awakened by an abrupt cry.

"Dadi, Dadi, is that you?"

"Go back to sleep, I'm not your Dadi," I yelled back groggily. "Wake up if you want to, I don't care, just let me sleep."

"But he there with me, he there."

I knew then, there was no escape. "Who was where?" Maybe if I joined in, I could keep this short. Otherwise he'd babble on for hours, keeping me up again while answering his own questions, like a chess game of nonsense.

"Dadi, he's in Cuba, in my dream when I'm just a kid."

I'd known since our days on the docks in Milwaukee that George Demas had been to Cuba. For a while he bragged about it, talked about cutting cane and the glory of socialist work. It was like he had religion. I was no capitalist. I knew the big money didn't represent me. But I was no commie either. They didn't like us gays any more than we were liked here. We're talking early '70s. But I didn't think that Gato knew George had been to Cuba. I knew for a fact I never mentioned it. George was the best payee Gato ever had—he never ripped him off, so why make Gato nervous?

"Yeah, I had a dream like that once, someone I knew now showing up in a dream about when I was a kid. A lady I knew appeared as one of the nuns at St. Stanislaw."

"No, Memo, it not like that. In the dream, Dadi's young. He has all his hair on his head and a big beard, he look like he come out of the mountains with Castro or something. He's not clean shaven and all grey and flabby like he is now."

"So where was he in your dream?"

"Dadi was in *mi tía's barrio, en Santiago de Cuba.*"

"You sure it was him?" I asked.

"You think I don't know my Dadi? His voice exactly the same, even when he try to talk espanish."

"OK. Why don't you start at the beginning. Can you remember?"

"Me and some buddies, we hanging around on the corner, you know, looking at and flattering all the girls.

"The street we on is very busy. I had my eye on the cars too, especially this one Buick, maybe '58, '56, chrome vents on the side, two-tone—sky blue on the top, sea blue in a wave at the bottom going up all the way to the blue-green mountain top of the *Sierra Madre*, turning purple as the sun set orange."

"Damn, Gato, you're talking like a poet. Keep going."

"Directing traffic was the finest woman we see all day. The black beret, you know, pushed to the side (*here he makes the motion with his hand to show the angles, first of the beret, then her breasts and hips*), the olive army uniform and combat boots. A pistol, look like 9 mm, strapped to her belt make her more sexy, and I'm getting hard.

"But then an old green bus pull up right where I'm standing. A lot of people get off the bus talking English. One of the *gringas* is light-haired, wearing an army uniform, except shorts real short so I can see the white of her thighs. Below a Che Guevara pin I see a nipple pointing through her army shirt.

"As I walk up to her (*Gato pantomimes his story with the bad-ass walk he learned on the streets of Chicago*), all of a sudden young Dadi is in my face. Of course I don't know then he be my Dadi now.

"'Who screw you, your boyfriend?' I say in English."

"'No, I am not her boyfriend, and no I am not screwing her.' But I could tell he wanted to, just like me. 'You're a sexist, leave her alone.' Then he's becoming old like Dadi now except his beard is grey and stringy, like Castro. Then he lecturing me just like he do now about my drinking, but all in espanish. He telling me how some people born in the United States are very poor but can't get government benefits, but *gusanos* who leave Cuba get supported by the government because the government don't like Castro.

"He's making me mad so I push him, but then the traffic cop she twists my arm and pushes me away. 'You stay away from our North American comrades. We have our eyes on you. We know about your brother in Detroit.'

"Dadi is yelling all in espanish about the Cuban refugees being paid by the government. And that's when I wake up," Gato concluded.

"You mean that's when you woke me up."

Gato laid back on his bed. He was sleeping and snoring before I knew it. As I reviewed the dream in my mind, I remembered back to a time George was talking about Cuba, down in the hold of a ship we were working. I asked him how he knew the Cubans liked their revolutionary government. Did he know enough Spanish to know what they were thinking? He told me that he understood what he heard better than he could speak Spanish. Except for the time he met someone with relatives in the United States, refugees of the Castro regime, to whom the US government was providing income. "I was angry. I told that boy off in no uncertain terms, and I did it all in Spanish, and my Spanish was never better."

I thought, Now I have to ask Gato if he has a brother in Detroit.

STANDING UP
GATO 2006

Today I'm a man. Not by beating someone up who disrespect me. Not by making a beautiful woman. No, I'm a man because I stand up for myself in court. I make them say they were getting rid of me for no reason having to do with me. I do nothing wrong. I do this without my Dadi. Maybe I do this because of my Dadi.

Dadi tell me he can't go to court with me. I have to go myself. He tell me which train to take to the Daley Center, where to get off.

Dadi, he don't take my bull either when I say, "What if I'm in the hospital?" He know I know how use the hospital to get out of a jam, like the alcohol program, or to stay out of jail, or maybe I just want three meals a day.

So he tell me I better show up or they will throw my stuff on the street in a week. They won't care if I'm in the hospital. And he say I better be sober. This is Saturday, court's on Tuesday. He say, not just Tuesday, but Sunday, Monday, and Tuesday. He could tell it was too late for me to be sober on Saturday. He smell my breath, he hear the way I talk.

Maybe he think I don't listen because I don't call him Monday night like he tell me. I don't drink Sunday and Monday even though I have first-of-the-month money in my pocket. I'm OK. So I say to myself, "I'm not calling Dadi. I'm not going to bother him and Mami."

I keep bothering them, maybe he say like he tell me two years ago to find myself another payee. Then he really hurt me. He say, "I'm not your Dadi."

But I don't call for a better reason. What, he think I can't make it downtown to the court by myself, that I don't know how to act in court? What? I'm in more courts than he can count. I can do this myself.

I don't like the train—too many stairs, too much noise, underground I don't know where I am. I might miss the stop and miss the court. So I leave real early, twelve o'clock for two o'clock court time.

I find the court, but I'm an hour early; doors are locked. I can't sit, I'm too nervous. Maybe if I have something to drink I won't be so nervous. Maybe I still have time. Dadi, he's not here, but I hear him, "You better be sober."

I see a Latina deputy. She looks fine in her uniform, all pressed, she got all the curves and angles I like in a woman. I ask her about court in Spanish, just like *mi tía* teach me.

"*¿Señorita, este es el corte de la vivienda?*"

"*¿Tienes su papeles?*" I hand her the papers. "*¿Tienes un abogado?*"

She tell me to follow her in when the court open, but she is all business. Too bad she's not interested. I see her diamond ring. Inside the court she make her way to the front, she stop and talk to another deputy, then a woman lawyer, then some old guy, his jacket not big enough to button. She signal me over with her chin and eyebrows.

"This is Mr. Abe Levine. He represents the owner, *el dueño de su edificio.*"

Looking up from his papers, he asks if Mr. Demas, George Demas, is coming."

I think, He know about Dadi?

Then he say he told Mr. Demas I could have thirty days.

In my head is my computer. One more check before I'm out. Dadi's sitting on this month's check. That's $1246 together. Five hundred, even $550, $1000, $1100 with security if Dadi borrow me the security before the first.

I nod. Maybe he think I don't know English. Deputy Salgado, she explain in Spanish. I nod again. I'm not sure to say OK or no. It seem Dadi talk to him already. Maybe that's why he want me to call last night. Maybe Dadi's coming to court. I'm looking this side, other side, front to back. The court is filling up. I can't see all of the seats because people are standing, talking to each other, till things go quiet. First the big Black sheriff come in. I hear, "Judge Rohmer." Everyone stands. After the judge come in, he sit at his high desk. Then everyone sit down. I'm in the first row behind the lawyers.

They call a lot of names before they call me. My stomach is nervous; maybe I still have time to go downstairs. "Cárdenas, Jesus, B&S Management, Incorporated." Abe Lincoln look my way, I go up and stand next to him in front of the judge. Lincoln is tall, fat, and white. I'm short, thin, and dark. The judge and Lincoln, or is it Levine, they talk. The judge look at me.

"Your honor, I pay my rent every month. My payee send the check. I do nothing wrong."

The lawyer Abe say something like, "This is just a thirty-day termination, surrender premises. No action by Mr. Cárdenas."

I like that he call me "Mr. Cárdenas."

The lawyer look down at his papers, turn some pages like he's looking for something. I wonder what. "No, I have no causal action here," says Lincoln.

The judge ask if anyone object to thirty days.

"I object. Thirty days for what?" Now I'm angry.

The judge tell me to calm down. He say, "Mr. Cárdenas, we're not sending you to jail. You have thirty days before an eviction."

"So the sheriff come in thirty days and take my stuff?"

Lincoln tell me I might have a week or two after the thirty days.

The clerk calls another name and another rental company. Different lawyers come in front of the judge. Lincoln nods for me to follow. Two years at that place over in two minutes. But I stand up for myself. That's what I tell Dadi when I call him tonight.

HIGH ROLLER
ALEXIA 2006

"Alex, this is Ada Salgado, remember, from the elections? I thought of you today because this Cuban guy was in court where I work today and he mention your husband name, George Demas. I wonder, Is that Alex's husband George? Anyway, call me, it's been such a long time, so call me: 773-555-2739. Hope you, Nick, and George are all right, if you still with George."

I listened to that phone message. How could I not remember Ada, even if it had been ten years since I last saw her? I consider myself a feminist, but I always picture Ada with those oversized hair rollers. At home, in meetings, she'd have her hair up in them. Sometimes even out in the precincts, her hair would be up underneath a colorful scarf—yellow, orange, purple, blue, flower patterns, diamond patterns. Perhaps the days were color coded.

We were partners even though we were in charge of different but adjoining precincts that voted in the same school. On weekdays and weekends, if our regular partners were not available, we'd walk the streets together. Typically I'd carry the poll sheet, Ada the campaign literature. If we were stopping at a building where neither of us knew anyone, we looked for clues about the voters inside. Names were important, but curtains were often our best clue. Flower-patterned curtains were favored by Puerto Ricans. Lace curtains the older residents. Sheets improvising as curtains told us the people were poor. Blinds, it would depend—thin or vertical had to be yuppies, while the wide, horizontal variety could belong to anyone.

Obviously the Cuban guy who showed up in her court—I knew she was a bailiff at the Daley Center—was Jesus. With my memories flashing before me and my curiosity looming about Jesus's day in court, I dialed her back right away.

"Ada? Alexia. I just got your message."

"Oh Alex, I'm so glad you called back. It's been such a long time. You in the same house?"

"Going on thirty years now."

"You're kidding; really? How about I come over now if you're not too busy."

"Seven thirty. That'll give me time to change."

On the dot the doorbell rang. George was home, so he went down the two flights to let her in. I could tell right away it was Ada. I could hear them talking as they got to the second landing.

"Yeah, they gave him thirty days. It'll be closer to forty before they actually evict him."

When we saw each other, Ada broke out in a smile as big as the rollers curling her hair under a gauzy orange scarf.

"Alex, you look so good," she said as she wrapped her arms around me.

Stepping back from Ada's hug, I gave her a look over. "Girl, you're trim as ever."

"Who you kidding? I must be ten pounds heavier than you last saw me. Sorry about the rollers."

"Now who's kidding? They're your trademark."

"Well, I have to look good in court, you know."

As we sat down at the dining room table, George moved to the kitchen and made himself busy with Mr. Coffee. I knew he'd be listening. He knew to stay out of our way, at least for a while.

"You heard about my sister, Elba? They didn't catch the cancer in time. It's three years now."

"I'm so sorry. No, I hadn't heard." I had, from Arianna, but I was embarrassed, having let the daily routine keep me from reaching out to Ada when I first did. "It must have been difficult."

"It was really hard. She had no husband. I was her only family in the States."

"Was your mother able to visit? She's still in Puerto Rico, no?"

"She had her own health problems, mostly just getting old. And things got bad so quick with Elba. She wasn't able to go to the island. She would have rather died there."

"Well, I know you were there with her to the end. I often envied how close Elba and you were. I never had a sister, and you know brothers, sometimes they are there for you, sometimes not."

"Kind of like husbands."

Our sadness-relieving laughter was interrupted by the husband in the house, bringing the coffee he brewed and the banana bread I baked the day before.

"How about men in general, aren't we all unreliable?"

"Oh George, we knew you'd be listening," responded Ada, puckering her lips, tilting her head, blinking a big eye straight at George. Then we were all laughing.

"Speaking of husbands, Ada, is that a new engagement ring?"

"You crazy? I wear that to keep the wolves away at the courthouse. Even your friend Cárdenas tried sweet talking me until he saw the ring. Actually, he kept it up after he saw it. Even asked me how long I had been married. Told him, 'None of your business.' Told him, 'Flatter me all you want, honey; next thing you'll miss your court call.'"

"How'd he conduct himself in court?" George wanted to know.

"He did all right for himself, except when he thought the judge was sentencing him to thirty days in jail. Almost got belligerent. But the judge was cool, winked at me, seeing I was doing some translating.

"Poor guy, how did you get mixed up with him? You're not in politics or community stuff anymore. Aren't you some kind of computer guy?"

"Have been almost fifteen years now, but Gato, that is, Jesus, he's been around the neighborhood forever."

"Hey, didn't he hang out a lot in the park paying chess and dominos with the Cubans from the senior building? I thought he looked familiar."

I told her the story of Jesus's "death" and resurrection, the payee arrangement, his string of housing crises over the last several years. But I didn't want Jesus to consume my conversation with Ada; he consumed enough of our lives.

"Ever see Albert?" For a while we'd seen Albert now and then in the neighborhood, at the Jewel, the Walgreens, the dry cleaner. Albert had been devoted to Ada, and that devotion gave him his energy, humor, self-confidence, and charm. Ada had the jewelry to prove his generosity: diamond rings, gold bracelets, and pendants. Their spacious apartment seemed to always have one new appliance or another and the best electronics. Albert, an assembly line worker in the '60s, had risen by the '80s to a management role for an electronics firm. He could easily afford the material things that Ada put so much stock in but for which he cared little. What he cared deeply for was Ada.

But once Ada's political connections landed her the deputy sheriff job, Albert found himself alone. Within a year, Ada and Albert were history, and she had herself a gold-colored brick bungalow with leaded-glass windows and beautiful oak woodwork in the Kelvin Park neighborhood. The furniture, appliances, and electronics from the old place moved in with Ada, everything except Albert.

Albert's complexion became pale, his step stiffened, his waistline expanded. But Ada, even after her sister's death, remained bubbly.

"Oh, I see Albert. We're still friends. He calls, says he wants to get back together, says he's a changed man.

"Matter of fact, that's one of the things I wanted to talk to you about. Seeing as how you're involved with Cárdenas, Albert might be able to help him. He's working for Hermosa Housing, they got some subsidized buildings. He might be able to get Jesus in there on an emergency basis."

She was on her cell leaving a message for Albert. "Honey, I'm over at Alex and George's house, in the old neighborhood. Call me. I need you to do a favor for me. George and Alex say hi and want to know where you been? Anyway, you know my number."

And she knew Albert's. At least this time someone else might benefit.

UNFINISHED BLUE LINE
MEMO 2006

I do some of my best writing on the train. If I know it's going to be a long trip, like to and from my mother's house in Berwyn, I make sure to bring my black composition book. There's the people, the scenery passing by, even underground, something about the rhythm of the train that helps me get into a writing groove and forget about my own troubles.

That day I was heading home, if you can call it that, to the stained mattress on the floor of Gato's studio for which he expected to get something from me in exchange. When it was not convenient for him or I was broke, I'd wind up sleeping in Humboldt Park. I spent most of my time outside that summer. That's why my clothes would get so bleached out, not from Mama's washing machine that I used when I went to see her maybe every six weeks.

The writing doesn't come quick on the train. There are a lot of scratches in that composition book, but there's also a lot of good poetry, too. I try to sit in the next to the last car, in the last seat before the conductor's area. From there I can scan the whole car, until it gets so crowded I can only reflect on the other passengers through their images reflected in the windows. On that day it wasn't until 18th Street that I caught my stride.

> *Riding on the train, riding on the Blue Line*

That's a start, I thought.

> *I read the faces like others read the Times.*

Not bad.

> *Days of stress drawn in brows,*
> *Nights of anticipation, fidgeting hands,*
> *Drooped eyes, bobbing heads sleeping*
> *Ears on edge listening for their stop*
> *Crowded in seats, standing braced against poles,*
> *Hanging from the bars,*
> *Swayed, sometimes jolted, side to side.*

Among those getting on at Lawndale was an African American teenager replete with denim shorts probably six sizes too big for his thirty-two-inch waist. As he headed away from the door, his shorts fallen down to the round of his cheeks, his plaid boxers were exposed. Similar arcs fell higher up on his slim body, gold bling around his neck, plastic cord from his ears ringing with the tinny sound of his cheap MP3 player.

I contemplated a verse about him, but rather than writing anything on the spot, I let it ruminate and weave through memories of my own teenage years estranged from my parents, especially my father.

At Polk Street Medical Center, a late fifties Polish woman, possibly from the housekeeping staff at Rush, got on and took the last seat in the car behind the teenager with the falling shorts. I wondered if she was from my first neighborhood near Pulaski Park or farther up Milwaukee Avenue in Avondale. See how I imagine things I couldn't possibly know.

> *Polish cleaning woman,*
> *hands tight around*
> *shopping bag on her lap,*
> *Whitening hair pulled back,*
> *On her mind, her daughter,*
> *Barely fifteen, soon to be a mother*
> *By a Puerto Rican.*
> *Why my granddaughter?*
> *I told her to watch out for that boy.*
> *I thought the Catholic School would help.*
> *How will I manage?*
> *She'll just leave the baby with me,*
> *How will I care for her,*
> *So tired, cooking, washing, scrubbing?*

I wanted to close my eyes so I could rest before the frenzy of the Loop. But as the train left UIC-Halsted, I noticed a middle-aged man and a teenager who had squeezed through the train's accordion doors. This wasn't father and son. The man's longing glances at the youth were all too familiar to me, as was the wary return gaze. I wondered if this were a return encounter or a first time. At least my first was with a schoolmate, not a teacher.

At LaSalle, an Indian woman in an orange and pink sari brushed past these two and grabbed the rail behind the second seat with her left hand. In her right hand she clutched a manila envelope to her chest. Had she been to the Immigration office at Clark and LaSalle, the one I went to with Gato to try to get him copies of his papers?

"Jackson, transfer to the Red Line" wakes me and my writing pen.

Amid the stream
Of white collar dulled minds,
An artist boards.
Obtuse angles delineate
This forty-something male,
Still brown straight hair
Falls at a slant
From retreating hairline,
Angled eyebrows,
Long nose, Adam's apple,
Elbows pointing, tilting posture,
Hands that think.

"Monroe, Madison." No one's getting off.

Madison Avenue, an ad man,
Pressed clean,
Pressed tightly to the window
By the too heavy
Carson's cosmetic girl.
Fumbling in her bag
Thinking I'm looking at her,
Looking down
To avoid staring eyes.
He's thinking he's so smart,

Bold ideas
Holding up the structure
Of an empty life.

"Randolph, Washington, Daley Center, transfer to the Red Line."

Three punks in Yankee caps
Coming from a courtroom,
Brims flat and askew,
Sox not good enough?
The hell with you.
In them, I know myself
Too well from twenty years ago,
Selling blow for gangs.
So cool standing by the doors,
Swaying larger than oversized jerseys,
Larger than the space should allot
Leaving less for clerks
Coyly avoiding a scene.

"Clark and Lake, Thompson Center, Transfer for the Orange, Green, Brown, and Purple Lines."

A dusty hard hat,
Steel-toed boot type,
Lucky Strikes rolled
In chest tight T-shirt sleeve,
Black lock curled on forehead.
Like me on the docks,
Fork lifting pallets
He's thinking he's pretty bad,

Shooting looks
There's a babe across the aisle
Filing her nails, chomping gum
Wondering why
He's giving her time of day.

It wasn't until days later that I was able to read again these verses I wrote. They helped me remember the before, but not the during. It was not until I was in the tunnel, choking on smoke, my head pounding, eyes tearing, that I knew more than the hands that lifted me, guided me past caged bulbs and numbered signs. And the first thing I knew was that I didn't have my composition book.

I stopped and tried to turn around, but others kept coming.

"You can't stop."

The voice had a familiar sound. Was it the one who asked, "Are you all right? Can you stand up? Let me help you."

"I have to go back. My notebook, I don't have my notebook."

"You can't go back."

I heard yelling and coughing. "Hey, what's the idea? Keep it moving."

Again the hands of the familiar voice were on my arms. "We all left things on the train."

We were moving forward again, too many people behind us to do anything else.

"That book isn't just anything, it's my everything."

"Let's get out of here. Then we'll talk to someone about your notebook."

It was getting brighter. Stairs loomed ahead, leading up through a shaft of light. Outside, the bright sunlight blinded me and accented the pounding in my skull. My legs gave way.

A vaguely familiar face was close to mine. The words and voice

I recognized, "Are you all right?" This was the first I could put a face to the voice. It had been so dark and smoky in the tunnel I could not see more than a silhouette of the person helping me. It was the man who I imagined to be an artist, the one with the long arms and angled features. But somehow he seemed more familiar than that.

I couldn't respond to his simple question. He stood up. "Paramedic," his voice boomed. "Paramedic. We need a paramedic here." In a lower voice, "Give him room, give him room to breathe."

I couldn't see much. Someone was shading my head with a jacket. Someone else cushioned my head with a bag of some sort. Legs with dark blue pants came into view. At the top of the trousers was a holstered gun. I heard an electronically muted voice. When awhile later a plastic mask was lowered to my nose, all I could see was the light blue shirt above the mask as I experienced a new kind of rush from oxygen entering my lungs.

I must have passed out. When I awoke I was in a hospital. The first thing I saw was the face of the familiar voice. This time he didn't ask, "Are you all right?" He just smiled.

THREE-RING CIRCUS
GEORGE 2006

It had been a long, busy day of work. Not a bad day. Matter of fact I had accomplished a lot, completing a prototype for a new way of defining metrics for the operations area of the company I worked for, Allied Imaging. My time on the Blue Line was longer than when I worked downtown, the counter commute toward the airport in the morning and back in the late afternoon had one advantage: I almost always had a seat. I'd read, do crosswords and Sudoku puzzles. I tried to leave work at work, but thorny problems sometimes caused my brain to itch. So on my way home, I might scratch a database design or shorthand the kind of complex SQL query that had become my specialty. It was that kind of day.

But by Jefferson Park, something seemed amiss on the Blue Line. The station's platform seemed crowded with outbound commuters waiting for the next train. The loudspeaker crackled with unintelligible messages. But when the doors shut on our inbound train, I lost any concern I might have had if our train had been delayed. I closed my eyes and instructed my ears to listen for only two words, "Western Avenue."

Indeed I woke up just past California as the automata announced, "Next stop Western Avenue." I exited there, though more often I got off at Damen. I needed the extra half-mile exercise, so I briskly walked the eight blocks. I was running a bit late, but nevertheless wondered whether Alexia would have dinner ready.

But as soon as I made it up the stairs to our apartment and shouted "hello" loud enough so it could be heard in the kitchen, the doorbell chimed and a second later the phone followed suit.

"Let it go; dinner's hot," Alexia rang out. "We don't need another three-ring circus around here."

"Nick, are you here? Can you get the phone? I have to see who's at the door."

"Can't you leave it? We're not expecting anyone. It's always something at dinnertime."

"I'm not going down. I'll look out the front window." I had to lift up the screen to do so, but even with my head out the window I couldn't see who was ringing the bell. "Who's there?"

"Dadi."

"Oh no, what does he want?" I said to myself, at first not able to see Gato. "Can you come back an hour from now? We're just starting to eat now." I could see him now, halfway down the limestone stairs.

"It's emergency. You got to come down."

"It's Gato. He says it's an emergency. I'll try to be quick."

"Pop, Tyrone is on the phone."

Tyrone Ford, his wife Alice, and their daughter Mindy had been our first-floor tenants for the last eight years. During that time they had become more than tenants. We counted them now among our best friends.

"Tell him I'll knock on his door when I'm done with Gato." I was starting down the stairs.

"He's not home, he's . . ."

"Just get his cell number."

Gato was there in his summer garb—baggy blue denim shorts, Hawaiian shirt. He seemed agitated. "Dadi, you watch the news?"

"No, I just got home."

"You take the train?"

"Every day. So what's the emergency?"

"Don't you hear about the train accident? The subway from downtown crash."

"I figured there was something happening. Listen, we're about to have dinner."

"Turn on the news . . ."

"Gato, I worked all day. I just want to sit down and have dinner with Nick and Alexia."

"Tell Mami. Memo in the accident. I see him on TV. He come out of the subway. Everyone all black. All of a sudden he collapse. Right on TV."

"You sure it was him?"

"What? You don't believe I know my own friend?"

"OK. We'll watch the news. I'm not sure there's anything we can do."

"What about the guy on the first floor, he here?"

"Tyrone? No, he's not home. Listen, I'm going upstairs now."

"He there too. He help Memo. That's what I want to tell you."

Then I remembered the phone call when the doorbell rang. "Wait here."

I ran up the stairs. "Nick, did you get Tyrone's cell number? Did he say where he was?"

"Here, I wrote it down for you. He said he's at Cook County Hospital. Something about an accident on the Blue Line and Jesus's friend Memo."

"Well, I'll be. Alexia, you hear anything about an accident on the Blue Line?"

"I turned BBM on right after Tyrone's call. Listen, it's coming on again."

"One hundred fifty transit riders have been brought to area hospitals after the rush-hour derailment of an outbound Blue Line train between Lake and Grand. A thousand passengers had to be evacuated after the last car on the train went off the tracks. A fire accompanying the derailment blackened the exit route with smoke as commuters walked single-file to an emergency exit near Clinton and Grand. The cause of the incident is being investigated."

"Gato saw it on the news. He saw Tyrone helping Memo. Did you talk to Tyrone?"

"I've been a little busy getting dinner ready. I could have used a little help." Alexia's exasperated expression turned to a worried look. "You think we better call Tyrone at the hospital? I wondered why he called us."

"Alexia, why don't you call him? I can't leave Gato hanging downstairs."

"OK, you get Jesus, invite him to dinner. Tell him it's his favorite, *habichuelas.*"

As usual, it took awhile for Gato to get up the stairs. He rested on the second landing. When we reached the third floor, Alexia was just hanging up the phone and Nick was watching the local cable news station.

"Pop, you just missed it. They showed Tyrone helping Memo out of the emergency exit. Their faces were covered with soot. Then all of a sudden Memo fainted or something."

"What did you find out, Alexia?"

"Tyrone is fine. It's Mamerto they're holding for observation. The smoke affected him pretty badly, but they're more concerned that he might have a concussion."

"Mami, you talk to Memo?" Gato asked.

"Just for a minute. He was a little groggy."

"So do you think we need to go there?" I asked.

"Ty says he can stay at least another hour. Alice and Mindy are visiting Alice's mom in Romeoville and won't be back until at least nine. He'll call us as soon as they decide whether they're going to admit Mamerto."

Nick and I arranged TV trays in the living room so we could watch the news while eating.

As we started eating, Gato surprised us. "That happen yesterday, I be in the hospital."

"How's that?" I asked.

"What? You don't remember I have court yesterday?"

"Of course we remember, Jesus," Alexia offered. "In fact, I talked to a friend of mine who told me you have least a month before you have to be out of your apartment."

A quizzical look came over Gato's face. "You got a spy down there?"

"No, just an old friend, Ada Salgado. She's a bailiff in the court."

"The good-looking deputy? The *Puerta Ricaña?* You know her?"

Nick shushed us all. "It's coming on the news now."

The phone ringing drowned out the "now."

"I'll get it, probably Ty," I whispered as I hurried to the phone in the kitchen. I caught it just in time to keep the call from going to the message machine.

"Ty?"

"George?" The voice wasn't Ty's. "It's Ada Salgado."

"Hold on, I'll get Alexia."

"No, it's about your friend Jesus. I talked to Albert. He said he could help him get into subsidized housing. I gave him your number."

"Wow, that's great news, Ada. Thanks. I'll tell him. I'll let you go now."

"George, wait. There is something I wanted to talk to Alexia about."

"Hold on then." I muffled the phone and shouted out, "Alexia, it's Ada Salgado. She wants to talk to you."

"Tell her I'll call her back."

Then I heard Gato. "Mami, let me talk to her, I think she like me."

"We've got to keep the phone open in case Ty calls about Mamerto."

I conveyed Alexia's message to Ada and came back to my spot on the couch with my TV tray and my lukewarm *habichuelas*. The news about the Blue Line accident was replaced by the latest Chicago sports blues.

After two spoonfuls the phone rang again. "Can you get this one, Nick? If it's Tyrone, I'll take it. Anyone else, take a message."

Another spoonful and a sip of water later and Nick is shouting from the kitchen. "It's Albert Salgado, says it important. Something about Jesus."

"I'll take it in here," I shouted back to Nick. "This guy can help you get into low-rent housing," I said to Gato.

Albert and I always got along, though we were never close. He was involved in politics because Ada was. He'd come to all of the meetings, drive Ada to the precincts she would canvass, but would rather sit in the car than talk to the voters. He put himself in their shoes. When he was home he didn't want to be bothered by the doorbell ringing, and he figured no one else liked it either. Now that I'm no longer into precinct politics I relate to Albert's point of view.

But on election day Albert was a great "passer." Whether it was his charm with the ladies or just that he knew almost everyone in the neighborhood, no one would get by him without taking a voting list with the punch numbers for our candidates. His technique of walking with the voters and between them and the other passers kept the opposition from getting their cards into the voters' hands.

When Ada and Alexia got together, usually at the Salgados, I was obliged to come along. Albert and I would drink beers, watching the Bulls in their pre-championship years. But we didn't talk much beyond the game in front of us.

"Jorge," he laughed, "how you doing? Better than your Cubs, I hope."

"Alberto, I'm good. How are you? But you know I've always been a Braves fan. Hey, I grew up not far from County Stadium. But you didn't call to talk baseball."

"No, Ada tells me you been helping this guy who's gonna need a place to live. I've been with Hermosa Housing almost five years now. If he's getting evicted and becomes homeless I should be able to get him in as an emergency case. Who is he, though? The name Jesus Cárdenas doesn't ring a bell. Ada says he looked kind of familiar."

"He's been around the neighborhood at least twenty years. I'm sure you'd recognize him. He knows just about everyone from the old days too."

"Hey, why don't you put him on the phone?"

I didn't have to crowd Gato while he was on the phone. I could have heard him from two rooms away, though the conversation was almost all in Spanish. Obviously Albert knew him as soon as he heard Gato's unique voice and his street name. Soon it was clear, Gato wasn't the only one laughing. Things quieted down a bit and I heard Gato say, "Berto, I'll have to talk to my Dadi. I see you in July."

He handed the phone back without saying anything.

Albert explained that he couldn't get Gato into one of their SRO units until September. He asked that we get in touch sometime in the middle of August and gave me his phone number.

After I hung up, I turned to Gato. He seemed dejected.

"Something wrong? Albert sounded pretty positive to me. Seems like you guys go back awhile. You know him from the park?

Gato burst back, "How come nothing ever go right for me? He say all I need is state of Illinois ID. I don't got that, just that parole card the immigration lawyer got me."

"That's something," I said as calmly as I could. "Let's take one step at a time. I think we can get your social security card with the parole card. With the two of them we should be able to get the state ID."

The phone rang again. Alexia, already in the kitchen cleaning up, answered it there.

"It's Ty. They're releasing Memo. Can you pick them up?"

"Tell them I'll be there in a half hour."

I looked at Gato. "You coming with?"

He nodded. I looked over at my *habichuelas* on the TV tray. They had to be cold by now. "So what," I said to myself. "I have about as much of an appetite now as a tightrope walker who just fell into the safety net."

Except I was playing the part of the safety net.

FIDELITY
ALEXIA 2006

On the eve of August 1, we first heard the news that Fidel Castro was stepping aside from the presidency of Cuba, and his brother Raul would serve as interim president. Speculation was that the older Castro had an intestinal disorder, perhaps cancer, requiring surgery. As ever, the official Cuban press announcement was short on details. But that did not stop the US media from speculating on reforms in the Cuban political system and changes in US-Cuban relations.

All of this interested George much more than it did me. He had been to Cuba in the early '70s and, though he had since soured on socialism and communism, he regarded Fidel Castro respectfully for standing up to the United States and for bringing healthcare and education broadly to the Cuban people, even if they lacked political freedom. George would argue that compared to other Latin American countries that had more "democracy," Cuba had much less poverty and a much smaller gap between the rich and poor.

My interest in politics was more local and national than international. My parents were Democrats and I was a Democrat. In

2006 there were two constants in my political outlook. I could not stand Mayor Daley and I absolutely hated George W. Bush. I had a visceral reaction to this president. His snicker and swagger revealed his arrogance, while his use of words unmasked his ignorance.

The imminent death, or not, of Fidel Castro would not alter my life. On the morning of August 1, 2006, I still had pages to edit, meals to cook, an eighteen-year-old getting ready for college, and a dog to walk. Being the first day of the month, I also had banking first thing in the morning for another wily Cuban, Jesus Cárdenas, who would be at our door at eleven a.m. looking for his monthly payment and money order to pay his rent. George was Jesus's SSI payee, but I was his banker, an arrangement that kept our first-of-the-month dinnertimes sane. By paying Jesus earlier in the day, even before his check came in the mail, we avoided George having to rush home from work to catch the bank before it closed. By paying Jesus earlier in the day, he'd be too soused and otherwise occupied to ring our bell just as we put dinner on the table. But there was no need for a rental money order that month. Jesus had been evicted two weeks earlier and once again was living on the streets, more accurately the grass of Humboldt Park.

Surprise it was then, shortly after seven a.m., while taking Bruno for his constitutional near Wicker Park, to hear that unmistakable shout as he crossed the street, "Mami, Mami." Upon reaching me, "You hear about Castro?" Here he was, Jesus Cárdenas, again homeless, still without identification, and he's up and about early in the morning wanting to talk about Castro.

"I thought you were staying in Humboldt Park."

"Mami, I am. But I have to come talk to you about Castro."

"Of course I heard the news; they're hardly talking about anything else on TV and radio. How did you find out?"

An exasperated look appeared on his face, a little surprised, a little hurt. "Mami, don't you think I listen to the news? I hear people in the park talking so I go to the bar with the espanish TV."

"Bruno hasn't gone yet. Walk with me. I want to hear what you think of the Castros."

"I take Bruno," Jesus commanded, seizing the strap from me without hesitation. We walked west along Schiller, as I did not want to crisscross George on his way to work. This would be my conversation with Jesus.

"So what do you think, Jesus, will Raul be better or worse than Fidel?"

"I feel bad, real bad. The little brother be much worse. Fidel, he's pretty good."

Now I was astounded. "I thought you left Cuba because things were bad for you."

"Yes, Mami, they real bad, just like they real bad for me now. I don't blame nobody but me that I'm on the street. You think I blame Bush I lose my ID and can't get the low rent?"

"So you didn't leave Cuba because of Castro?"

"That's what I tell the US. How else I get my benefits? I even tell Dadi that before I know him so good. But Mami, I always tell you the truth. I can't lie to you. You too good to me."

"So why did you leave then?"

"I screw up, Mami, excuse my language, but I screw up. I don't listen to nobody. You know my family always have trouble. But I don't even listen to *mi Tía Felicita*. So I get into trouble and then I have to leave." Gone was his earlier defiance and playfulness. Jesus's face was as long as Bruno's.

"What did your aunt suggest?"

"She tell me the revolution be good for me, to stay in school, to work hard. Now I know she right. Some boys like me study hard, go to school, become doctors, engineers. OK they not rich like they be here, but they not bums in Cuba or bums here, like me."

"Will you tell me, what was it that made you leave Cuba?"

"Mami, I don't like to talk about it. But you ask, I can't refuse."

He stopped walking, as if he was in pain, but he didn't pull out his inhaler. Conveniently Bruno had some interesting smells to keep him occupied.

"Mami, I tell you my family have troubles. My father leave our family. He say he wanted to keep his job at the Guantanamo base, but my mother's sister, *Tía Felicita*, she's with the revolution. That is why he say he leave. But *mi madre*, she know he have another woman.

"We have nothing. With five children, my mother, she can't work. The new government's no help, especially when the CIA invade *Playa Giron*, you call it Bay of Pigs. I'm the oldest; I have to do something. I start stealing, first small things like fruit from the market, some milk, right from the goat. I don't get caught; I keep stealing. I think I'm so smart I can steal a pig and have the butcher cut it up. He say no. Then I try to sell it to a truck driver; he refuse too. Why I don't think to roast it for *lechón* first? It roast on the *asador* behind our shack when the police drive up in a jeep. I hear them talk to *mi madre*, and I start to run through the cane fields until I can run no more. Then I lie down still, like a rock.

"When night come, I take the long way to my friend's house. I make some noise, so he come out and I call out his name, 'Pedro.' I tell him what happen. He get some *cerveza* and then we talk all night.

"Pedro, he the one suggest we escape to the United States. I say we can't do that 'cause we don't have no money. But he say we don't need much, just a little boat. Maybe he already have this idea 'cause he has it all in his mind. He say if we go to *Habana*, he have a friend there. He say his friend can get us work, construction. Then we have enough to buy a boat. He tell me his friend want to leave Cuba too.

"But I'm not so sure. I tell him my family need me. He convince me. He say, 'They need you in Castro's jail? You crazy.'

"Dadi can tell you the rest of the story, if he not already tell you. But I tell you one more thing. I tell you I'm no tief. Once I'm here in United States, I do plenty bad things, but I don't steal from nobody. I'm in a gang, I sell drugs, shoot at people, beat up people, but I'm no tief."

Jesus's confession left me without a response. One the one hand I was touched that he opened up to me; on the other, doubts lingered as to his veracity. This extension of his teenage escape story pained him, making him vulnerable. But once again, it clashed with the US Immigration and Citizen Services version of a *Mariel* émigré.

I changed the subject. "I have an idea. What are you doing now?" I asked, as if Jesus had his appointments penciled in his calendar book. "You want to go to Gus's for breakfast?"

"Mami, I don't want to bother you. I come back at eleven for my money."

"No, you come to breakfast. We can drop off Bruno at home and pick up the car. At Gus's we'll listen to the latest news, maybe hear what others have to say about Castro. Then we can go to the bank together."

His face brightened a bit. "Mami, can you give me $20 from my check? I want to treat you."

"No need . . ." He cut me off.

"I don't pay, I don't go."

"OK, OK."

When we arrived at the restaurant, in Greek I greeted Yianni, behind the counter, and his wife Dena, waiting on customers, with a hearty "*Yia sas.*" Jesus nodded to a few customers, one of whom responded boisterously, "What's the haps, Gato, *qué pasa*? Hey, I see your *jefe* Fidel has stepped down."

"He ain't my *jefe*. Uncle Sam sign my check." Jesus laughed as he slapped hands with a middle-aged, balding African American, who then extended his hand to me.

"You must be Gato's Mami. I'm Amos. He talks all the time about you and his Dadi. I met George back in the day at Cortez Arms, that fleabag Max Caldwell called a hotel and then ran down to the ground. You seen it, Gato? He's got it all gutted out. Ms. Demas, that's your name, right? You look a bit familiar. You involved in politics? Wait, now I remember, you were doing voter registration with Lady Love for Harold back in '87. Wo, that's almost twenty years ago. You ever see Ms. Love anymore? I heard she moved out of the neighborhood, keeping her nose clean. Hey, Auggie," Amos yelled across the room to a fat, orange-vested Streets and San worker, "this here's Mrs. Demas; she knows Lady Love." With that, soft drink in hand, he sauntered over to Auggie's table, sat down, and continued his nonstop chatter, except at a lower volume.

Gus's Corner was an old-style snack shop, with red, turning stools at the grey-patterned counter, stainless steel-framed booths along the front and side windows and along the wall. Tables filled the middle of the room. All the cooking was done right in front of the counter sitters. Stacks of precooked bacon awaited final searing for BLTs, omelets, and over-easies, tinging the air with a smoky aroma. Always brewing coffee helped waken the early morning clientele.

Besides Yianni, Orlando, a tall, muscular Puerto Rican was at the grill. Orders were yelled from Dena to Yianni to Orlando and barked back in Greek to Dena when they were ready to be parsed out to the diners at the booths and tables.

A booth opened up that gave us a good view and listening post to the TV, tuned to the morning news on a local channel. The expression "all politics is local" rang true that morning on WGN as

215

members of the Chicago Cuban community were interviewed about the events in Cuba.

"Look Mami, that's Hector they talk to. He from my hometown."

"Nothing's gonna change," Hector said matter-of-factly. "One day Fidel Castro will be running Cuba from the grave."

The camera panned to a restaurant in Logan Square and school board member Elvira Castillo. "We in the Chicago Cuban community are heartened by this news. It's only a matter of time before the Castros are history and the exile community in the United States will be able to reunite with our families on the island."

"What she really say? The rich Cubans in the states want to take back Cuba," said Jesus.

Amos shouted from his spot next to Auggie. "They need to talk to you, Gato. You tell 'em like it is."

Dena took our orders at the commercial break. "Alexia, you planning a trip to Greece this year?"

"More likely we will go next spring. Perhaps the euro will come down by then, make it less expensive for us," I responded, adding, "If it were up to Jesus, we'd be going to Cuba, to visit his relatives."

"Gato, what you think, you be able to go back now?" Dena spoke to Jesus with a familiarity that bespoke how long they had known each other, in fact how long everyone at Gus's seemed to know each other.

"I don't want to go back. I just want Mami and Dadi to go there. My aunt is real sick, might not last too long."

Dena crossed herself in the Greek Orthodox way (Catholics do it backward). "I know. My mother, my brother, I not able to see them before they die, too much work here, and then it too late. Alexia, you go to Cuba, you could get in trouble, no?"

"George would have to go himself, but I don't think he will.

Jesus, he always has his big ideas. Of course, there's nothing wrong with dreaming."

By then Yianni was yelling at Dena again, so she hustled back to the counter to pick up the next omelets and sandwiches ready from the grill.

Maria Ramos and daughters Isabel and Ana, six and eight, sat at the table next to us. The Ramoses were a family George and I got to know, our lives crossing frequently at Gus's. Tomás must have been running late that morning from his graveyard shift handling freight for Federal Express at the airport. Isabel had a book of stickers and Ana a coloring book. Our food hadn't come yet, so I went over to check out the girls' artistry.

Perhaps it was my attention to someone else that brought Jesus to begin sulking, slouching down in his seat, looking up at the ceiling, then moving his legs apart and in, repeatedly. I didn't return to the booth until I saw Dena coming with my BLT and fries and Jesus's scrambled eggs and hash browns.

At the same time, Tomás entered, said hello to Yianni and Orlando, shook hands with Auggie, who was now on his way out, and winked at Dena. But for me there was just a nod, for Jesus not even a backward glance. He kissed each girl on the top of the head, and pecked Maria on the cheek. He was talking to her in a hushed voice and gesturing to an empty table at the far end of the room.

"The girls are all settled; let's just stay here," I heard Maria say to Tomás while I pretended to focus on the weather forecast.

"Hear that, Jesus? It's going up to 85 today." He didn't respond. He just kept eating his eggs, though somewhat half-heartedly.

Without saying a word he got up and walked over to Tomás, who stood up as well. Jesus reached into his pocket. I couldn't tell for sure, but I think he slyly showed Tomás the $20 bill I had given him so he could "pay" for breakfast.

"Too little, too late," I thought I heard Tomás say to Gato through the din of the restaurant. But I didn't have to strain to hear his next words. No one else in the restaurant had to either. "Stay away from me and my family. Matter of fact, why don't you take your thieving ass back to Cuba? We don't want parasitic worms any more than the Castros do."

Without looking at anyone Jesus turned, crumpled the twenty, and threw it toward our booth, kept walking right out of Gus's, and began crossing North Avenue. A car horn's blare rousted him from his zombie-like trance, enough so he could flip off the driver and the rest of the world.

Tomás picked up the crumpled bill. "Looks like he wanted you to have this, Mrs. Demas. You know me, Maria, and the girls all like you and George. But I don't know why you give that guy the time of day."

Tomás sat down again and started eating his pork chops as if nothing had happened. Leaving behind my food I went out the diner door. "Jesus, Jesus, wait," I yelled so that I might catch him, already across the street and down the block toward Damen Avenue. At first he acted like he didn't hear me, but when I yelled again he stopped and turned, reaching out to a lamppost for support, his knees seeming to buckle under him. A beer bottle was in his other hand. Where it came from I didn't know.

When I reached him, almost out of breath myself, he spoke first. "You hear what he call me? He call me a tief. He think I stole some tools from him when I help him build somebody a deck. But Mami, I no lie to you, I tell you I'm no tief."

Looking him straight in his eyes, I tell him, "Jesus, I believe you. But why did you try to pay him?"

"Mami, a couple of time Tomás let me work for him, he do side jobs for people in the neighborhood. The last time, it was hot, real hot. I can't breathe. I tell him I have to leave early. So he pay me and I go to the hospital."

"Was that in June? I remember you called us from St. Mary's."

"No, I think last September. When I get out, everyone tell me Tomás looking for me. I think he has more work for me. Then I see him. He mad, real mad. He ac-c-cuse I take his power drill and nail gun. I tell him the truth, I don't have them. He tell me I owe him $160, and he just drive away. I don't see him again until today. I tell him I can pay him little by little. But you see what happen."

"Can I talk to him for you?"

"No, *compañera*, you and Dadi, you do enough for me. I don't want you to lose your friends count of me."

"OK, *compañero*," I replied, smiling inside at these new salutations that we would use from then on when speaking directly to each other.

A couple of days later, I paid Yianni for the breakfasts we hardly ate.

ON HOLD
GEORGE 2007

Editor's note: Found in our mailbox, in a wrinkled envelope, addressed simply, Mami and Dadi Demas, in a crooked hand. Inside, on a single sheet, typewritten, most likely on the old Smith-Corona portable Alexia gave Memo Rodriguez, a note from Gato.

George Demas
May, 2007

Dadi and Mami,

    I know you mad at me. You have my respect, so I am sorry. I know I messed up. Dadi, you try to help me. You take off from work to take me for my ID, and I don't show up. I call, I tell you I'm too *borracho*. Dadi, you start yelling, say you be too drunk to cash my check and hang up. I know you don't drink much. But there is a reason I'm drinking that morning. Mami and Dadi, you have each other. Who do I have? What do I have? Nothing. Nobody. No place to live since the sheriff evict me, except the park. But the day before it rain real bad, thunder, lightning all day and night. All my stuff got wet in the shopping cart. The blue plastic you give me come loose with the wind. I'm trying not to spend too much since I don't pay no rent no more, and you holding most my money. But I have no choice that night to go to that hotel at Chicago and Pulaski. $28 a night for a room with roaches. But you know who's there? Alicia from the Cortez Arms. She so happy to see me, she take my room number and come back when she done for the night, real early in the morning. You have each other, and since I stay in the park, I have nobody to keep me company, you know what I mean. And in the morning, before I have to be out by noon, I get something to drink and Alicia and I, we remember the old days. And so I can't go with Dadi.

I know this sound like excuses and I'm sorry 'cause I have the utmost respect for my Mami and Dadi. But seeing Alicia bring me good luck. She tell me of a place I can rent a room. It's on North and Central Park. Only $110 a week or $425 by the month. I need one month security to pay the lower rent. When I get my pay on the first I have enough with what you holding. But the owner says he just have one room open now, so I need the money fast. Maybe you can loan me the $200 I'm short now.

I have one more thing I'm sorry about. When I go back to get my things from where I chain my cart, my ID, the parole card from immigration, it so wet it fall apart, you can't read my name. I know you tell me to get it covered in plastic, what you call it, lemonade it? But I can't find no place that do that. Walgreens don't have the machine no more. But if I can rent this place on North then I don't need ID for the low-rent apartment.

Say hello to my brother Nick.

Your other son,
Gato

That son-of-a-gun. Even an apology—and he needs to apologize all right—he turns into a negotiation. Always has to be something in it for him.

Well, I wasn't going to argue, I wasn't going to lecture. Either would take more effort than he deserved. I was going to give him the $200 in advance, even with the chance that he might squander it. I just wanted him out of my hair, out of our lives, as much as we could. I knew a complete excision was unlikely. The plus side was he had found a place on his own, without my involvement. All we would have to do is cash his check and get him a money order for his rent. And I was going to tell him, no more $40 advances. Either he could make do with the money left over, after his rent was paid, or he could hustle what he needed or borrow from someone else.

I was his chump for the last time. And one more thing: I wasn't going to seek him out to give him that $200. He'd have to come and get it. We'd have it ready, give it to him—whoever answered the door, Alexia, Nick or I—and tell him when to pick up his money order and whatever remained after he paid us back the advance, and be done with him for a month.

That's how I felt then. Looking back on it, I can still feel the anger all along my neck, rising over my scalp, turning my forehead and face red. That sense of anger.

As it turns out, this minimal arrangement with Gato was as much as I could handle for several months, as my job at Allied Imaging exerted new pressures on me and in turn the rest of the family. Interestingly enough, either because he knew this was a time to keep his distance from me or because he settled into his own relatively low-key winter cycle, we only did see him once during each of the six months my life seemed to be on hold because of the job.

Since 2005 I've been managing a team of database developers at Allied Imaging, a diagnostic and industrial X-ray firm that has grown significantly with the advent of digital X-rays. A few months after Gato stood me up, our group was charged with developing a data warehouse on a tight six-month deadline. The data warehouse would integrate data from the three legacy companies now merged as Allied Imaging.

A data warehouse is not built in six months. But try telling that to the senior executives at Allied Imaging. Our approach had to be to deliver a big enough chunk of work to whet their appetites for more. Naturally we weren't given the budget we thought we would need. But we'd make do with the staff we could afford: myself as data architect, a quality assurance analyst, and three contract developers recently extracted from India.

As data architect I had multiple roles: understanding and clarifying business requirements, analyzing data, designing data warehouse tables that would house the data uniformly in structures optimized for reporting, and creating specifications for the developers.

I wound up working long hours, starting early, eating lunch at my desk, connecting remotely from home on evenings and weekends. Even when I was not working overtime, I was drained by the work or consumed by problems to be solved. I'd doze off exhausted, trying to relax watching TV, yet upon waking would have trouble falling asleep in bed, thinking of ways to reconcile the data from two or three legacy systems. Or I'd be jarred awake from an on-the-job dream or with far-fetched solutions to the issues at hand.

The rest of my life seemed to be vanishing. I dropped out of the Greek classes Alexia and I were taking at our church. Alexia continued. Workouts at the gym weren't happening, and my gut was expanding. The little housework and cooking I might have done before the work crisis became none. Tensions between Alexia and me grew. The holidays passed. Thanksgiving was a minimal affair, no guests, not even Gato. Christmas and New Year's? I was barely able to take an extra day off before each, let alone the entire last two weeks of the year.

More than once, Alexia, frustrated with my unpresence and the glazed look that hid my internal thought processes, flared up at me. "Why don't you just stay at work?" Or on a weekend, "Go to work, you're not here." Jostled, I might engage for a while, but then I'd drift off, back to the data warehouse.

On the job our deliverables were set at months four, five, and six of the project. The first was a disaster. Reports had to be pieced together manually from source data because of the deficiencies of the data warehouse. Luckily the audience for these reports was internal to the company.

Before the second round, there was an IT reorganization. I now reported up through a new director, Vishnu Riganasara, a guru of digital X-rays. Whether he knew anything about data warehousing was unclear. His concentration was on the new enterprise application, dubbed "Imagine," not our mere "reporting environment." All V.R. needed from me was a weekly status report on progress toward our milestones. This regurgitation of project status seemed more important to him than our actual client-facing reports.

I could have used the organizational changes as an excuse for the botch we made of the month five deadline, but I didn't. For a couple of days I holed myself up in a recently vacated office not far from my cube. I was low-key, even self-effacing in conference calls, and blamed no one but myself, as I had become the chief bottleneck of the project.

At home, I was still blind to the accumulating dust and dog hair. But Alexia sensed how down I was and took a new tact. She prodded me to analyze what went wrong. Then drawing from her own well of organizational experience, she made some suggestions: Ask your team to meet without you for a "lessons learned" session;

speak individually with your peers from the business side to get their feedback. A couple of nights later, when I told her what I heard from my colleagues, Alexia smiled. "It sounds like you've taught them well; now let them step up to the plate. Challenge your staff to take on some of the analysis and design tasks you've been doing. God and I know how stubborn you can be."

Calm descended upon me with Alexia's words. I saw a path ahead and, more importantly, knew again Alexia's heart and support through this hard time. That night we shared tender moments and I slept through the night without waking.

My newfound even keel kept me afloat through the next month without a loss of intensity. Indeed the hours were as long as ever, but the whole team shared the load and overcame our most substantive obstacles. The data had to be ready for our biggest client's quarterly report, and it was—on time, correct, and all processes automated.

Our sighs of relief must have been heard all the way from our office near Cumberland and Higgins on Chicago's far northwest side back to the neighborhood. Walking home from the "L" that balmy, early spring evening, as I passed Wicker Park, a familiar voice beckoned my attention. "Dadi, Dadi."

A month earlier I would have kept walking, without looking for him. How could my anger toward him have abated in the midst of my angst-filled career challenge? But that evening, I did turn, and there he was, Jesus Cárdenas, our Gato, across the street, his arms spread, palms turned up, matching the smile on his face, matching the smile on mine.

HIP STIR
GEORGE 2007

"Thank you, Dadi, for crossing the street. My legs not working so good." Indeed his left leg seemed to be bearing all his weight.

"What's going on? Are you all right? God it's been so long since we've spoken."

"I know you don't want to see me. You too busy with work. Mami tell me. And you mad at me. I'm sorry I disrespect you."

"No, no, Gato. I'm the one who needs forgiveness. I can be such an asshole."

"You got that right." He smiled and winked.

"But how are you feeling? I think Alexia said something about you being in the hospital at Christmas, or was it Thanksgiving?"

"You don't remember because you don't visit me. Mami, Nick, they come. They don't tell you?"

"Gato, I was so wrapped up in my job, I didn't make time for anything. But that's over now and you still haven't told me how you are."

"I'm in the hospital three times. First it's for my asthma. Then

I have pneumonia and some other infection. Now it's my leg. It hurt real bad whenever I walk. I try to walk, it burn from up here," he points to his right hip, "down to my foot."

I motion to the bench fifteen feet away, inside the southeast entrance to Wicker Park, and take a few steps toward it. As I do so, I see the grimace on Gato's face as he struggles to follow me.

"Damn, that looks bad. What does the doctor say?"

"Dr. Uribe, he say he don't know. He say I got to get an orth-orth-o-pedic opinion. I say those beds too expensive. No, he says, I got to see a specialist, for the bones."

"Did you go to see him?"

"It was a lady doctor, Dr. Dominguez, same building as Uribe. Even in the waiting room she make me nervous. I'm thinking she going to make me take my pants off. I'm thinking, 'What if she good looking.'"

"Gato, you're crazy. Ever since I met you, you've been trying to get women to do more than look at you, though not with much luck."

"You laughing at me? I'm afraid I might get hard when she touch me."

"Well? Did she have to throw some cold water on you? Didn't you trust Dr. Uribe? He sent you to an orthopedic surgeon, not Ms. Dominican Republic. So what happened?"

"The doctor, she good. And she a *Cubana*. Once I meet her I'm not nervous. She ask me a lot of questions. What's my disability, what drug I taking? Did I have a bad fall, any broken bones any-where? And she ask me about Cuba, where I from. You know what? She from Santiago like *mi tía*. She don't know my uncle, but she hear the name.

"Then she ask me why I left. I tell her what the papers from immigration say. And she asked me did they give me injection when

I in jail. Did they give me something with a long name. I don't re-member, so I say, I think so."

"Then what?"

"She look at my leg, she feeling around my hips."

"So you did have to take your pants off," I said, shooting back at him one of his sly smiles.

"Dadi, you think this funny. She send me for an X-ray, same day in the same building. When I'm done they send me back to her office. She show me the picture of my hip, my right hip.

"She say it no good, the right one. It de-de-teri-or-or-ate. She say I need a new one.

"I say, 'What? I don't think so. You ain't cutting my hip out.' Then she surprise me. She tell me I'm right. I have to go Cook County Hospital.

"Now I'm mad. I ask her why I have to go to Cook County? St. Mary, that my hospital. But she tell me Medicaid won't pay St. Mary's enough. So she give me the paper to take to Cook County. She say it a good idea someone else go with me.

"Dadi, you go with me?"

I knew instinctively this was not something I wanted to do, but I needed time. "When is the appointment? Do you have the referral on you now?"

"Re-referral, what you mean?"

"The paper for Cook County." In a déjà vu moment, he reached into his back pocket and pulled out a crumpled piece of paper. Actually he handed me three papers. I looked at the first two. Both were medical device orders—one for a walker, the other for a wheelchair. The last, for the Fantus Clinic at Cook County Hospital, was an orthopedic consultation. There wasn't a specific time for the appointment, but the hours of the clinic were eight a.m. to one p.m., Mondays, Tuesdays, and Thursdays.

There was no way that I wanted to go with him to that appointment. He already seemed reluctant to have an operation, and I didn't want to waste a whole day going down there. Less than a year ago we were supposed to go to the Loop for his state of Illinois ID, and he had blown me off. Why should I tempt fate again?

There was a larger reason I didn't want to go. I've known people who had hip replacement surgery. These operations are, by now, more or less routine, surgically. But more important than the surgery is the four weeks of near daily rehab—call it more aptly "work"—afterward. No way would Gato have the discipline to follow through, assuming he was able to get to the rehabilitation facility. Healthwise, he's always looked for the magic bullet—an inhaler, some pills, a couple of days of rest in a hospital to mask his substantial health issues.

And would any doctor agree to the surgery if he or she knew he was an alcoholic? Would they want to see their work and the taxpayers' Medicaid dollars go to waste when the new hip was jarred out of place in a drunken fall or brawl? No, quite simply, Gato was not a good candidate for a hip replacement surgery, and I wanted no part of building up his hope for a new miracle of modern medicine.

Not knowing how to be honest with him, I stalled for time. "Let me check my calendar and talk to Mami," I told him. "I'll let you know when you pick up your money next Thursday."

"Dadi, can you drop it off? I'm not getting around too good. My hip hurts like a son-of-a-bitch."

"We'll see. You call me the night before. Maybe one of your friends will give you a ride."

Sensing my growing irritation, he changed subjects. "Hey Dadi, you hear about Memo?"

"What's he got to do with anything, unless maybe he could go down with you to Cook County."

"That's what I try to tell you. Memo got religion now." Gato paused. He must have known I'd need time to absorb that information. "His church help people all kinds of ways."

"Memo has religion? He goes to church?"

"Why you not ask him yourself? He right there by the fountain. Memo," he shouts, "Dadi want to talk to you."

The man Gato shouted to, sitting at a bench with his back to me, turned and rose. It was a new Memo. Clean, new clothes fit him smartly, making it obvious that he had shed fifteen to twenty pounds. Likewise, his hair was short and neat, accompanied by a trim mustache and goatee. All in all he looked quite distinguished.

I sure did want to talk to Memo, and I knew Alexia would as well.

REDEEMING HOPE
ALEXIA 2007

When I called the phone number Mamerto gave George, a woman answered, "Redeeming Hope Outreach Ministries. How can I help you? *¿Cómo puedo ayudarle?*"

"I am trying to reach one of your participants, Mamerto Rodriguez, Memo Rodriguez. Do you know him?" I asked.

"Mr. Rodriguez is one of our associate ministers. I will connect you."

Associate minister? I wondered as the phone rang three times before being picked up.

"Memo Rodriguez, how may I help you?"

"Mamerto, this is Alexia Demas."

"Ms. Demas, I've been expecting your call. Excuse me for a moment, please.

"Luis, Felipe, excuse me. I have to take this call. I'll just be a few minutes."

I could tell his hand was loosely covering the phone's mouthpiece, yet his tone must have assured Luis and Felipe that they were important too.

"Alexia, it has been many eventful months since we last talked."

"Yes it has. You sound great. Associate Minister; I'm impressed."

"Don't be. Our church has dozens of associate ministers; anyone who works or volunteers at least twenty hours a week in one of the eighteen ministries of the church has the title."

"And you're in the outreach ministry?"

"Well, that's the overall name. Listen, Alexia, I need to resume the meeting I was having. But I have an idea. Why don't you come to one of our services and we can have coffee or breakfast afterward?" In the spirit of ecumenicalism I readily agreed. Plus, any church that could engage Mamerto as it obviously had, I wanted to see myself in order to understand its appeal.

George agreed to go with me but was skeptical. "It's going to be one of those evangelical churches that pushes the conservative agenda. What's worse is that it's in the Hispanic community. I've heard about that church, what's it called, Redeeming Money?"

"Well, I don't want to hear about it, I want to keep an open mind," I said as George thumped off to do some "research" on the Internet.

Redeeming Hope occupied an old movie theater on North Avenue, just west of Humboldt Park. I'd been on a few dates at the Von Humboldt, though I don't remember any of the films Ed Stone and I "saw" from the balcony, where the main attraction was the battle of the hands, bras, and breasts. I'd make sure that George and I sat on the main level.

When we arrived for the nine a.m. service, I was immediately struck by the changes the church had made to the old structure. From the street, the surrounding shops masked the size and depth of the Von Humboldt. But despite its aristocratic name, it was dwarfed in size, décor, and reputation by Chicago's numerous "Movie Palaces." Inside it had been drab, with a stale smell tinged with popcorn and too many spilled Coca Colas. Outside its once boxy white marquee, lined to hold the names of then-playing features in black, block letters, had been replaced by a curved, sky-blue façade whose large scrolled letters proclaimed Redeeming Hope and underneath in smaller letters, Reverend Jorge de la Cruz. The lobby seemed airy and fresh as it, too, was painted sky blue. Its beautiful hardwood floor, which extended into the curved balcony staircases, obfuscated the previous flooring I remembered, bathroom-style octagonal tiles.

As we entered the assembly, a friendly usher directed us to two of the few remaining seats. I could hardly reconcile the old with the new. In the old days the theater had always been dark; before and after shows, only the exit signs and a few bare bulbs lit the place, making it seem like a cavernous tomb. Once again, the bright paint job changed everything; though I was a bit surprised that the tall walls were painted light grey and not sky blue. The stage, rebuilt in hardwood matching the lobby's clean lines, was at least twenty-five feet deep, and toward its back left was a set-up for a band: amplifiers, drums, keyboard, and microphones. Yet there were no thick curtains to dramatically reveal a huge screen. Instead, three computer-fed projection screens—front, right, and center—welcomed the congregants in Spanish and English, and connected the facility to its past.

Gazing around, I took in the assemblage, the worshipers of Redeeming Hope. Every facet of the community was present from teenage mothers with their babies in arms, to *abuelas* and their extended families in their Sunday best, to street youth in ones, twos, and threes wearing "He is our Hope" T-shirts. Hispanics were clearly the majority, but African Americans and whites were well represented, often as husbands or wives in the predominantly Hispanic families or in their own families and groups, with Hispanics interspersed. In other words, race seemed to be left at the door.

I must have had my head turned to the rear when music started up from the stage. And there he was, Mamerto Rodriguez, looking sharp in a linen *guayabera* shirt and well-pressed black slacks playing bass, behind and to the left of a soulful lead guitarist. Entering rhythmically from stage right, five women in tight but floor-length pastels vocalized the band's number, a spotlight following the gold-haired, lead *Puerta Ricaña*. The projection screens lit up in, you guessed it, sky blue. Words appeared simultaneously as the Redeeming Hope version of the Pointer Singers eased into their song:

> *Whenever you are feeling blue*
> *Whenever chaos surrounds you*
> *Remember there is only one*
> *Who will always be there for you.*

> *Jesus is the one*
> *He is the only one*
> *He will always be there*
> *Always be there for you.*

> *Whenever you are all alone*
> *And your man has abandoned you*
> *Ask the Lord to open His arms*
> *He will take you into His heart.*

> *Jesus is the one*
> *He is the only one*
> *He will always be there*
> *Always be there for you.*

Your troubles may drive you to drink
Or lead you to forbidden drugs
But only His love will fill you
Fill your emptiness forever.

Jesus is the one
He is the only one
He will always be there
Always be there for you.

For twenty minutes the Lord's quintet belted out their songs of redeeming hope and moved in step with each other. By their second
number the assemblage was standing, swaying, singing along, arms
waving. Two rows in front of us a twenty-something Hispanic with
prison tattoos on his arms and neck jabbed his right arm high in the
air, index finger extended each time any lyric like "He is the one"
lifted from a song's chorus. I contemplated what brought a young
man like that, unaccompanied by anyone else, to church on a summer Sunday morning.

My thoughts and unfocused gaze were interrupted by a familiar voice, Mamerto's. "Let's hear it for our remarkable Redeemers,"
who, rather than bowing, lifted up their arms toward the sky-blue
ceiling. "And if you think they are something, here come our children." And just like that a stream of forty or so eight- to twelve-
year-olds ran up the stairs stage left while the band struck up a
high-spirited number reminiscent of "We are the World." Within
seconds we were witnessing a riotous romp of singing and dancing,
arms thrust left then right high in the air. As a group, the children
pulsed in concentric circles in and out and then transformed themselves into a spiraling snake. They were the stars as video cameras
captured their excited faces and choreographed movements onto the

projection screens, right, left, and center. Parents proudly shouted out their names as the children in song promised their abstinence from violence, drugs, and sex and proclaimed their love for the only one, Jesus Christ. "Very entertaining, quite a production," George said quietly to me as the spotlights retreated with the children and then went out briefly.

Before I could reply, a single spotlight shone its light on a commanding presence, the Reverend Jorge de la Cruz. "Lord Jesus Christ, don't we have some talent here at Redeeming Hope." He was slighter in stature than I had imagined, but his height, gold complexion, dark gleaming eyes, and impeccable silk suit fit his reputation. "And I'm not just talking about our remarkable Redeemers and our engaging children. Look at the workmanship that renovated our house of worship. Every plank laid, every nail hammered by a member of our faith community.

"Brothers and sisters, *hermanos y hermanas*, do you know why I am talking of our church's talent today? It is because today we celebrate the Pentecost, when the Holy Spirit descended upon the Apostles, the true first Church of our Lord Jesus Christ. The fire the Holy Spirit breathed into the life of the Apostles and the teachings of Jesus Christ became their talent. And we call ourselves Pentecostals because we, too, must have that talent to live and breathe life, not just into our church but into our families and our communities. Because sisters and brothers, *hermanas y hermanos*, our families, our communities, indeed our country have been put to sleep and need to be woken up as if our homes were on fire, and they are. In our neighborhoods our young people are at war with each other, killing each other over who will control the distribution of drugs, the drugs that pacify our people, poison our bodies, and destroy our souls."

"Still finding this entertaining?" I whispered to George.

"Actually, a bit surprising," he answered.

"But we must beware the false prophets. Yes, we wish that not a woman among us would ever abort a human spirit within her womb. But abortion is not the problem. Rather it is our young women, looking for love, as the song says, 'in all the wrong places.' Everlasting love can only be found in our salvation, in accepting Jesus Christ into our hearts. Likewise the homosexual. Of course we believe that marriage is a blessed union only between man and woman, but we cannot turn our backs on these sisters and brothers, who also look for love in the wrong places. But do we succumb to the fearmongers who say they cannot raise children when we know they have always helped to raise the children of our extended families as aunts and uncles and second mommies? They too can receive salvation by accepting Jesus as the purpose of their lives. Aren't we all sinners? Didn't Christ die on the cross for our sins? Can anyone among us cast the first stone?"

This was his lead-in to the Lord's Prayer. As the parishioners rose, George and I experienced something we had never heard before. The Lord's Prayer, recited simultaneously in multiple languages, English and Spanish of course, but if you listened carefully, a Polish voice or few. Vietnamese? We looked at each other. George shrugged, "What the heck," and we "forgave those who trespass against us" in Greek.

"*Hermanas y hermanos*, sisters and brothers, *adelphes kai adelphi*, in the name of the Lord, we speak in all the tongues of the world." Had he heard and recognized our voices, or had a certain associate minister prepped him of our presence? "Our speaking in tongues, isn't this our hope for the future, that people the world over can unite in the house of the Lord?"

My mind began to wander off again, wondering again about our associate minister, how the passion *de la Cruz* must resonate for him. I remembered the words from Mamerto's narrative, in his essay or at our kitchen table, about his years at the Polish Catholic paro-chial school, or in his dealings with Jesus's gang. "I was tolerated, not accepted." And, once again, I heard his voice, in the present.

"Thank you, Reverend de la Cruz. Lord, have mercy; Lord, have mercy; Lord have mercy. Lord, give us hope. Lord, accept our humble prayers." He had the cadence, he had the tone. Had Mamer-to finally found his calling? "Newcomers to Redeeming Hope, those of you ailing in body or soul, those of you who have not yet accepted Jesus Christ as your personal Savior, this is the time in our service where Reverend de la Cruz walks through our aisles to accept you as born again, to put his hands to your hurt and heal. Stand now if you want to be saved."

Quiet befell the congregation. Several rows in front of us, first one, then another and another, rose in their seats or moved to the aisle. Necks craned to recognize the supplicants. Then, at the same moment, our jaws dropped as George and I saw him, not his swag-gering self, but twisted, bent-over aluminum, hospital-issue walk-er, dragging himself from one of the last rows on the opposite side of the hall right toward de la Cruz. Jesus Cárdenas and the pastor stopped as they reached each other. The pastor, towering over Jesus, stretched his arms to grasp each of his shoulders. He didn't shake them but held them firmly, and as he did Jesus seemed to straighten, standing taller an inch at a time. When Jesus let go of the walker, de la Cruz bent toward Jesus's right ear to whisper, but his lapel mike allowed the whole congregation to hear his plea, "If you are ready to accept Jesus Christ as your personal Savior, you must only say His name." Jesus's silence did not deter Reverend de la Cruz, who repeat-ed his challenge in Spanish.

Now it was Jesus's voice coming through the church's sound system. "*Señor, Jesus Cristo*, I accept you as my Savior. Forgive me for all of my sins." With that, de la Cruz playfully kicked the walker away and stepped from Jesus, standing on his own now, as straight as we had ever seen him.

"Walk tall, my brother. Please join Associate Minister Memo Rodriguez on the altar." As Jesus strode toward the front of the congregation, I had to blink. Was I imagining a hint of his old swagger? But I didn't have to imagine what George was thinking of the reborn Jesus Cárdenas, who almost five years earlier we "resurrected" from death by Social Security.

"You got to be kidding. I bet you your Memo put him up to that," George said in less than a whisper.

I shushed him but whispered back, "If Mamerto put Jesus up to this for our benefit, I'll be done with the both of them."

On the altar the associate minister and Jesus hugged sincerely, with Jesus whispering in his friend's ear. What was he asking Memo Rodriguez, "How'd I do?"

Others joined them on the stage-turned-altar, none quite as dramatically as Jesus, and most, more humbly. The tall pastor helped the last of the saved up the few stairs and addressed not the whole assemblage but the new members of his flock, "Blessed are the meek, for you shall inherit the earth." With a simple gesture, Reverend de la Cruz indicated the meek should sit in the seats behind and to his left.

"Christ is in our midst. From Matthew 25: Come, you blessed of My Father, inherit the kingdom prepared for you from the foundation of the world: for I was hungry and you gave Me food; I was thirsty and you gave Me drink . . ."

My inner self smiled. This is why I'm a Christian. I glanced at George, looking skeptical, as de la Cruz continued, as if speaking directly to him.

"The righteous will answer Him, saying, 'Lord, when did we see You a stranger and take You in, or naked and clothe You? Or when did we see You sick, or in prison, and come to You?' And the King will answer and say to them, 'Assuredly, I say to you, inasmuch as you did it to one of the least of these My brethren, you did it to Me.'"

"Brothers and sisters, *hermanos y hermanas*, today there are congregations in our country where this same gospel will be read, and few if any will know what it means to be hungry, thirsty, homeless, or imprisoned. But not in our congregation. We know this pain and we have faith in Him because we know that though he was the Son of God, he was here on earth as a man, and he, too, knew this pain. And when we see those here who today accepted Jesus as their Savior, as so many of us have, we come together as a congregation and we care for each other in body and soul. And as we do this for the least of us, we are doing it for Him. Amen."

ACCEPTED
ALEXIA 2007

After the Redeeming Hope service concluded, George had to nudge me to get me out of my seat, so absorbed was I in streams of thought bouncing from one to another, provoked by what I had witnessed that morning. Thinking of the young people immersed in messages of hope made me think back to a troubling time in my own youth.

Early in 1977 my father passed away. He had not been well for several years as diabetes took its toll. Knowing that a loved one will pass in the foreseeable future does not lessen the blow when it actually happens. By June, my marriage to Ed Stone fell apart, and he moved out. On the first of August, everyone in our building was given notice of a pending condominium conversion—before the end of the month, a week before the term was to start at *Casa de West-town*. Our funding from UIC was pulled as part of the university's overall budget cuts. I wondered, Would I have been swayed by the message of Redeeming Hope if I had encountered it then as a vulnerable young woman?

I also reflected on this church, not as a religious institution,

241

but as a cultural production, with starring roles for young women and children, band members, the sick and troubled. How much this church was in the present, how much it was in contrast to our orthodox services and its link to the ancient past. Yet wasn't our church's liturgy at one time modern and controversial? And didn't that day's Pentecostal homily reach back to the beginnings of Christianity? Hadn't I wandered from the orthodox church (from the time my parents passed until Nick was born), disenchanted that it was not in sync with the times? Were the congregants of Redeeming Hope, most of whom had left the Catholic Church, not just disenchanted but looking to be uplifted in a message that pulsated with the currents of modern life?

When George and I entered the lobby, we found ourselves among swirling congregants leaving one service and arriving for the next. I was anxious. "George, I don't know that I can get together with Mamerto now and discuss his conversion. I haven't had a chance to resolve any of this in my own mind."

"Honey, take a breath. And don't worry about Gato. I'll dispatch him if necessary. I think we've had enough of one Jesus today and already too much of the other."

Still not sure of myself, I saw Mamerto near the opposite exit, talking with two young men. Lurking nearby, but not part of the associate minister's conversation, was Jesus. He wasn't talking to anyone. At first he didn't see us through the crowded lobby, but he edged his way toward us when the sea of worshippers parted, just enough to let him through.

"Mami, Dadi, Memo tell me you be coming today. I am so happy you see me accept *el Señor en mi corazón.*"

Mamerto was right on his heels, leaving his party behind. "Alexia, George, thank you so much for coming to Redeeming Hope today. It was an inspiring service, as Gato can attest. Unfortunately,

Gato told me that he cannot join us for breakfast."

"*Compañera*, they invite me to the Outreach Ministry. They make a picnic in the park this afternoon. So I say I help." Going over to George's side, Jesus gives him a head feint, indicating they should speak privately outside. I am alone with Mamerto.

"Do you think he was for real today, Mamerto?"

"With Gato it's hard to tell what's real and what will stick. Time will tell. I am hopeful. Look what He has done for me."

"Mamerto, you have always had a strength within you; now you have found a way to realize it."

"God willing."

Without Jesus, George reentered the church lobby, and the three of us agreed to go for breakfast at Gus's Corner, where Yianni and Dena welcomed us heartedly. But all eyes were on Mamerto, their former short order cook. "Memo, you look good. What, you win the lottery?" Yianni asked.

"Better than that, Yianni. I won the Lord's blessing."

"Well," Yianni answered, perhaps not quite translating Mamerto's St. James English, "whatever you win, congratulations."

The Sunday morning rush at Gus's was thinning out, so we were able to find a quiet booth along the side windows. George, sensing I wasn't sure where I wanted to start the conversation, jumped in, as he was apt to do, without much tact. "Reverend Jorge de la Cruz," he started, letting his best Spanish pronunciation roll from his lips before pausing a second, "he's quite a charismatic and powerful preacher, isn't he? And I hear he's quite powerful in the community. All the northwest side Hispanic aldermen take his influence seriously."

"George," I interrupted, before he could do some preaching of his own, "I don't think we're here to talk about Reverend de la Cruz."

"It's all right, Alexia. Let's put it all on the table," said Mamerto. "George, there was a reason back in the day we called you Just George. You were always talking about justice. Well, Reverend de la Cruz is about justice, too. But his justice starts with spirituality, not politics. His justice starts with a deep belief in Jesus Christ, praise be His name, not unlike that of Martin Luther King. And he is very effective, because he's not just talking the talk. The outreach ministries are actually doing something. In Uptown, you would have called them survival programs. You probably don't know this, but when the reverend was a young boy, his family lived in Uptown, and they benefited from the programs of *las Panteras Negras*. It is said that Jorge de la Cruz was very observant as a child."

George was fidgeting. He probably wanted to cut in, but Mamerto wasn't done yet. "There are a lot of rumors out there about the reverend. Some say he married his wife in order to take over her father's church. Some say he has a child by another woman. Others say he's taking Bush's faith-based money and buying fancy clothes and living high. All these rumors prove he's effective. If he weren't, why would so many want to bring him down?

"There's another rumor I personally know is not true, that he's having a gay relationship with his new associate minister, Memo Rodriguez."

"I'm sorry, Memo," I offered.

"No need; everyone knows I'm gay. That's what I love about the reverend and Redeeming Hope. I am accepted for who I am. But do you know who is spreading these rumors? Not the politicians. Yes, they would like him to go away. No, it's the other evangelicals who claim homosexuality is an abomination in order to distract everyone from their own immorality. What's really going on is that they are jealous of what the reverend has built, precisely because he accepts himself and everyone else as a sinner, capable of being redeemed."

"And that's how you feel, Mamerto, redeemed?" I asked.

"Yes, but much more. Don't forget the other half of our name. I am hopeful, not just for myself, but for everyone in the community. Look at Gato. He probably can't tell you coherently what happened this morning, but perhaps he was moved at the moment, just as I was the Sunday after Thanksgiving." Uncannily, Mamerto was reading my mind. "I do know I didn't put him up to it, as you are thinking."

That was George's opening. "Well, I can tell you he's not going to any church picnic today. He just borrowed forty dollars off his next check. Oh yeah, he'll be in the park today, but with a different congregation."

Mamerto was ready. "My new name for you would be Cynic George, except I have hope even for you."

"That I'll join your church? I wouldn't bet on it, Memo, excuse me, associate minister."

Just then Dena arrived with our food, cutting the building tension like a knife through warm butter. I was having my usual BLT, George a stack of pancakes and a side of ham. "Memo, you only want toast and coffee? You sure you don't want anything else? No wonder you looking so thin." Dena corrected herself, "I mean trim. What about a Denver omelet? Orlando cook them almost as good as you."

"No, Dena, I'm saving my appetite for the church picnic. Matter of fact, why don't you, Yianni, and Orlando join us after you close up? We'll be right off North Avenue in Humboldt Park; can't miss us. Just look for the sky-blue banner with our church's name, Redeeming Hope."

AA
GATO 2007

"Good morning, everyone. My name is Karl, and I am an alcoholic."

Many voices. "Hi, Karl." *Fewer voices.* "Good morning."

"Yes, it is a good morning. Every day I wake up and remind myself that I am an alcoholic is a good morning, and it helps me make the day a good day.

"I'll try to be short today. Already some of you let me know you have something to say, and I see some new faces who I hope will have courage to tell us something about themselves. I say courage with all honesty. For me it was the hardest thing I had ever done up until then, nineteen years ago.

"Like everyone here, my path has not been a straight one. Lots of zags. Lots of zigs." *Some chuckles.* "Backward, that's how we go sometimes. For me lots of times. But just the other day I was reminded of something that keeps me moving forward. It was a little thing, really. My cable TV was breaking up. I couldn't watch anything—not HBO, not the regular cable like the movie channel, not even the networks—for more than a minute when the little boxes would show up all over the screen. I was irritated. I pay a lot for that cable, though not nearly as much as I used to spend in the bars. But this had happened before, so I knew some things I could do, or change, myself. So I unplugged the cable box for a minute and started it up again. No help.

"Now I got on the phone to the cable company. I had to go through their stupid menu system, and then had to wait about ten minutes before a real person got on the phone. I was more irritated, but I knew that by myself I couldn't change the cable outfit's lousy customer service. So why get mad? That's when I used to drink, whenever I got mad, and I used to get mad a lot.

"Finally, Customer Rep Louise gets on the phone with her syrupy voice and asks me my phone number even though I had to punch it in as soon as my call was answered. Another stupid little irritant. Still not worth getting mad about. She goes through all the troubleshooting routines, including the unplug the box trick I already did. Patiently I tried it again, 'cause she says she boosted my signal. After unhooking the set, I come back to the phone. We had been disconnected. This had happened before too, and I knew, despite them asking for my phone number twice, Louise was not going to be calling me back.

"In the old days, I would have been steaming and would have popped a couple of cans from the fridge by now. But I remembered I had the power to change the situation. All I had to do is call up the cable company again, and this time, cancel my service. But I liked the shows on HBO, I liked the better reception, and I liked the greater choice. So I didn't call back, I didn't cancel my service. Like Tony Soprano, I said 'Forget about it,' and came here to the meeting.

"Now, I'd like to ask, is there anyone here today who would like to say something for the first time, to use that courage God gives us to change our lives?" *Several seconds of silence, some coughs, chairs moving.* "Yes, go ahead and introduce yourself."

"My name is Felix."

Many voices. "Hi, Felix."

"My friends call me Gato."

Again, many voices. "Hi, Gato."

"I am alcoholic. I don't have a drink in six days."

Applause, a single shout out, "Way to go, Gato."

"Excuse me, but I'm no good at talking to a big group. But thanks to *el Señor*, I am here. Believe me, it's hard, real hard to be here. It's hard for me to not drink today. I wake up and I want to drink. So I have to do something to keep busy. I pray to *el Señor*. That don't take too much time and I don't pray so good. It's been so long. So I have to go somewhere. I can't stay in my room; I don't have a room; I sleep in the park. I have to get out of the park because everyone in the park, they drink.

"I come here and drink coffee, and talk to people even if I don't know them. They let me bum smokes. I listen to everyone else, like me alcoholic. So thank you, everybody.

"I have some people, especially my Mami and Dadi, I have to tell I am sorry. They not my real Mami and Papi; they already dead in *Cuba*. I call them Mami and Dadi 'cause they help me a real lot. You know, one time Social Security say I'm dead, so I get no check. I can't pay rent and I got no room, like now. But Dadi get my check back, and Mami let me stay with them. They find me a room once I get my back pay. Dadi, he get my check now. One time he take off work to try to help me get ID and I don't show up. Mami, she take me for breakfast and I almost get into a fight 'cause I owe someone money.

"My friend Memo, he want to find me a place to stay, but he say I have to stop drinking.

"So, with help from *el Señor*, I try. I try again today to stay sober."

Applause.
"*Sí se puede, Gato.*"
Clicking noises and pauses on the tape.

"Hello, my name is Gato, I am alcoholic."

"Hi, Gato."

"I don't drink now three days. I'm sorry I drink a few days ago. I think my friend find a room for me, low-rent housing, but he say I need picture ID. I get mad. How I gonna get ID when I don't have ID? All day I'm worrying about ID, where I'm going to sleep 'cause the radio say a storm coming. I run into Alicia, she have a friend I can stay with, but he's drinking, so I drink too.

"But then Saturday I go see my Dadi to get some money. He don't know I'm drinking again, he say he take me to get ID, he has papers from Social Security. He say we can go one day next week. Sunday I go to Memo's church and I will pray real hard. At the church, the singing make me feel good. So I don't drink since then. Monday we go for the ID.

"Thank you, *Señor*, for giving me the strength to not drink today."

Applause.

"Gato, my name is Karl."

"Hi, Karl. I remember you from the first day I talk here. I like what you say up there. It help me a lot. About the things you can change and the things you can't."

"I learned that the hard way, up and down, just like you're going through. Listen. I used to work for the secretary of state at the State of Illinois Building. You know, where you get driver licenses and ID."

"Yeah, I been there. Turned me down 'cause I didn't have the right papers."

"Well, that's what I want to tell you. You can get the right papers right down Clark Street at the Social Security office. Just give them your social security number. You know that, don't you?"

"Three-five-three . . ."

"You don't have to tell me; tell them. And ask for your approval letter."

"I show the approval letter, and they still don't give me ID."

"No, not the one they send you each year that tells you your pay. You're right, that one won't work. This approval letter is more of a computer printout, a bunch of facts, like your date of birth, where you were born, address. You show the secretary of state's office that printout, they'll give you ID. Make sure you tell your Dadi when you go there on Monday."

"What, you mean if I know this I can have my ID five years ago? Nobody tell me. They don't tell me at Social Security, they don't tell me at secretary of state office. Dadi, he supposed to know this."

"Well, Gato, you just got the inside scoop. Maybe we can't change the rules, but we can change what we know about the rules and use them to change our circumstances. You know what I mean?"

"You making sense, Karl. Thank you; you got my respect."

"Gato, you'll see. Good things happen when you come to these meetings. We're drunks, but we've been around, we know a lot, and we go to bat for each other. You'll do the same one day."

"I will, I will."

Again clicking noises and pauses on the tape.

"Good Morning. My name is Gato. I am alcoholic."

"Hi, Gato."

"It's two days since I have a drink. I'm sorry. I drink again for a couple of days. I have something to celebrate. I think I can just have a beer or two. I celebrate 'cause after five years I finally get my state of Illinois ID. Look, I show it to you."

Near silence for a few seconds.

"Hold it higher, Gato, so we can see it."

Other voices, not in unison. "Congratulations, Gato."

"Way to go."

"I want to thank Karl, he tell me how I can get it. And my Dadi, he go with me downtown to Social Security and State of Illinois Building. Really I thank everyone here. If I don't come here, Karl don't tell me how. Or I'm drinking every day and Dadi don't take me.

"I know I can't drink. I start again. Memo won't help me get the low-rent apartment. And I need it real bad. The park is no place to sleep. It's no place, especially you need a new hip and you need to stop drinking. And I want to stop drinking.

"Thank you, *el Senor.*"

More clicks and pauses, then more clicks

I am on the street now. The meeting, it go long today. And after, Karl want to talk some more. He say he can be my sponsor. I tell him Dadi, he my payee, so I don't think I need a sponsor. I'm lucky the batteries don't run out on this recorder. I need the tape so I can prove to Memo I'm not drinking, if he no believe me. If he say I'm not doing too good, I say at least I try. I try real hard.

Now I got too much time, and I'm hungry like a son-of-a-bitch. I can go to Marta's, but that too close to the park. Or I can go to Mariela's and get a Cuban sandwich. I can be quick. And then after three I can check into the Logan Hotel on Milwaukee. I got enough for maybe two nights. I need a shower real bad. My hip hurting real bad, so I got to get off my feet and sleep.

"Gato, yo, Gato."

Low voice. "Oh shit, I got to watch it now."

"Gato, my man. Where you been?"

"I'm around all the time. What about you, Amos? I don't see you in the park. I don't see you nowhere."

"Just got out of lockup. Some old warrant. They drop it, though. Police, he don't show. You heading somewhere?"

"I'm thinking I go to Mariela's for a sandwich."

"Oh yeah, they make the best Cuban sandwich. I'd go with, 'cept I'm short, you know what I mean?"

"Yeah, I know, you mean me to buy you lunch."

"You know it'll come back to you, Gato. Matter of fact, I got almost 'nough for a quart. You in?"

"Amos, I'm not drinking."

"Since when, this morning? Ever see a cat that don't scratch?"

"Why you mess with me? I tell you I don't drink today."

"OK, Gato, but this half pint has your name on it." *Pause.* "That's good. Have some, or you on life number nine or something?"

"Listen, Amos, I'm sick."

"I can see you leaning on that walker again. What, that religion wear off like a bad high and your hip hurting that bad?"

"I'm alcoholic sick."

"Tell me something I don't know. You don't want any, that's cool, won't come up again. Matter of fact, you want some of this pint, too late."

Silence except for a passing car, then a bottle rattling on the ground.

"You still gonna help me with that quart, right?"

"You think I made out of gold? You want a quart and lunch? Hey, what's that in your pocket? What? You already have a quart?

Amos, you son-of-a-bitch."

"Watch your tongue, Gato, or I really won't give you any."

"Now I need some. Too much bull in one day."

Hiss of a quart bottle opening.

URGENT REQUEST
MEMO 2007

Editor's note: Late summer 2007 was an eventful time for Jesus. It seemed after all these years, things were falling in place for him. He was attending AA meetings and they seemed to be helping him reduce, if not completely stop, his drinking. He was able to obtain his state of Illinois ID, and that became the key for his getting an offer for a subsidized apartment. Mamerto Rodriguez, at the time Associate Outreach Minister of Redeeming Hope Pentecostal Church, lit the way for Jesus's new life and was in touch with us with the good news as well as the bad.

First we received copies of his letters to Hermosa Housing and a couple of other agencies. As you will see from the second letter he sent us, it was Hermosa Housing that responded to his efforts, perhaps because of the web of personal connections between Jesus, Mamerto, George, myself, and Albert Salgado, Hermosa's Director of Residential Services.

The first letter mentions that Jesus is in need of hip replacement surgery. Accompanying Hermosa's offer letter was a personal note from Mamerto to me regarding Jesus's health.

Alexia Demas
September, 2007

Redeeming Hope Outreach Ministries
1690 Humboldt Boulevard
Chicago, IL 60647
July 23, 2007

Mr. Alberto Salgado
Hermosa Housing
3244 W. Armitage
Chicago, IL 60647

Dear Mr. Salgado,

To confirm our conversation of July 12, Jesus Cárdenas has
an urgent need for housing, preferably subsidized housing. An
orthopedist specialist has deemed Mr. Cárdenas a candidate for hip
replacement surgery. Yet he is homeless. On at least two occasions
he was found sleeping on the stairs of a transient hotel where he
would sometimes spend the night. Police were called to the scene,
and he told them the pain was unbearable, that he could not make
it up to his room.

Unfortunately, he is on a long waiting list at Cook County
for the needed operation. As you can infer, Mr. Cárdenas would
need placement in a building with an elevator.

Over the last decade, Mr. Cárdenas has been homeless
several times, often because of circumstances beyond his control.
Twice the buildings he was living in were sold for renovation
or condominium conversion. For another period of time he was
homeless because the Social Security Administration mistakenly
terminated his benefits when his check was returned because his
payee was deceased.

Mr. Cárdenas's situation is made more urgent now due to various medical conditions in addition to hip deterioration, including asthma, chronic emphysema, and alcoholism.

On a positive note, since seeking out the outreach services of Redeeming Hope Pentecostal Church, he has been regularly attending meetings of Alcoholics Anonymous. In addition, for the first time in many years he has obtained a state of Illinois picture ID. Lack of such identification about a year ago put his application for subsidized housing from your organization on hold, after his SSI payee, George Demas, brought him to your office.

I have known Jesus Cárdenas, as I believe you have, for many years. Perhaps as we have aged, each of us in our own way has learned that we can no longer live loose or live without purpose. I found my way through Christ; Jesus is finding his through the Alcoholics Anonymous community. Through your purposeful activism with Hermosa Housing, your agency can now give Jesus additional peace of mind by providing him with decent, affordable housing as he struggles for his dignity and health.

I have been in touch with Mr. Demas, and he assures me that as soon as Jesus is situated in an apartment through Hermosa Housing that he will guarantee prompt payment of his rent.

Upon receipt of this letter, please call me at 773-899-9595 to let me know a convenient time that Mr. Cárdenas can come to your office to present his state of Illinois identification to you.

Once again, let me thank you for your service to the community. Please let me know if there is any way I can help you expedite this matter.

Sincerely yours,
Mamerto Rodriguez,
Associate Minister
Redeeming Hope Outreach Ministries
Cc: Mr. and Mrs. George Demas

Hermosa Housing
3244 W. Armitage
Chicago, IL 60647
August 20, 2007

Mr. Jesus Cárdenas
c/o Associate Minister Mamerto Rodriguez
Redeeming Hope Outreach Ministries
1690 Humboldt Boulevard
Chicago, IL 60647

Dear Mr. Cárdenas,

I am pleased to inform you that your application for subsidized housing through Hermosa Housing has been reinstated. In addition, your reinstatement has moved you to your previous position at the top of our waiting list in our single-room-occupancy category.

As a result, we can now offer you a studio apartment at our Dignity Apartments, 2600 N. Central Park starting October 1, 2007. Be assured that Dignity Apartments has a recently installed elevator. Your rent, for the remainder of 2007, will be 30 percent of your monthly income of $623, or $187 per month. Your rent will be adjusted for 2008 according to the cost of living adjustment to your SSI benefit.

Please contact me at 773-555-9988 to arrange a viewing of the apartment and to finalize arrangements for your tenancy.

Mr. Cárdenas, again, we are pleased to welcome you to our community of residents at Dignity Apartments.

Sincerely yours,
Alberto Salgado
Director Resident Services
Hermosa Housing

August 24, 2007

Alexia,

Why is it so often that bad news accompanies the good? Indeed, the ways of our Lord are mysterious. Now at the very moment that Gato has secured a really decent and affordable place to live, the orthopedist now states that he needs his left hip replaced as well as the right. Nonetheless, this fact will not move him up on the near two year waiting list at Cook County. Perhaps this additional diagnosis influenced our friend Alberto's decision to move Gato to the top of the list, enabling him to get the current opening at Dignity Apartments.

Gato and I go back a long way, as I told you that time at your kitchen table. There was a time when we thought we were on the top of the world. Really we were engaged in some pretty bad stuff. Of course, each of use fell on hard times, though for different reasons. For a while we were out of touch. But our struggles for survival brought us back together, this time not as "business" associates, but in my mind as brothers. Neither of us had real brothers we could rely on. Mine would have nothing to do with me once he found out my ways. Gato's brother died several years ago now.

So I fear the worst for him. Even though we are close, I cannot know what is in his heart, whether he has truly accepted Jesus Christ as his Savior. Only Jesus and Jesus know that. But I believe he has a good heart no matter how much he acts destructively, usually as his own victim.

How Gato will manage for two years waiting for the hip replacement surgery is an unknown. His asthma, emphysema, and a diseased liver won't make the wait any easier and could jeopardize his hip replacement candidacy because his diminished immune system may make it too risky. I can only put my faith in God, that He will give Gato one new opportunity now that he seems to be finding his way.

Gato was a little embarrassed to give you this news himself and asked me to let you know. He is moving into his apartment on October 1 and eventually, once he is settled, he would like to have us all over for a Sunday dinner. Please call me when you receive this so we can talk more about these new developments.

My prayers are with you, George, and Nick, as well as with Gato.

Your friend,
Memo

SUNDAY DINNER
GEORGE 2007

I would never have imagined a Sunday dinner prepared by Gato at an apartment of his own big enough even to have a table and clean enough that Alexia would feel comfortable there. But that's what happened after he moved into the subsidized housing that had so long eluded him.

Alexia and I were the first to arrive, and as Gato would say, "It smelled good, real good." The "it" was rice cooking with chicken, bubbling in a large cast iron pan on the stove. In a smaller pan were sweet plantains, cooking in minimum oil on a low flame. Among her favorite Caribbean foods, they brought a smile to Alexia's face as she surveyed the stove top, then more broadly the tidiness of the apartment. The mint green clothed table was set with matching china, silverware, and glasses for five. Already on the table, lettuce tossed with cucumber and tomatoes, and limes halved on a small plate next to the salad's big bowl. Her eyebrows rose as she turned to me.

"*Compañera*, you like what you see?" Gato asked from behind a white, waist-level apron that protected his sharply pressed slacks.

He was leaning against the counter within which the four-burner stove stood. But not far away was a new walker, the blue kind that doubled as a chair.

"*Compañero*, I'm impressed. How'd you do this?"

"Low rent. And Amos. He working at the Salvation Army store. He tell me some good stuff coming in from some rich lady, she die in the suburbs. He tell me to get there early so I can get the best. He say he get me a good price on everything I buy. I even get this walker; it like brand new."

"You really picked some nice stuff, Jesus. And everything smells delicious."

"Maybe as good as your cooking, Mami."

The doorbell rang. It took a second to register the sound. Gato had a doorbell.

"Dadi, must be Memo. Buzz him up. It's by the door."

A minute or so later, I opened the door for Memo.

"Just George," he greeted me with a smile, reaching out his hand and shaking mine firmly. "Alexia, isn't this place something? Gato, my mouth was watering more every step up the stairs. Lord Jesus Christ, look what you have done."

"Memo, you better pray I don't overcook the food." Gato laughed; we all laughed. "Hey why you not take the elevator?"

Tears were welling up at Alexia's eyes as she and Memo hugged. Then quiet overtook the room, each of us grasping the un-likelihood of the moment.

Gato broke the silence, as he brought a pitcher of water to the table. "Sit down, everyone; the food is ready."

"Let me help bring things to the table." Not waiting for her offer to be refused, Alexia brought over the plate of plantains, while Gato, with potholders in both hands, carried the heavy cast iron pan to the table.

Memo held out his hands so that Alexia and I could join his and in turn join Gato's to say Grace. "Lord, we are blessed to be in your presence and in the presence of our loved ones. We are blessed for the food you make bountiful to us and the good health you bestow upon us. Lord, give us the strength to overcome our weaknesses, for thou are the path to our salvation. Amen."

"Mami, Dadi, Memo, please fill your glasses so I can make a toast. I hope you don't mind, I only have water." The pitcher was passed and we all raised our glasses.

"To my friends, you make all of this possible to me. I owe you everything. You have my respect and you have my love for as long as I live. ¡*Salud!*"

"Thank you, Gato, and now a toast to you." I raised my glass again.

"You are a loyal friend, the best a payee could ask for . . ."

"Excuse me, friend? Don't you mean, son?" That sly smile of his was all over his face.

"If you let me finish my toast, I was going to say, you are like a son, whether you are older or younger than us. *Yia mas!*"

Alexia shot me a look and then turned the conversation. "Jesus, who is the fifth place for? Should we be waiting before we start to eat?"

"I invite my daughter Marisol. First she say she come, then she say she be late, so start without her. I don't think she is going to come."

"I'm sorry. I hope you won't be disappointed."

"Mami, I can't blame her. I'm not there for her; she growing up."

"Don't be too hard on yourself, Gato," Memo added. "When she had problems with her uncle's friend, you tried to help. And remember, your ex, she didn't want you around, except when she needed something."

"You right, Memo. She always got her hand out, even though she know I got nothing. She teach Maribel the same thing. Maybe it's good she not come today. She probably think I got money 'cause now I have the low rent."

"Well, don't worry yourself. Your number one focus has to be your health. Isn't that right, Alexia?"

"Yes, Jesus. Mamerto is right. We were all feeling so good a few minutes ago. Let's enjoy the food you prepared, Jesus."

We three guests dug in with gusto, and indeed the food was as *sabroso* as it smelled. Gato ate slowly, probably because it was hard to eat with so few teeth. But every once in a while he'd ask one of us, "You like, Mami? Is good, no, Dadi? What you think, Memo?"

Of course we responded back with the compliments he sought. Alexia saw an opportunity. "It's so good to see you happy like this, Jesus. You know a positive attitude is more important than medicine."

"They say laughter is the best medicine, except when Dadi telling the joke." Gato grinned again.

"Well, did you know I'm now an executive at my company?" I countered.

"What? You try that one on me again? Yeah I know what kind of factory you work at, and believe me, I don't take no bull from you."

Memo looked a little confused. "Did I just miss something?"

Alexia replied, "One of George's tired jokes; you don't want to hear it."

I used this mild rebuke to excuse myself to go to the washroom. I could hear the conversation, at least until I flushed the toilet.

"Well, let's stick to the subject of health," Memo suggested. "When is your next appointment?"

"Friday, eleven in the morning. You should know, you make it."

"Is the appointment with the orthopedist or Dr. Uribe?" Alexia asked.

"Orth-orth-o-pedist?" Gato would sputter at words not familiar, or when nervous.

Meanwhile I strolled around the large studio, looking for something but nothing in particular, without being too obvious, as their discussion continued.

"Dr. Uribe, Gato," Memo replied. "It'll be awhile before you see the orthopedist again. You'll need to be higher on the waiting list. Dr. Uribe wants to keep you as strong as he can until then."

Alexia tried to encourage Gato too. "And you're already doing your part, trying to quit drinking, cutting back on the smoking."

"I tell you before, Memo, I don't let them cut me."

"I thought you wanted the new hips, that you can't bear the pain. There's no magic wand that's going to replace them," Memo said.

And then I saw it. On the shelf of the night table next to the bed was a tape recorder, unbelievably the same tape recorder we had given Gato five years earlier for Christmas, with hopes he might record his story. More unbelievably, a little red light and the slowly turning tape indicated everything being said was being recorded.

As the others continued their conversation, I found myself vacillating in my reaction to the tape recorder. How ridiculous, I thought. But then I started to get angry. What a lot of nerve for him to tape us behind our back! Had he done this before?

"Why I have to wait so long for Cook County? How come I can't have the operation at St. Mary Hospital? What, now I'm not good enough for them? I got the medical card."

"That's not what it's about, Gato. You have to have private insurance for that kind of surgery at St. Mary's," said Memo.

"Mami, maybe I don't make it. You think I can last two years? You think I make it under the knife?"

His fear was out there. Silence prevailed uncomfortably. One thing for sure, this was not the time for me to play "got you."

MIRACLE SPRGS HOTEL S
10625 PALM DR
DESERT HOT SP, CA 92240

03/01/2017   09:45:49

CREDIT CARD

VISA SALE

CARD #	XXXXXXXXXXXX6230
INVOICE	0001
SEQ #:	0001
Batch #:	001596
Approval Code:	06486C
Entry Method:	Swiped
Mode:	Online

SALE AMOUNT $75.00

CUSTOMER COPY

NO PARTY
GATO 2007

"Bye, Mami. Bye Dadi. Memo, I see you later."

Muffled voices coming from the hallway. Door closing, deadbolt lock latching.

"I have to find my bottle."

Cupboards opening and closing, each one louder than the last. Drawers slammed shut.

"*Jesus Cristo*, where I put that bottle? Why I invite them? All they do is talk about my hip surgery. What they think I want to hear about that? I know, between the mattresses. Damn it, where I put it? The closet, that's it. I hide it in my jacket sleeve. Nobody think about that."

Rustling sounds.

"That's good, real good. That Maribel. Why I invite her? I know she not going to come; she don't care I need a new hip. She don't care even if I going to die soon. All she care I say I don't have no money now. She think I got money, because I got low rent."

Pause. Sound of bottle put down on table. Burp.

"I got only $90 left to last me three weeks. Almost all gone. On what? Table, bed, dishes."

Pause.

"TV, DVD player."

Pause. Exhale

"Pots, pans."

Pause. Burp.

"Forks, spoons."

Pause.

"Knives."

Pause. Exhale.

"Glasses. I buy everything for this party."

Pause.

"Lots of food. All fresh."

Pause. Bottle put down on table, then stumbling, then bottle breaking on floor.

"Now I got no beer. All I got, dirty dishes and pots in the sink."

Shattering dishes, stumbling, more shattering dishes. Metal-sounding object hits the floor. Something hard hitting a wall.

"I got nothing. I got nothing."

Bed wheels sliding across the floor. Then a thump.

Minutes of silence.

Knocking on the door. More knocking.

"Gato? Gato? Are you in there? It's Carlos from next door."

More knocking. Unrecognizable talking at the door. Knocking.

"Gato, Eddie and I heard a lot of noise. Can you hear us? Gato, you all right? We're going to get the manager to open up. Hold on, Gato, we'll be right back."

About a minute goes by. Deadbolt unlocking.

"Gato. Oh my God, he's out cold and bleeding. Eddie, call 911. Then call Alberto from Hermosa Housing."

Water running.

"Hang on, Gato. You're still breathing. I'm going to clean you up a bit."

Silence, just some slight sounds, occasional breathing.

"Carlos, OK, I called 911 and Alberto. Alberto can't make it, but he's calling Gato's friend Memo, you know the one from the church. How's he doing?"

"Well, at least the cuts aren't deep. He must have cut himself on some of the broken dishes or the bottle. His pulse is pretty weak, though."

"You see that over there, Carlos?"

"Not sure what you're talking about."

"There's a tape recorder running on that little shelf next to the bed."

"Shut it off. I don't want anyone thinking we did anything wrong."

"Got it . . ."

DECISIONS, DECISIONS
GEORGE 2007

That same Sunday night, about ten p.m. Memo called. Gato was in the hospital, Swedish American to be exact. Memo was already there, having been called by Hermosa Housing. By the time Memo arrived at the emergency room, Gato was no longer unconscious, merely incomprehensible. "Surprise, Surprise," was my immediate response. Perhaps I shouldn't have been so sarcastic, given the gracious dinner Gato had just hosted for us. Gracious, that is, except for the tape recording bugging every word. There was no diagnosis and no prognosis yet, so I asked Memo if he'd call me in the morning, relieved that he was there, not I.

Gato's hospitalization gave me an excuse to work from home the next day. When the phone rang, my only surprise was that it wasn't Roela from my office, but a nurse from the Intensive Care Unit at Swedish American. "Mr. Demas, I think you better come here to the hospital. We're having trouble with Mr. Cárdenas, and you are the only one he has authorized to receive any information regarding his situation." I wasn't inclined to rush over there; I'd have to

268

blow off a standing work meeting. I wasn't convinced that I should go until I talked to the attending ICU resident or, more accurately, tried to talk to her. Dr. Grandheim's thick German accent made it difficult to understand exactly why Gato was in the ICU.

It was good Alexia decided to come along with me. As soon as we arrived, it was clear something was wrong. There was a hubbub around Gato's bed. Two nurses and a security guard were trying to bind him to the bed, but Gato was resisting. An officious Nurse Ratchet type approached us. "Mr. Demas, Mr. Cárdenas is being belligerent. He won't let us take care of him." As she talked, she'd look at me, look back at Gato, and then back at me with an inquisitive look on her face. "You're not really his father, are you?"

Walking her away from the bed, I straightened her out right away, giving Alexia a chance to go to Gato's side. I could see she was holding his hand, talking calmly to him. The other nurse and security guard pulled back, seeing that Gato was finally responding to someone. I dispatched Nurse Lupino to get Dr. Grandheim, and joined Alexia at the bedside.

"Gato, how are you doing?"

He responded faintly. "Dadi, Mami, they got my money." He was trying to sit up and pivot himself off the bed. But the restraint on his right hand made it impossible for him to do so.

Alexia again tried to calm him. "Jesus, we're here now. We'll make sure your money is safe."

Now he was crying. "Mami, nobody know where's my money. It's not in the plastic bag with my stuff."

"Gato, here's your wallet," I said, holding it up after discovering it in a pocket of the sports team jacket I found in a blue bag sitting on the windowsill.

"The money, it's not in the wallet. It's in my pants. Where my pants?"

Alexia asked the security guard where the rest of Gato's clothes were. He answered, "I checked it out earlier when he was fussing about his money. That blue bag, that's all they brought up from the emergency room. They say some fella from a church came by and was talking to your friend last night. Maybe he has the money and his clothes."

I called Memo, but he said he never saw any of Gato's belongings the night before. So I approached the security guy. "Listen, I realize you weren't on duty last night, so whatever happened to his stuff isn't your fault."

"You got that right. Come with me down to the ER. Let's see what I can find. You'll have to stay in the waiting area, though," Guard Jackson Phillips told me. Before we headed down the two floors, I asked one of the attendants to ring the ER for me when Dr. Grandheim became available.

I was waiting for twenty minutes and starting to get anxious about the time because I had told them at work I'd only be gone from my home office about two hours, so I asked the ER receptionist if she could check on the guard. She tried calling someone but didn't get through. After another twenty minutes of my foot tapping, her phone rang. "Dr. Grandheim can see you in the ICU now."

"It's about time. Can you please tell Phillips to bring whatever he finds up to the ICU?"

I was a little turned around making it up to the ICU. I don't think I took the short cut the security guard took. Nurse Lupino was talking to a fortyish woman with short, dark brown hair. Dr. Grandheim, I presumed, had her back turned to me. As I approached from behind, she appeared to have her own tapping foot syndrome. Lupino introduced us, "Mr. Demas, this is Dr. Helga Grandheim." With that, Lupino headed toward Gato's bed.

Luckily Grandheim was more comprehensible in person than

over the phone, though her thick accent turned Vs to Fs, Ss to Zs, Ws to Vs, and so on. "Haff they found the Cárdenas fortune yet, Mr. Demas?"

For a second I considered a quick comeback, but my time was shorter than my fuse, and I really didn't want to get off on the wrong foot. "Actually, no, they have not found his money yet. But forget that for now. An hour and a half ago when you first called, it seemed rather urgent."

"It is, Mr. Demas. Since Mr. Cárdenas has signed the HIPAA release for you and your wife, I can be very direct about his condition."

"Thank you, doctor. The nurse didn't explain what it was that Jesus didn't want them to do. He's very concerned about his money; it's all he has until the first of next month, still three weeks away."

Grandheim replied, "I realize that's no small matter for a guy like Cárdenas. Between his breathing problems and the alcohol withdrawal we do not have time to waste. The IV we have in his arm is not working effectively. He was admitted with lacerations on his head, alcohol seizures, difficulty breathing, and dehydration. Because of his alcohol dependency and especially because of his chronic pulmonary condition, we need to insert a central line from the femoral vein near his groin to deliver his medicine directly to his heart. From there it will be distributed quickly to the rest of his body. We need to do this quickly or he can lapse into convulsions or even a coma. That's what they were trying to do when he put up a fight.

"Even after he is stabilized, we will need to monitor him for a few days here in the ICU, as there are complications that are possible from central intravenous therapy, including infections and blood clots. But through the same line we can effectively monitor his blood levels."

Out of the corner of my eye, I saw Guard Phillips walking through the hall with another blue bag. "Doctor, let me see if his money is in that bag. If it is, I am sure Jesus will cooperate."

Phillips and I went through the bag together, neither of us trusting the other. I immediately saw the clothes Gato had worn the day before. They were rumpled, stained with blood, and reeking of alcohol. I went right for the slacks. Sure enough, there was a thin roll of money deep inside the right pocket. When my count could go no higher than $88, the guard prescribed our next step. "Let's go see what he wants to do with that money."

As soon as we showed him the money and told him how much, the anguish on his face seemed to disappear. "Dadi, you want to take it?"

"I'd rather not, Gato. I may not be around when they release you. Let's get it locked up in security, get a receipt for it, your wallet, and your IDs. Then whether or not I'm here when you need it, it'll be here."

Phillips took care of the paperwork while I worked on Gato. "Listen, my friend, the doctor says your condition is very serious. You know they can't find any really good veins in your arms."

"I know, Dadi. I have too many needles all the time I go to the hospital."

"So they want to put one in through your groin."

"What, they going to put a tube in my dick? I don't think so. That hurt like a son-of-a-bitch."

"No, not there, Gato; here," and I showed him on myself where the IV would be inserted.

"If you say that's what they need to do, OK. You in charge of me."

"OK, I'll tell the doctor. She wants them to do it right away. But I'm not in charge. This is your life, not mine. You think I'd let you make decisions about my health, I don't think so." With a smile I went over to Dr. Grandheim, who, upon my news, immediately dispatched Nurse Lupino again with the central line IV order.

"One more thing, Mr. Demas. We will need you to sign papers so that in an emergency you will be authorized to make decisions on behalf of Mr. Cárdenas if he is not able to do so himself."

"What kind of decisions?"

"For example, DNR, do not resuscitate."

"Wait a minute, doctor, all I am is a friend and his SSI payee. I don't think I should be making life or death decisions on Gato's, I mean Jesus's, behalf."

"You do not need to decide now, but you must think about it. Maybe, once he is more stable, Mr. Cárdenas will be able to sign the DNR himself. But if not, and you do not, we will have to make the decisions ourselves."

As she handed me her card, she asked, "Do you have any other questions, Mr. Demas?"

Of course I had other questions, but I didn't have time, and it was clear she didn't either. We'd be sticking around until the procedure was complete and Gato was settled. My day was already shot. For not the first time, I wondered how much longer we could continue in our current role with him. Now I wondered if we would have to assume even greater responsibility.

Gato's stay at Swedish American lengthened. We called daily to get an update from the doctors and stopped in every other day. On our second pop-in, Gato seemed alert and was up to his old tricks, flirting with the nurses and attendants. A different attending physician, Dr. Pho Nguyen, glancing at Gato's chart, told us he should be moved to a semiprivate room within the next day, and that Gato had signed the DNR form.

Alexia asked if he really knew what he was signing. "How did you explain it to him?" she asked.

"I can't tell you for sure. It was Dr. Grandheim who obtained the consent. She'll be on duty tonight if you want to call her."

I intended to call in the evening but fell asleep watching *Double Indemnity* on one of the classic cable stations. The telephone rang as the wounded Fred McMurray was confessing his crime into a Dictaphone. I staggered to the phone as if I were McMurray and didn't recognize the caller's name. The accented voice told me it was Dr. Grandheim.

"Mr. Demas, I'm afraid Mr. Cárdenas has taken a turn for the worse. After you left this morning, his breathing became irregular and painful. A CT scan revealed a clot in his lung. We had to put him on thrombolytic medicine to dissolve the clot. If he responds well to this treatment, tomorrow or the next day, we'll switch him to a less aggressive blood thinner."

The following day, Saturday, we went to the hospital in the afternoon, not knowing what to expect. But as soon as we got off the elevator, we heard Gato . . . flirting with one of the nurses. While I went to find Dr. Grandheim, Alexia went to Gato's bedside, and I could hear their comradely exchange of greetings, "*Compañero.*"

"*Compañera.*"

As usual, I had to wait awhile for Dr. Grandheim, but based on Gato's improved mood, my own lightened. But Grandheim dashed my hopes as soon as she turned her attention from her charts to me. "Mr. Demas, don't be lulled by your friend's good cheer. We've given him a mild sedative. If he gets agitated, he could loosen the clot before it dissolves."

"I see," I responded. "Are you having any luck with the clot?"

"Like I said, it has not dissolved yet. Which brings me to my next concern, and your next decision. Even if the clot dissolves, he will have to stay on blood thinners, and we cannot release him to go home right away, especially to the kind of place he lives, with no one to care for him. Unless you are willing to take him into your home, we will have to send him to a nursing home where they can monitor his blood levels."

I'm the one who would need sedatives if we were to let him stay with us again, I thought, while saying to Grandheim, "I told you we are not his real parents, no matter what he calls us. As for a nursing home, that's going to be a tough sell. If you can assure me it would just be temporary, a month or so, maybe he will agree."

"Mr. Demas, I can't assure you of anything. If the blood is too thin he could bleed out, if too thick he could have another clot."

"Well, I'll talk to him. I can't promise you anything."

Before I talked to Gato, I pulled Alexia aside while one of the nurses was changing his IV drip. She was more adamant than I. "I may call him *compañero*, but no way is he going to be our *cohabitante*. Once was enough. Matter of fact, I'm thinking you've been his payee long enough. We're not equipped to deal with all his problems. Did you ever think you might be able to pay more attention to what's going on with your mother in San Diego if you weren't so involved with him? I shouldn't have to remind you of her health issues."

Alexia had my attention, but Gato called, "Dadi, Mami." We turned around and approached him. "Mami, Dadi, you don't have to worry about me. I already tell them I'm not going to no nursing home. You got no freedom there."

"Gato, if they say you need to go to a nursing home, you're going. We don't have time to fool around with you and your freedom."

"Dadi, I go there, they take all my money but $30 a month. And I will lose my low-rent apartment."

"Easy come, easy go."

"Dadi, don't be cruel."

"How's this for cruel?" I snapped back. "Let's say you go home and your medicine isn't right. You keep drinking, you fall again. You know what's going to happen? You're going to bleed to death internally. I don't want any part of that. Memo can be your payee."

"Dadi, you going to fire me?"

"George, this is a hell of a time to bring this up. Jesus, no he's not going to fire you. Right now we're worried about you, and George has a lot going on at work. Getting Memo involved is a good idea. His church must have some ties to the Hispanic nursing homes near Humboldt Park."

"Gato, I'm sorry. Alexia is right. Let us get to work with Memo and see what we can find out."

"Dadi, Mami, I mean no disrespect."

Gato started to get tired; perhaps another dose of sedative was having its effect. So Alexia and I went home, where I spent the rest of the afternoon on the phone. Memo was happy to be of help, but Swedish American would not talk to Memo because he wasn't on the authorized contact list. Finally I reached Nurse Lupino, who promised that once Gato woke up again, she'd have him sign the papers so Memo could talk to the doctors. Meanwhile, each time Memo made contact with another nursing home, he reported back to me. Then Lupino called and put Gato on the phone so I could explain why she needed his signature. "No, the paper is not releasing you to the nursing home." Not yet, I said to myself.

GOING THE DISTANCE
GEORGE 2007

Jesus Cárdenas was pronounced dead by Swedish American later that night. Apparently, even in the hospital, his blood thinner was not thin enough and the clot in his lung enlarged rather than dissolved. The ensuing stroke was massive, his body unable to take it, too compromised by poor liver function, reduced lung capacity, and who knows what else.

As I listened to the details of Gato's demise, delivered by Nurse Grandheim to our home phone, my mind wandered first to events earlier in the day, then earlier in the week, and then over the last several years. Unlikely remembrances came to mind, like the two of us spiraling the neighborhood in my car looking for places for him to live, or seeing him in the hospital for the first time so skinny. Some things that came to mind made me angry, like his contempt for the immigration lawyer who was trying to help him, or his standing me up for a trip downtown to get his state of Illinois ID. But other recollections put a smile on my face: playing chess in the yard (also known as kicking my ass) or his flirting with our holiday guests, including my mother. The more I smiled, the sadder I became. Gato had become a fixture in our lives, and no matter how frustrated he sometimes made us, there was a sweetness that sometimes penetrated, his beautiful crooner's voice, a twinkling in his eye, a real sincerity when he would say, "You picked me up from the gutter."

"Mr. Demas . . . Mr. Demas?" A distant voice interrupted my travels in time and space. "Mr. Demas, do you have any other questions?" The questions I had about Gato Cárdenas, indeed those I had about our relationship, would not be answered by Dr. Grandheim. "Mr. Demas, will you be making the arrangements for Mr. Cárdenas's remains?" I suggested that Memo Rodriguez would be the capable hands for this task.

Hanging up the phone, I turned to Alexia, sitting up in our bed, having listened as much as she could, knowing what had happened. Crossing herself, she prayed quietly, "Lord Jesus Christ, have mercy on his soul. May his memory be eternal." We hugged, holding each other up, each of us crying in our own way. Perhaps because Alexia sobbed convulsively, while I cried inwardly, she was able to compose herself first.

"George, we've talked about this. We knew that he would die sooner or later and that it would not be pretty. You think he wouldn't have died in a nursing home? Remember, he told us he'd rather die on the street than in a hospital?"

"I know you're right, Alexia. But maybe we could have handled things differently with him, you know from the start. We could have tried to get him into AA much sooner. Maybe his health wouldn't have been so bad if we had gotten him to stop drinking."

"And the smoking too? We're no miracle workers, George. Even if we had made it a full-time job dealing with him, and thank God we didn't, would it have really helped or would it have just enabled him?"

Just then Nick knocked on our bedroom door. "Mom, Pop? Is everything all right?" When Alexia told him, he immediately convulsed into tears that only his mother could comfort, leaving me alone with my grief, memories, and even a few conclusions.

Over the years we had learned to accept Gato for who he was—a man with troubles, but a man who had made a place in our lives. His calling us Dadi and Mami, even before we were more than casually involved in his life, was a bit prophetic. Inasmuch as he was childlike, our relationships to him were parentlike. I lectured him, trying to get him to give up habits that were not going to change. Alexia tried to engage him more, listen more, hoping he would open up. But she also set the rules, even if I had to enforce them.

Well before we knew his end was near, we realized that his mysteries would remain so. In fact, there was nothing in his behavior to suggest anything but that he was a Mariel refuge. Castro, with wicked brilliance, in one stroke rid his society of thousands of parasites, unleashing them on his enemy to the north. We came to believe Gato was one of them. Everything about him smelled Mariel, including the official papers, despite his initial tale of escaping on a boat when he was only fifteen, almost twenty years before Mariel.

These perceptions would change with Hector Barrera's arrival at our door two days after Gato's passing. I invited Hector up, but he didn't want to leave his car parked by the fire hydrant. I knew Hector from my days teaching GED in the housing project. He wasn't a student; he had received his diploma while in jail. But we used to talk politics, and now and then he'd send me a student. On that day he was in no talking mood.

He handed me a small black backpack, saying only, "Gato wanted you to have this." With that he turned and went down the porch stairs to his car.

I yelled to him, "What should I do with it?"

He shouted back, "Listen."

Inside were about a dozen tape cassettes, mostly unmarked, a few with years scribbled on them, the latest 2006, one or two from 2002. Another tape we found with the tape recorder, when Albert Salgado of Hermosa Housing let us go through the things in Gato's apartment.

For several nights, Alexia and I listened to the tapes, starting from the earliest year. We soon realized that he had taken me up on my suggestion that he record his story, though the telling wasn't what we would have imagined.

LAST TAPE
GATO 2007

Mami, you remember Dadi give me the little tape recorder. Actually, I first use it when I stay with you waiting for my back pay. Then he give it to me for Christmas and say I should tell my story. You know how much I appreciate what you and Dadi do for me, so if Dadi say tell my story, I do it. All these years when I think about it, I record something. Maybe after you listen to the tapes, you and Dadi can tell the rest of my story. Now it is our story because now I'm part of your family.

I think this is my last tape. I hope Hector give you all the tapes. Maybe he tell you and Dadi to listen to this one last. Even you listen first, it's OK. I hope you believe what I tell you.

Soy enfermado y muy cansado. By the first of the month I proba-bly be dead, real dead, not like Social Security dead. Make sure Dadi return my check.

Now I must tell you the truth, what you and Dadi never figure out. Not from immigration, not from Social Security, the army, from *nadia.*

Mami, you met me first registering voters at the rooming house. Lady Love tell you I have a voter card. Then when I stay at your house, you think I'm sleeping, but I am awake. I listen to you and Dadi talk. You say there is no Jesus Cárdenas on the voter list for the rooming house. You even find the list and read the addresses on Hoyne, 1408, 1412, 1414, 1420, and finally 1432. I remember the names you read like it was last night. Aguirre, Domingo; Barber, Amos; Bell, Samuel; Cárdenas, Felix; Carlton, Paul. Then you say "Felix Cárdenas, but no Jesus Cárdenas."

Mami, I am Felix Cárdenas. Why you think they call me Gato? Jesus Cárdenas was my brother. But now I'm Jesus Cárdenas too. I know I confuse you. But I have no choice until now when the only thing that matters is I give you the respect I owe you for everything you and Dadi do for me.

Back then when it happen, I don't think straight. The gangbangers kill my brother. They shoot at me, but they hit him. Who know they shoot at me or they shoot at him? Even though I was nine years older, we look like twins—same size, same build, both of us dark. In 1988 he visit from Detroit, come to Chicago to see his big brother. They suppose to kill me.

You think you see me at the bottom when Social Security say I'm dead? No, I am even lower then, even before they kill Jesus. You know, I tell you before, I am Latin Lord. I tell you I go to jail. I told you I only have one lung 'cause someone stab me. But I don't tell you; that's when I lose my nerve. So I can't drive no more for Carlos, Lady Love's man and number one Latin Lord. I'm too nervous. No one trust me. Some think I'm a snitch. Not Lady Love. She know it's just my nerves, but she lose power when Carlos go up to Stateville. So I have no friends. I'm not earning 'cause I'm not driving.

That's when I first figure out I can make the hospital my hotel. My one lung is bad anyway 'cause of the smoking and the asthma.

The hospital get me the medical card so welfare can pay them. One time I get the idea and call my brother in Detroit. If he visit me, maybe he decide to stay. Maybe we can share his check. See, he have his own problems.

He no hero when he come from Cuba. He no swim to shore from a sinking boat. He one of the *Marielettas*, the *maricóns* and the ones Castro send from the jails and the mental hospitals in 1980. And if Castro no make you crazy, the US camp in Arkansas for the Cuban boat people, it make you more crazy. You see the papers from Immigration, the mental diagnosis they give Jesus. When they release him, he go to Detroit; he think I am there.

I go to Detroit when I get out of Nam. A Black guy I'm tight with over there say the car factories hire vets and pay good money. I work there one day. I survive Vietnam, you think I want to kill myself working that Dodge assembly line? I stay there awhile, but that city too Black. You know I ain't against them, I got more Black blood than anything else, but Cuban Black, and my people speak espanish. I remember Carlos from Vietnam. He from Chicago. He tell me I ever come to Chicago, look him up. He tell me just ask for him at the Lumari Club on Division.

But Jesus, he go to Detroit and he stay. He don't know where else to go. He's twenty-seven. Later I find out from *Tía Felicita* he's in Detroit but not doing so well. He find a job, then lose it. Can't hold a job. She tell me he got no luck with women. He even try to commit suicide. That's how he get on SSI. Once in a while I write, but I don't want him coming to Chicago till I check him out.

I really make it then as Lord Carlos's number-one driver. I have the clothes, the women, the jewelry. I have rank, no one mess with me, not even from the other gangs. So one time I take two fine ladies—one for me, one for Jesus—to Detroit in my '84 Trans Am. When I see him, he was a punk. I'm not sorry for him; he embarrass me. I make some excuse and take my women back to Chicago.

But then I lose my nerve. I am so low, he's the only one I can call. He can afford a bus to Chicago. I can't go there. So he come. In one week he's dead on the streets, in my arms, and all I can think about is his ID and his check. I grab his wallet and slip mine into his pocket and split before the police come. I don't think no one see what I do.

I know this will not fool the gang members who think I'm a snitch. But I need that check bad, even if it less than $500 a month back then. Only Lady Love can make them get off my back. I lay low at the rooming house where I live. Everybody there know me just as Gato. I pay my rent with cash to the manager. The landlord, he's out in the suburbs. He don't care as long as he get his money. You remember? Lady Love she live on the other side of the alley, just down the block. So one night I sneak to her place, give her the signal I always give Carlos. She don't want me at her place, so she take me out in her big Buick, cover me up with bags of laundry. She drive me clear out of the city to some place Carol Stream, some kind of place she and Carlos go to be alone.

Before she go back to Chicago, we go to the supermarket for food, cigarettes. She pay. With my own money I get a six-pack. I look on the way back so I remember the streets, the stores, gas stations in case I need something else. Luckily her house has a TV. Otherwise I go nuts, no one to talk to. I don't know nobody out there. No phone either. She says no phone, no taps.

That's when I start drinking. I don't drink much alcohol before that. I'm feeling bad about my brother and I'm lonely. You know me, always talking to someone. Always flirting with the ladies. The next day I finish the six-pack and I find the 7-Eleven we pass on the way home. This time I buy a twelve-pack. It last three days. I'm smoking a lot, too. I don't forget how Jesus look bleeding and how I leave him on the street; maybe he not dead when I take his wallet. Now I'm going out every day to get more beer, more cigarettes. I'm hardly cooking.

The house a mess when Lady Love come back. I don't know how many days she gone. She start cussing me right away, calling me motherfucker and a son-of-a-bitch. It hurt bad when she say she wish the gangbangers find me before she go down to Stateville and tell Carlos what's happening so he can put out the word to let me be.

I feel bad, real bad. I can't say nothing to her. I can't look at her. She pop open a can of Miller beer and take a couple of hits. Pop open the rest of the cans and pour them down the sink. Then she sit down on the couch, start watching soap operas. She shout at me, saying we ain't going nowhere till this place is as clean as a whistle.

I clear out all the garbage, wash all the dishes, sweep the floors, take the sheets off the bed. In a low voice I say, "Miss Love, I'm done."

Without looking at what I do, she yell again, this time that the house smells like my *putas*. I mop the floors using Mr. Clean, scrub the toilet with some white foamy stuff. Slowly she get up. She click the remote and nod her head to say, "Let's go."

In the car she don't talk; she got some oldies on. She shut off the radio. She tell me I'm not in the family, you know, the gang, no more. She drop me off at the Greyhound and tell me to go to Detroit so I can pick up my brother's check and tell Social Security I move to Chicago so they send the check to the rooming house. She give me a form all filled out to make Tony the rooming house manager my payee. The last thing she says I remember exactly. "You come back and mind your business. If I need you, I know where to find you." That was it, real cold. Maybe it's like Dadi says sometimes, that I need tough love. I think now Lady Love give me tough love.

Mami, believe me, now I tell the truth. Dadi, I know you listening, too. I know you going to put holes in my story. But if Mami believe me, then you believe Mami.

I'm tired now. Real tired. You tell Nick he always be my brother and study hard.

RECUERDE
ALEXIA 2007

How ironic. Jesus Cárdenas pronounced bureaucratically dead by Social Security in 2002, while the real Jesus died by homicide in 1988, his identity taken over by his brother Felix. Should I now think or speak of him as Felix because in death his real name was revealed? That didn't seem right. George had an answer for my dilemma. "Call him Gato, like everyone else." George was right. Gato never seemed comfortable being called Jesus.

Jesus, Gato, Felix: the name didn't matter. This stranger who had become such a part of our lives, a vexing one at that, had made it into my heart. Any small cue, and I'd remember his sly smile or that winking gleam in his eyes, and tears would come into mine.

Memo, who preferred his street name to his given name Mamerto as well, was planning a remembrance for Gato in Wicker Park for the day after Thanksgiving. When he told us this, I remembered the photo in a local community paper that Gato had shown us. It was of five or six guys, including Gato and Memo, gathered in a circle in Humboldt Park, beer bottles in hand, drinking to a homeless man who had been murdered in the park a few days earlier. Memo wanted to carry this tradition forward for Gato.

Nick, George, and I walked the few blocks to the park, not talking, taking in what was likely to be the last nice day of the fall with cold and snow forecast for the weekend. I wasn't sure what to expect of this street people's memorial. Would many people show up? Do people just talk quietly among themselves, or do they speak out their words of remembrance?

Thoughts kaleidoscoped through my mind: Gato running across the street shouting, "I'm dead, I'm dead;" seeing him all cleaned up when he took a shower that first night he stayed with us; seeing him in the park on Sundays when we would go to the farmer's market; running into him just last year, right after Fidel Castro stepped down as president of Cuba. It was on this occasion that he really opened up to me and that we started calling each other *compañero* and *compañera*. Since then I've felt good that I gained that level of trust with him, a level George had never achieved.

Not far from the southwest entrance of Wicker Park, clumps of people, maybe thirty in all, stood or sat at the chess tables and the long green benches. These were not the now dominant class of park denizens, the yuppies with children in the newly rebuilt playground, or the frolicking flirters, canine and human, at the eastmost point of the park's triangle, Wicker Bark, or the slim blondes sunbathing. These were the people with long connections to the neighborhood, and this was still their corner of the park, though usually in smaller numbers than there that day.

As we got closer, I recognized a few faces and shapes. Arianna and I must have seen each other at the same time. Walking unsteadily with a cane, followed by a bearded Hispanic man I did not recognize, she took a few steps toward me. I closed the distance and we hugged. We hadn't seen each other since that time she came to our apartment and saw Gato's picture on the wall.

"Sun-o-a-gun, it was only a matter of time when Gato's nine lives were up," she drawled. Her companion had stopped to talk to someone else. Although George hung back, Nick came up to us.

"Nickie, I always said you took after your moms, and now you got the looks to prove it." Nick was uncomfortable as she wrapped her huge frame around him and pulled his head down to kiss his cheek. "Smart as ever, I bet. How many degrees you got? Still playing that fiddle?"

George sidled up, saving Nick from having to answer her questions. "Hello, Arianna. I'm actually happy to see you."

"Don't think you're going to pump me for information about Gato. You'll hear what I got to say if I get a chance to pay my respects."

"No, I've made my peace with Gato. I'll let it be."

George, seeing Alberto of Hermosa Housing, continued farther into the park. Memo and I caught each other's eye, but seeing Lady Love he stayed right where he was. A forty-something Hispanic, good looking and trim, with wavy, jet-black hair approached.

"Lady Love, my respects."

"Hector, long time no see. You know Alexia Demas? Alexia, this is Hector Barrera."

"Mrs. Demas, it is an honor to actually meet you. I've only seen you from a distance. Gato would point you out. He'd say. 'That's my Mami.' You were a real friend to Gato. You know, we grew up in the same neighborhood in Guantanamo. George and I met a long time ago, when he was teaching GED up in the projects."

"Happy to meet you as well, and thank you for the package you dropped off." He shook his head ever so slightly and furrowed his brows. It seemed he was trying to tell me to say no more about the tapes he had left with George earlier in the week. Arianna meanwhile perked up her ears. Sensing she wasn't going to miss a word between Hector and me, I changed subjects. "It's a nice turnout for the memorial."

"You kidding," Arianna interrupted. "Considering Gato knew everyone and everyone knew Gato, you could say hardly no one's here." Arianna going negative; some things never change.

"You'll see, they're still coming," Hector countered. "You bring something to share?"

"You're not going to see me drinking in the park," she said. "I ain't giving them any excuse to take me in. You see Romano over there, I wonder if it was that faggot Memo who told him. And if you don't recognize someone, probably some new narc."

I'd had enough of her. "Arianna, I see someone I need to say hello to. Hector, George said he gave you our number. Please call us. We'd like to see you again."

As I walked away, I thought I heard her say, "I bet she does." Then from a distance I could see their conversation getting more animated. She was angry. I could only imagine her asking Hector about the tape she made of her visit to our home.

By then, Memo was trying to encourage people to gather near the fountain. Several minutes later, people were gathered to some extent. George, Nick, and I had regrouped together, my arm laced through George's and into his warm jacket pocket. Memo stood on the arcing ledge of the fountain and raised his voice. "Brothers and sisters, we are here today to remember our friend Gato Cárdenas. I never knew Gato to be much of a churchgoing man, though he went a few times in recent months, but I do know that when in need he would pray privately to the Lord. In the cover of darkness, thinking I was asleep, he would start, '*el Señor*, I know I have sinned.' So let us pray."

Memo started the Lord's Prayer in Spanish, and several others joined in.

Padre nuestro que estás en los cielos
Santificado sea tu nombre . . .

"It is a tradition among those of us of the streets that when one of our own passes, that we pass a bottle or two and remember our departed friend."

Clusters of mourners were already passing bottles, each person raising it up to say, "For Gato" before taking a swig and sharing it with the next. Memo raised a quart of Miller that someone had given him and held it high without drinking.

"Gato was my brother, more so than my own flesh and blood. It didn't start that way. At one time it was just business. We bought or sold the same goods, lived by the law of supply and demand. But when we were both living on the streets, we learned to watch each other's backs, and he accepted me for who I was, a *maricón*. And if anyone thinks because we often crashed together that he was that way, then you didn't know Gato."

Amid a chorus of laughs, a female voice rose, "Gato was my man, quite a man."

"You got that right, sister, and a charmer at that." Bottles went up.

The first woman, a slight Latina, had made her way to the front of the crowd. "My name is Alicia. A lot of you know I've had a lot of men. So when I say Gato was quite a man, I'm not just talking like that. He looks out for me. More than once he protects me. But you know he cooks for me, too, and he's a good cook, and he sings to me, treats me like a real woman." Tears were running down her cheek, and she paused to wipe them. "See, I'm talking like he's still with us, 'cause for me he is." Alicia wasn't alone in her tears, so George gave me his handkerchief.

Memo was about to say something else when a familiar-looking African American man stepped forward. "Gato and I, we been all around this neighborhood together. You know what I mean? How many places we been moved from to make way for the yuppies—three, four? I lost count. But I could count on Gato. He was from Cuba, I'm from down South, so sometimes he don't understand me and sometime I don't understand him, but we spoke the same language. You know what I mean? God bless you, Gato."

"We hear you, Amos," someone shouted.

A few more people spoke, each saying something good about Gato. One Wicker Park regular extolled Gato's chess playing, another his clever ways of hustling, yet another, his storytelling.

When Sergeant Romano went to the fountain's edge, a handful in the crowd started heckling. "We don't need any police here. Get out of here."

Romano stood his ground. "There's just one thing I want to say, to clear the air if any rumors persist. Gato was no snitch."

Hector Barerra was next. He told the story of how, as a teenager, Gato left Cuba on a leaky boat. When word reached the neighborhood in Guantanamo, where he was already known as Gato, he became a hero to the young boys. About ten years later a group of them, including Hector, followed Gato's example. Naturally, since Hector heard Gato was in Chicago, he made his way here as well.

As Hector spoke, George meandered up. I knew he wanted to say something, though he didn't tell me so.

"I don't know why Gato always called me Dadi. But that's how it was. I know that many of you only know me as Gato's Dadi, and that's OK too. My wife Alexia and I really got to know Gato when Social Security said he was dead, just over five years ago. Once they get it in their system that someone is dead, that's a hard one to turn around."

"You got that right," somebody called out.

"And Gato had no ID either. But we straightened them out. That was the easy part. There was no straightening out Gato. He had his ways, and you know what? Maybe we're better off because of his ways. He was one of those people who was down but never out. Some would say he was from the bottom of the barrel. But an old friend once said, the strongest beers come from the bottom of the barrel. Gato had some weak spots—drink for one. But he had a strong survival instinct, so his street name matched his nine lives perfectly.

"We came to be friends. All of us in our family and Gato. More than that, he became a member of our family. Maybe not the cousin you want to see every day, but the one a holiday wouldn't seem the same without. So we'll miss Gato, but we know our lives were richer and more real having known him."

As George was finishing, I saw Arianna making her way up to the edge of the fountain. But then a commotion came from the other side of the fountain area. A big black SUV pulled up and an entourage of sharply dressed men got out of the vehicle and surrounded the tallest among them, who I recognized immediately as Reverend Jorge de la Cruz. As they approached, Memo walked toward them, and Arianna retreated back into the crowd of mourners. When I last saw her, Arianna was once again accompanied by the bearded man. I wondered, Was it Carlos, her husband, finally out of prison?

Memo shook the reverend's hand, walked with him to the front of the congregants, and introduced him. "Please welcome Reverend Jorge de la Cruz of Redeeming Hope Church." But Memo's rising voice did not rouse the crowd. More than a few walked away shaking their heads; others took a few more hits on their bottles. Someone said loudly, "This is bullshit." But I for one was paying attention, surprised the controversial reverend would show up for a street person's memorial.

"Brothers and sisters, *hermanas y hermanos*, I only met Jesus

Cárdenas once, but when Memo mentioned he passed and that there would be this memorial, I told him I wanted to say a few words. Jesus came to our church on the holy day of the Pentecost, just six months ago. When the infirm were called to be healed, Jesus stood up, struggling to reach me with his walker. As I do with all such supplicants, I put my two hands on his shoulders and asked him quietly and directly, 'Are you willing to accept Jesus Christ as your Savior?' He looked up at me and said, 'Yes I am,' adding with a twinkle in his eye, 'Are you?' Strange as this seemed, I answered without hesitation, 'The Lord Jesus Christ is my Savior.'

"At that moment I increased the pressure of my hands on his shoulders, and as I did I could feel this bent, hurting man straighten himself, rising taller. Yet I felt something more. I felt an energy coming from him into me and then an aura of peace enveloping my soul. I swear in the name of Jesus Christ that what I am telling you is true.

"When he stood independently alongside of me, as strong as any man his age, I felt such joy that I was impelled to kick his then-unneeded walker away from him. Then Jesus walked toward the altar to share what I thought was a new faith, like the others accepting Christ that day. But the words of Matthew 24:44 came upon me and made me wonder whose faith was new and whose everlasting? 'Therefore be ye also ready: for in such an hour as ye think not the Son of man cometh.' Will not the second coming of our Lord come as unexpectedly as Jesus Cárdenas came into each of our lives? Thank you for letting me share my experience with Jesus, your friend Gato."

I was dumbstruck by how de la Cruz's words affected me. On the one hand I felt he was talking directly to me, but the other hand was much weightier. In my mind I saw the icon of Jesus on the cross that both my mother and my mother-in-law, Dimitra, had on their dressers. It was this Jesus that held my faith, the Son of God both fully God and fully human, a God who knew personally the pain, suffering, and temptations of the people, even people like Gato, perhaps especially people like Gato. If our God is humanlike, then must not all of us, especially the meek who will inherit the earth, have God within them?

Earlier on the way to the memorial, and again listening to George speak, the thought foremost in my mind had been how this stranger had become so much a part of our lives. Now I realized how much he had changed our lives. Some changes were obvious, others less so and unconscious. Thrust into having to help another with his basic survival needs, we became less obsessed with our own daily routine. Our circle of acquaintances grew to include some in Gato's circle, most notably my long-lost promising student, Memo—and look how much Memo had changed. Had Gato influenced his turn from drugs to spirituality and community activism as he had influenced a greater involvement in our own church's Feed the Hungry program?

What was most clear was that I would miss my *compañero*. His absence would leave a void in my life and, I was sure, in George's as well.

EPILOGUE
GEORGE 2007

It was Friday, the 30th of November. As I headed south along Damen Avenue from the "L," I observed how the plowed snow from Wednesday evening's fall was already turning grey and hard. No wonder, the temperatures had not risen above twenty the last two days. Yet I managed to get to work and back with my leather jacket and a sweater underneath rather than breaking out the down coat before winter even became official.

It was getting dark when I left work, darker still when I walked up the stoop. Inside the vestibule I crouched to sort through the mail of our three households. Two envelopes down was the familiar blue envelope addressed to me, for Jesus Cárdenas. Catching my eye next to the government's postage imprint was a checkbox to the left of the emboldened words.

☐ **IF RECIPIENT DECEASED**
check here and drop in nearest mailbox

The same, once marked and returned five and a half years earlier, had thrust the then officially dead Jesus Cárdenas into our lives quite unexpectedly and unforeseeably even until this day, when he was now quite deceased.

But I didn't linger on the envelope or the checkbox. Instead I grabbed our pile of mail, wiped my feet thoroughly, and headed up to our third-floor home. No sooner had I kicked off my shoes in the foyer, laid the mail and my briefcase on the table, and yelled, "I'm home" over the news radio Alexia was listening to in the kitchen, when the doorbell rang. Instinctively I shouted again, "I'll get it, it's probably Gato," even though, or perhaps because, just minutes earlier the blue envelope and its checkbox had reminded me he was no more. "Whoever it is, I'll be right back," I shouted to Alexia.

So with shoes untied I hustled down the stairs to be startled by a slumping silhouette through the inner and outer door panes. As I descended further, a second silhouette appeared. When the streetlight caught the first face, I was startled again. The face was Gato's minus the mustache, plus teeth, sum total a female. Startled thrice, the shadow behind had the same face, only the hairstyle was different.

I opened the door.

"Mr. Demas?"

"Yes?"

"I'm Marisol."

"I'm Maribel . . . Cárdenas."

"We got a message from our grandma saying our Papi died. She said you might have something of his for us," said Marisol.

"Now I get it. Whenever your Papi mentioned a daughter, sometimes he'd call her Marisol and other times Maribel. Are you twins?" Neither of the young women responded.

"Wait a second. You look so familiar. Of course you take after your father quite a bit, but there's something else."

"That's 'cause you used to know us," said Marisol.

"You just haven't seen us in fifteen years," said Maribel, her laughter joined in seconds by her sister's.

"Grandma Love, you know, Lady Love, used to bring us here when we were little. We played with your Nick," Maribel added, as I realized that Alexia was coming down the stairs to see what was taking me so long.

"Alexia, come see who's here. It's Arianna's grandkids, Sol and Belle. But that's not all. They're Gato's daughters, Marisol and Maribel."

ACKNOWLEDGMENTS

Without the encouragement and regular critiques of new and re-
vised chapters by members of my writing group, *Citizen Cárdenas*
would not have materialized. So thank you Bob Boone, Bob Lawrence, Marlene Marks, Dan Shaffer, Susan Mullen, Pavell, Chuck
Kramer, and Samantha Hoffman for helping me shape the book and
its characters. I hope I contributed as much to your works with my
comments as you did for mine.

I initially decided to publish the book serially on the Web, so
that friends and family could follow the progress of the story and
provide feedback. I always knew I had to make changes when several
readers had similar reactions to the same chapter. I will mention only
one reviewer by name: my mother Jeanette Cole Malinow. She loved
the chapters with insights into Chicago politics and the intricacies
of the various bureaucracies Gato had to traverse. Jeanette also
provided me a great self-publishing example, her memoir, *My Nine
Lives*, which came out in 2008 about a year after I started writing
this work. Jeanette was still alive when I completed my first draft in
2011, but passed away before being able to read a published version
of *Citizen Cárdenas*.

Of course, others in my family were supportive as well. Son Matthew offered early encouragement and arranged to have a friend host my website. Son Sam read draft four in just a few days. For him, the story was a page turner.

Judith Gallagher, a friend, served as my developmental editor. Judith asked tough questions and posed interesting challenges to me when we met at her western Pennsylvania home in 2011. Through her organization, Ligonier Valley Writers, she also introduced me to new electronic trends in self-publishing. As a result, I was more aware of the playing field when I searched for a self-publishing company, ultimately choosing Minneapolis-based North Loop Books. Everyone at North Loop Books and parent company Hillcrest Media have been real professionals. These companies have lived up to their promise of helping authors publish, own, and be compensated fairly for their work.

My wife, Patricia Stahl, played a significant behind-the-scenes role in the writing and publishing of *Citizen Cárdenas*. Before a single word was written, Pat and I were partners in helping the man who would become the inspiration for Gato Cárdenas overcome many difficulties, especially with the red tape poor people face while struggling for survival. But that's only the beginning. As a voracious reader, she knows a good read from a bad one and gave me names of other such readers to add to my mailing list. As a life-long editor in the publishing industry, she's provided advice every step along the way even when the recipient (me) was bullheaded. With her compassion in the lead, we continue helping our friend who, despite a Social Security declaration and this author's fiction, remains very much alive.

Steve Cole
Fall 2015

ABOUT THE AUTHOR

Like many people of our time, Steve Cole has reinvented himself more than a few times. Until he retired in early 2014, he had been a database developer and data architect in the health care industry. As a young man, after quitting college, he worked in factories, on the docks of Milwaukee, and in communities in Milwaukee and Chicago as a community advocate and political activist. From 1976–1986, Steve wrote articles for a community magazine, *Keep Strong,* and a biweekly newspaper, *All Chicago City News.* Steve and his family have lived in their Chicago three-flat for 30 years. They travel frequently to Greece to visit relatives and have made learning Greek a family project. They are also active in St. Basil Greek Orthodox Church and, in particular, its prison ministry.